THE SEABOARD PARISH

George MacDonald

EDITED BY DAN HAMILTON

A Quiet Neighborhood
The Seaboard Parish
The Vicar's Daughter

PROPERTY OF
MARS HILL GRADUATE SCHOOL
LIBRARY
2525 220th ST SE, Suite 100
Bothell, WA 98021
(425) 415-0505 x 109

WITHDRAWN

PR
4967
S4
1985

MacDonald, George,
The seaboard parish /

A DIVISION OF SCRIPTURE PRESS PUBLICATIONS
USA CANADA ENGLAND

Mars Hill Graduate School

1 0000205

VICTOR BOOKS BY GEORGE MACDONALD

A Quiet Neighborhood

The Seaboard Parish

The Vicar's Daughter

The Last Castle

The Shopkeeper's Daughter

The Prodigal Apprentice

Third printing, 1986

The Seaboard Parish was first published in England in 1868.

Library of Congress Catalog Card Number: 84-52365
ISBN: 0-89693-329-6

© 1985 by Dan Hamilton. All rights reserved
Printed in the United States of America

No part of this book may be reproduced without
written permission, except for brief quotations
in books, critical articles, and reviews.

VICTOR BOOKS
A division of SP Publications, Inc.
Wheaton, Illinois 60187

CONTENTS

INTRODUCTION

George MacDonald (1824-1905), a Scottish preacher, poet, novelist, fantasist, expositor, and public figure, is most well known today for his children's books—*At the Back of the North Wind*, *The Princess and the Goblin*, *The Princess and Curdie*, and his fantasies *Lilith* and *Phantastes*.

But his fame is based on far more than his fantasies. His lifetime output of more than fifty popular books placed him in the same literary realm as Charles Dickens, Wilkie Collins, William Thackeray, and Thomas Carlyle. He numbered among his friends and acquaintances Lewis Carroll, Mark Twain, Lady Byron, and John Ruskin.

Among his later admirers were G.K. Chesterton, W.H. Auden, and C.S. Lewis. MacDonald's fantasy *Phantastes* was a turning point in Lewis' conversion; Lewis acknowledged MacDonald as his spiritual master, and declared that he had never written a book without quoting from MacDonald.

PROLOGUE

I am seated once again at my writing table in the little octagonal room, which I have made my study because I like it best. It is rather a shame, for my books cover over every foot of the old oak paneling. But they make the room all the more pleasant, and after I am gone, there is the old oak, none the worse, for anyone who prefers it to books.

My story will be rather about my family than myself now. What was once one, and had become two, is now seven. Ethelwyn—or Wynnie—is the eldest, and is named, of course, after her mother. Constance—Connie—followed her, and after that Dorothy, whom we often call Dora. And our two boys, Harry and Charlie, came to us last.

I intend to relate the history of one year during which I took charge of a friend's parish, while my brother-in-law, Thomas Weir, took the entire charge of Marshmallows.

ONE

CONSTANCE'S BIRTHDAY

It was a custom with my family that each of the children, as his or her birthday came round, should be king or queen for that day and—subject to the veto of Father and Mother—should have everything his or her own way. Let me say for them, however, that in the matter of choosing the dinner—the royal prerogative—it was almost invariably the favorite dishes of others that were chosen, and not those especially agreeable to the royal palate. (Members of families where children have not been taught that the great privilege of possession is the right to bestow, may regard this as an improbable assertion.) But there was always the choice of some individual treat, determined solely by the preference of the individual in authority.

And Constance, for her eighteenth birthday, had chosen "a long ride with Papa."

On her birthday morning, a lovely October day with a golden east and clouds of golden foliage, there came yet an occasional blast of wind which smelt of winter. However, I do not think Connie felt it at all as she stood on the steps in her riding habit, waiting for the horses. She had been at school for two years and had been home a month that very day. She was as fresh as the young day, for we were early people. Breakfast and prayers were over, and it was nine o'clock.

"O Papa! Isn't it jolly?" she said, merrily.

"Very jolly indeed, my dear," I answered, delighted to hear the word from the lips of my gentle daughter. She very seldom used slang, and when she did, she used it like a lady.

She was rather little, but so slight that she looked tall. She was fair in complexion, with her mother's blue eyes and long, dark, wavy hair. She was generally playful and took greater liberties with me than any of the others, but on the borders of her playfulness there was a fringe of thoughtfulness. She enjoyed life like a bird—her laugh was merry and her heart was careless. Her sweet soprano voice rang through the house as she sang snatches of songs—now a street tune from a London organ, now an air from Handel or Mozart. She would sometimes tease her elder sister about her anxious and solemn looks, for Wynnie had to suffer for her grandmother's sins against my wife, and she came into the world with a troubled heart.

"Where shall we go, Connie?" I asked, the same moment as the sound of the horses' hooves reached us.

"Would it be too far to go to Addicehead?"

"It is a long ride."

"Too much for the pony?"

"No, not at all. I was thinking of you, not the pony."

"I'm quite as able to ride as the pony is to carry me, Papa. And I want to get something for Wynnie. Do let us go."

"Very well, my dear," I said, and raised her to the saddle—if I may say *raised*, for no bird ever hopped more lightly from one twig to another than she sprang from the ground to her pony's back. In a moment I was beside her, and away we rode.

The shadows were still long, and the dew still pearly on the spiders' webs, as we trotted out of our own grounds into a lane that led away toward the high road. Our horses were fresh and the air was exciting, so we turned from the hard road into the first suitable field and had a gallop to begin with. Constance was a good horsewoman, for she had been used to the saddle longer than she could remember. She was now riding Sprite, a tall well-bred pony, with plenty of life—rather too much, I sometimes thought when I was out with Wynnie, but I never thought so when I was with Constance. Another field or two quieted both animals, and then we began to talk.

"You are quite a woman now, Connie, my dear," I said.

"Quite an old grannie, Papa," she answered.

"Old enough to think about what's coming next," I said.

8

"O Papa! And you are always telling us that we must not think about the morrow, or even the next hour. But, then, that's in the pulpit," she added, with a sly look up at me from under the drooping feather of her pretty hat.

"You know very well what I mean," I answered. "And I don't say one thing in the pulpit and another out of it."

She was at my horse's shoulder with a bound, as if Sprite had been of one mind and one piece with her. She was afraid she had offended me and looked up at me anxiously.

"Oh, thank you, Papa!" she said, when I smiled. "I thought I had been rude. I didn't mean it. But I do wish sometimes you wouldn't explain things so much. I seem to understand you while you are preaching, but when I try the text by myself, I can't make anything of it, and I've forgotten every word you've said."

"Perhaps that is because you have no right to understand it."

"I thought we all had a right to understand every word of the Bible."

"If we can. But last Sunday, for instance, I did not expect anybody there to understand a certain bit of my sermon, except your mamma and Thomas Weir."

"How funny! What part was it?"

"Oh, I'm not going to tell you. You have no right to understand it. But tell me what you are so full of care about, and perhaps I can help you there."

"Well, you often say that half the misery in this world comes from idleness, and that you do not believe that God could have intended that women, any more than men, should have nothing to do. Now what am I to do? What have I been sent into the world for? I don't see it, and I feel very useless and wrong sometimes. I don't want to stop at home and lead an easy, comfortable life, when there are so many to be helped everywhere in the world."

"Is there anything better in doing something where God has not placed you, than in doing it where He has placed you?"

"No, Papa. But my sisters are quite enough for all you have for us to do at home. Is nobody ever to go away to find the work meant for her? But you won't think that I *want* to get away from home, will you?"

"No, my dear. I believe that you are thinking about duty. What God may hereafter require of you, you must not give yourself the least trouble about. Everything He gives you to do, you must do as well as ever you can. That is the best possible preparation for what He may want you to do next. If people would but do what they have to do, they would always find themselves ready for what came next.

"But there is one more thing. It is not your moral nature alone you ought to cultivate. You ought to make yourself as worth God's making as you possibly can. Now I am a little doubtful whether you keep up your studies at all."

She shrugged her shoulders playfully, looking up into my face again. "I don't like dry things, Papa."

"Nobody does."

"Nobody? How do the grammars and history books come to be written, then?"

"Those books are exceedingly interesting to the people who make them. Dry things are just things that you do not know enough about to care for. And all you learn at school is nothing to what you have to learn."

"Must I go all over my French grammar again?" she sighed. "Oh, dear! I hate it so."

"If you will tell me something you like, Connie, instead of something you don't like, I may be able to give you advice. Is there nothing you are fond of?"

"I don't remember much in the way of schoolwork that I really liked. I did what I had to. But there was one thing I liked—the poetry we had to learn once a week. But I suppose gentlemen count that silly, don't they?"

"On the contrary, I would make that liking the foundation of all your work. Besides, I think poetry the grandest thing God has given us, though perhaps we might not agree about *what* poetry was a special gift of God. Most poetry is very thin, and it is time you had done with thin things, however good they may be. I must take you in hand myself, and see what I can do for you. I hold that whatever mental food you take should be just a little too strong for you. That implies trouble, necessitates growth, and involves delight."

"I shan't mind how difficult it is if you help me, Papa."

We went on talking a little more in the same way, and at length fell into silence—a very happy one on my part. I was more than delighted to find that my child was following after the truth, wanting to do what was right in the voice of her own conscience and the light of that understanding which is the candle of the Lord.

We were going at a gentle trot along a woodland path—a brown, soft, shady road, nearly five miles from home. Our horses scattered the withered leaves that lay thick upon it, between the underwood and the few large trees that had been lately cleared from the place. There were many piles of sticks about, and a great log lying here and there along the side of the path. One tree had been struck by lightning and had stood till the frosts and rains had bared it of its bark. Now it lay white as a skeleton by the side of the path and was, I think, the cause of what followed.

All at once Sprite sprang to the other side of the road, shying sideways. Then, rearing and plunging, he threw Connie from the saddle across one of the logs, and then bolted away between the trees. I slid from my horse, and was by Connie's side in an instant. She lay motionless; her eyes were closed, and when I took her up in my arms she did not open them. I laid her on the moss, and got some water and sprinkled her face. Then she revived a little, but fainted again in pain.

Very shortly, a woodsman came up and asked how he could help. He had been cutting firewood at a little distance, and had seen the pony careering through the woods. I told him to ride my horse to Oldcastle Hall and ask Mrs. Walton to come with the carriage as quickly as possible. "Tell her," I said, "that her daughter has had a fall from her pony and is rather shaken. Ride as hard as you can go."

The man was off in a moment, and there I sat watching my poor child. She had come to, but complained of much pain in her back and found that she could not move. Her face was dreadfully pale and looked worn with a month's illness. All my fear was for her spine.

At length the carriage came, as fast as the road would allow, with the woodsman on the box directing the coachman. My wife got out, as pale as Constance, but quiet and firm. She asked no questions; there was time enough for that afterward. She had brought plenty of cushions and pillows, and though we did all we could to make an easy couch for the poor girl, she moaned dreadfully as we lifted her into the carriage. We did our best to keep her from being shaken, but those few miles were the longest journey I ever made in my life.

When we reached home, we found that Wynnie had readied a room on the ground floor for her sister, and we were glad indeed not to have to carry her up the stairs. Before my wife had left, she had sent the groom for aid, and a young doctor named Turner was waiting for us when we arrived. He had settled at Marshmallows as general practitioner a year or two before. He immediately began to direct her care, and helped us lay her on a mattress. It was painfully clear to all that her spine was seriously injured, and that she probably had years of suffering before her.

I left her at last, with her mother seated by her bedside, and found Wynnie and Dora seated on the floor outside, one weeping on each side of the door. I called them into my study and said to them, "My darlings, this is very sad, but you must remember that it is God's will. As you would both try to bear it cheerfully if it had fallen to your lot to bear, you must try to be cheerful even when it is your sister's part to endure."

"O Papa! Poor Connie!" cried Dora, and burst into fresh tears. Wynnie said nothing, but knelt down by my knee and laid her cheek upon it.

"Shall I tell you what Constance said to me just before I left the room?" I asked.

"Please do, Papa."

"She whispered, 'You must try to bear it, all of you, as well as you can. I don't mind it very much, only for you.' So, you see, if you want to make her comfortable, you must not look gloomy and troubled. Sick people like to see cheerful faces about them. I am sure Connie will not suffer nearly so much if she finds that she does not make the household gloomy.

"We will do all we can, will we not," I went on, "to make her as comfortable as possible? You, Dora, must attend to your little brothers, so that your mother may not have too much there to think about."

They would not say much, but they both kissed me and went away.

My wife and I watched by Connie's bedside on alternate nights, until the pain had so far subsided, and the fever was so far reduced, that we could allow Wynnie to take some care of her. Connie's chief suffering came from keeping nearly one position on her back, and from the external bruises and consequent swelling of her muscles.

It soon became evident that Connie's new room was like a new and more sacred heart to the house. At first it radiated gloom to the remotest corners, but soon rays of light began to mingle with the gloom. Bits of news were carried from there to the servants in the kitchen, in the garden, in the stable, and over the way to the home farm. Even in the village, and everywhere over the parish, I was received more kindly and listened to more willingly, because of the trouble my family and I were in. In the house, although we had never been anything else than a loving family, it was easy to discover that we all drew more closely together in consequence of our common anxiety.

Previous to this, it had been no unusual thing to see Wynnie and Dora impatient with each other, for Dora was wild and somewhat lawless, though profoundly affectionate. She rather resembled her cousin Judy, whom she called Aunt Judy, and with whom she was naturally a great favorite. Wynnie, on the other hand, was sedate and rather severe, more severe, I must in justice say, with herself than with anyone else. It was soon evident not only that Wynnie had grown more indulgent to Dora's vagaries, but that Dora was more submissive to Wynnie, while the younger children began to obey their eldest sister willingly, keeping down their effervescence inside and letting it off only out-of-doors.

TWO

THE SICK CHAMBER

In the course of a month, Connie's pain was greatly reduced but the power of moving her limbs had not yet begun to show itself.

One day she received me with a happy smile, put out her thin white hand, took mine and kissed it, and said, "Papa," with a lingering on the last syllable.

"What is it, my pet?" I asked.

"I am so happy!"

"What makes you so happy?" I asked again.

"I don't know," she answered. "I haven't thought about it yet. But everything looks so pleasant around me. Is it nearly winter yet, Papa? I've forgotten all about how the time has been going."

"It is almost winter, my dear. There is hardly a leaf left on the trees—just two or three disconsolate yellow ones that want to get away down to the rest. They flutter and try to break away, but can't."

"That is just as I felt. I wanted to die and get away, for I thought I should never be well again, and I should be in everybody's way."

"Well, my darling, we are in God's hands. We shall never get tired of you, and you must not get tired of us. Would you get tired of nursing me, if I were ill?"

"O Papa!" And the tears began to gather in her eyes.

"Then you must think we are not able to love so well as you."

"I know what you mean. I did not think of it that way. I was only thinking how useless I was."

14

"There you are quite mistaken, my dear. No living creature ever was useless. You've plenty to do."

"But what have I got to do? I don't feel able for anything," she said, and again the tears came to her eyes, as if I had been telling her to get up and she could not.

"A great deal of our work," I answered, "we do without knowing what it is. But I'll tell you what you have to do: you have to believe in God, and in everybody in this house."

"I do, I do. But that is easy," she returned.

"And do you think that the work God gives us to do is never easy? Jesus says His yoke is easy, His burden light. People sometimes refuse to do God's work just because it is easy. Sometimes this is because they cannot believe that easy work is His work, and so they accept it with half a heart and do it with half a hand. But, however easy any work may be, it cannot be well done without taking thought about it. And such people, instead of taking thought about their work, generally take thought about the morrow, in which no work can be done any more than in yesterday. Do you remember our talk on that dreadful morning? You wanted something to do, and so God gave you something to do."

"Lying in bed and doing nothing!"

"Yes. Just lying in bed and doing His will."

"If I could but feel that I was doing His will!"

"When you do it, then you will feel you are doing it."

"I know you are coming to something, Papa. Please make haste."

"You must say to God something like this: 'O Heavenly Father, I have nothing to offer Thee but my patience. I will bear Thy will, and so offer my will a burnt offering unto Thine. I will be as useless as Thou pleasest.' Depend on it, my darling, in the midst of all the science about the world and its ways, and all the ignorance of God and His greatness, the man or woman who can thus say, 'Thy will be done,' with the true heart of surrender, is nearer the secret of things than the geologist and theologian."

She held up her mouth to kiss me, but did not speak, and I left her, and sent Dora to sit with her.

In the evening, when I went into her room again, having been out in my parish all day, I began to unload my budget of small events. Indeed, we all came in like pelicans with stuffed pouches to empty them in her room, as if she had been the only young one we had, and we must cram her with news.

After I had done talking, she said, "And you have been to the school too, Papa?"

"Yes. I go to the school almost every day."

"You'll have to take up my teaching soon, as you promised—you know, Papa—just before Sprite threw me."

"Certainly, my dear, and I will begin to think about it at once."

She was quite unable for any kind of work such as she would have me commence with her, but I used to take something to read to her every now and then, and always after our early tea on Sundays. And it was in part the result of Connie's wish that it became the custom to gather in her room on Sunday evenings.

This custom began one Sunday evening as I was sitting beside Constance's bed. The twilight had deepened nearly into night, and the curtains had not yet been drawn. There was no light in the room but that of the fire. Now Constance was in the way of asking what kind of day or night it was, for there was never a girl more a child of nature than she.

"What is it like, Papa?"

"It is growing dark," I answered. "It is a still evening, and what they call a black frost. The trees are standing as still as if they were carved out of stone, and would snap off everywhere if the wind were to blow. The ground is dark, and as hard as cast iron. A gloomy night, rather—it looks as if there were something on its mind that made it sullenly thoughtful. But the stars are coming out one after another overhead, and the sky will be awake soon. Strange, the life that goes on all night, is it not? The life of owlets and mice and beasts of prey and bats and stars," I said, with no very categorical arrangement, "and dreams and flowers that don't go to sleep like the rest, but send out their scent all night long. Only those are gone now. There are no scents abroad, not even of the earth, in such a frost as this."

"Don't you think it looks sometimes, Papa, as if God turned His back on the world, or went farther away from it for a while?"

"Tell me a little more what you mean, Connie."

"Well, this night now, this dark, frozen, lifeless night, which you have been describing to me, isn't like God at all, is it?"

"No, it is not. I see what you mean now."

"It is just as if He had gone away and said, 'Now you shall see what you can do without Me.'"

"Something like that. But I think the English people enjoy the changeful weather of their country much more than those who have fine weather constantly. It is not enough to satisfy God's goodness that He should make us able to enjoy them as richly as He gives them. Now can you tell me anything in history that confirms what I have been saying?"

"I don't know anything about history, Papa. The only thing that comes into my head is what you were saying yourself the other day about Milton's blindness."

"Ah, yes. I had not thought of that. I believe that God wanted a grand poem from that man, and therefore blinded him that he might be able to write it."

"It was rather hard for poor Milton, though, wasn't it, Papa?"

"Wait till *he* says so, my dear. We are sometimes too ready with our sympathy, and think things a great deal worse than do those who have to undergo them. Who would not be glad to be struck with such blindness as Milton's?"

"Those who do not care about his poetry, Papa," answered Constance, with a deprecatory smile.

"Well said. And to such it never can come. But, if it please God, you shall love Milton before you are about again. You can't love one you know nothing about."

"I have tried to read him a little. I am only sorry that I am not capable of appreciating him."

"There you are wrong again. I think you are quite capable, but you cannot appreciate what you have never seen. You have a figure before you in your fancy which is dry, and which you call Milton. But it is not Milton, any more than your Dutch doll was your Aunt Judy, even though you named her so. But here comes your mamma—and I haven't said what I wanted to say yet."

"But surely, Harry, you can say it all the same," said my wife. "I will go away if you can't."

"I can say it all the better, my love. Come and sit down here beside me. I was showing Connie that a gift has sometimes to be taken away before we can know what it is worth, and so receive it right.

"As long as our Lord was with His disciples, they could not see Him right—He was too near them. Too much light, too many words, too much revelation, blinds or stupefies. They loved Him dearly, and yet often forgot His words almost as soon as He said them. He could not get it into them, for instance, that He had not come to be a king. Whatever He said, they shaped it over again after their own fancy. Their minds were full of their own worldly

17

notions of grandeur and command. Therefore He was taken away, that His Spirit might come into them—that they might receive the gift of God into their innermost being. After He had gone from their sight, they looked all around—down in the grave and up in the air—and did not see Him anywhere. And when they thought they had lost Him, He came to them again from the other side— from the inside. And His words came back to them, no longer as they had received them, but as He meant them. They were then always saying to each other, 'You remember how. . . . ' whereas before they had been always staring at each other with astonishment while He spoke to them. So after He had gone away, He was really nearer to them than before.

"And so the world and all its beauty has come nearer to you, my dear, just because you are separated from it for a time."

"Thank you, dear Papa. I do like to get a little sermon all to myself now and then. But should we not know Jesus better now if He were to come and let us see Him, as He came to the disciples so long ago?"

"As to the time, it makes no difference whether it was last year or two thousand years ago. The whole question is how much we understand—and understanding, obey Him. And I do not think we should be any nearer *than* if He came amongst us bodily again. If we should, He would come."

"Shall we never, never, never see Him?"

"That is quite another thing, my Connie. That is the heart of my hopes by day and my dreams by night. To behold the face of Jesus seems to me the one thing to be desired. The pure in heart shall see God. The seeing of Him will be the sign that we are like Him, for only by being like Him can we see Him as He is. But when we shall be fit to look Him in the face, God only knows."

"Papa, could we, who have never seen Him, know Him better than the disciples?"

"Certainly."

"O Papa! Is it possible? Then why don't we?"

"Because we won't take the trouble. Whoever wants to learn must pray and think and, above all, obey—that is, simply do what Jesus says."

There followed a little silence, and I could hear my child sobbing. And the tears stood in my wife's eyes—tears of gladness to hear her daughter's sobs.

"I'll try, Papa," Connie said at last. "But you will help me?"

"Next Sunday. You have plenty to think about till then."

"But," said my wife, "don't you think, Connie, this is too good to keep all to ourselves? Don't you think we ought to have Wynnie and Dora in?"

"Yes, yes, Mamma. Do let us have them in. And Harry and Charlie too."

"It would be all the better for us to have them," said Ethelwyn smiling.

"How do you mean, my dear?"

"Because you will say things more simply if you have them by you. Besides, you always say such things to children as delight grown people, though they could never get them out of you."

"Well," I said, "I don't mind them coming in, but I don't promise to say anything directly to them. And you must let them go away the moment they wish it."

"Certainly," answered my wife. And so the matter was arranged.

THREE

A SUNDAY EVENING

On the following Sunday evening when I went into Connie's room with my Bible in my hand, I found all our little company assembled. There was a glorious fire, for it was very cold, and the little ones were seated on the rug before it, one on each side of their mother. Wynnie sat by the farther side of the bed (for she always avoided any place or thing she thought another might like), and Dora sat by the chimney corner.

"The wind is very high, Papa," said Constance, as I seated myself beside her. "I am afraid I do like it when it roars like that in the chimneys, and shakes the windows with a great rush. I feel so safe in the very jaws of danger."

"But tell me, Connie," I said, "why you are *afraid* you enjoy hearing the wind about the house."

"Because it must be so dreadful for those who are out in it."

"Perhaps not quite so bad as we think. You must not suppose that God has forgotten them, or cares less for them than for you because they are out in the wind."

"But if we thought like that, Papa," said Wynnie, "shouldn't we come to feel that their sufferings were none of our business?"

"If our benevolence rests on the belief that God is less loving than we, it will come to a bad end before long, Wynnie. Then your kindness would be such that you should cease to help those whom you could help! Either God intended that there should be poverty and suffering, or He did not. If He did not intend it, then we should sell everything that we have and give it away to the poor."

20

"Then why don't we?" said Wynnie.

"Because that is not God's way, and we should do no end of harm by so doing. We should make so many more of those who will not help themselves, who will not be set free from themselves by rising above themselves. We are not to gratify our own benevolence at the expense of its object, not to save our own souls by putting other souls into more danger than God meant for them."

"It sounds a hard doctrine from your lips, Papa," said Wynnie.

"Many things will sound hard in so many words. If people should have everything they want, then everyone ought to be rich. There was once a baby born in a stable, because His poor mother could get no room in a decent house. Had God forsaken them? Would they not have been more comfortable somewhere else? Ah! If the disciples had only been old enough, and had known that He was coming, would they not have gotten everything ready for Him? They would have clubbed their little savings together and worked day and night, and some rich women would have helped them, and they would have dressed the baby in fine linen, and got Him the richest room their money would buy, and they would have made the gold that the wise men brought into a crown for His little head, and would have burnt frankincense before Him. And so our Manger Baby would have been taken away from us. No more the stable-born Saviour, no more the poor Son of God born for us all, as strong, as noble, as loving, as worshipful, as beautiful as He was poor! And we should not have learned that God does not care for money; or that if He does not give us more of it, it is not that it is scarce with Him, or that He is unkind, but that He does not value it. He sent His own Son not merely to be brought up in the house of the carpenter in a little village, but to be born in a stable of a village inn. We need not suppose, then, because a man sleeps under a haystack, and is put in prison the next day, that God does not care for him."

"But why did Jesus come so poor, Papa?"

"That He might be just a human baby; that He might not be distinguished by this or that accident of birth; that He might have nothing but a mother's love to welcome Him, and so belong to everybody; that from the first He might show that the kingdom and favor of God lie not in these external things at all. Had Jesus come among the rich, riches would have been more worshiped than ever. See how so many who count themselves good Christians honor possession and family and social rank. Even in the services

21

of the church, they will accumulate gorgeousness and cost."

"But are we not to serve Him with our very best?" asked my wife.

"Yes, with our very hearts and souls, with our wills, with our absolute being. But all external things should be in harmony with the spirit of His revelation. And if God chose that His Son should visit the earth in homely fashion, in homely fashion likewise should be everything that enforces and commemorates that revelation. All church forms should be on the other side from show and expense. Let the money go to build decent houses for God's poor, not to give them His holy bread and wine out of silver and gold and precious stones. I would send all the church plate to fight the devil with his own weapons in our overcrowded cities and in our villages where the husbandmen are housed like swine, by giving them room to be clean and to breathe decent air from heaven. When the people find the clergy thus in earnest, they will follow them fast enough, and the money will come in like salt and oil upon the sacrifice."

"There is one thing," said Wynnie, after a pause, "that I have often thought about. Why was it necessary for Jesus to come as a Baby? He could not do anything for so long."

"First, Wynnie, all of us come as babies, and whatever was human must be His. And are you sure that He could not do anything for so long? Does a baby do nothing? Ask Mamma there. Is it for nothing that the mother lifts up such heartfuls of thanks to God for the baby on her knee? Is it nothing that the baby opens such fountains of love in almost all the hearts around? Was not Jesus going to establish the reign of love in the earth? How could He do better than begin from babyhood? He had to lay hold of the heart of the world; how could He do better than begin with His mother's? Charlie, wouldn't you have liked to see the little Baby Jesus?"

"Yes. I would have given Him my white rabbit with the pink eyes."

"That is what the great painter Titian must have thought, Charlie, for he has painted Him playing with a white rabbit."

"I would have carried Him about all day," said Dora, "as a baby brother."

"Did He have any brother or sister to carry Him about, Papa?" asked Harry.

"No, my boy, for He was the eldest. But you may be sure He

carried about His brothers and sisters who came after Him."

"Wouldn't He take care of them, just!" said Charlie.

"I wish I had been one of them," said Constance.

"You are one of them."

Then we sang a child's hymn, and the little ones went to bed. Constance was tired now, and leaving her with Wynnie, we too went to bed.

About midnight my wife and I awoke together. The wind was still raving about the house, with lulls between its charges.

"There's a child crying!" said my wife, starting up.

I sat up too, and listened. "It is some creature, I grant."

"It is an infant," insisted my wife. "It can't be either of the boys."

We were out of bed in a moment and into our clothes. I got a lantern, hurried out, and listened. I heard it, but not as clearly as before, and set out as well as I could judge in the direction of the sound. I found nothing, for my lantern lighted only a few yards around me, and the strong wind threatened to blow it out. My wife was by my side, all the mother awake in her bosom.

Another wail reached us from a thicket at one corner of the lawn. "There it is!" Ethelwyn cried, as the feeble light of the lantern fell on a dark bundle under a bush—the poor baby of some tramp, rolled up in a dirty, ragged shawl and tied round with a bit of string. It gave another pitiful wail, and Ethelwyn caught it up and ran off to the house with it, up to her own room where the fire was not yet out.

"Run to the kitchen, Harry, and get some hot water."

By the time I returned with the hot water, she had taken off the child's covering, and was sitting with it wrapped in a blanket, before the fire. The little thing was as cold as a stone, and now silent and motionless. We had found it just in time. It was a girl— not more than a few weeks old, we agreed. Her little heart was still beating feebly, and we had every hope of her recovery. And we were not disappointed, for she began to move her little legs and arms with short, convulsive movements.

"Do you know where the dairy is, Harry?" asked my wife. "Bring a little of this night's milk and some more hot water. I've got some sugar here. I wish we had a bottle."

I executed her commands faithfully. By the time I returned, the child was lying on her lap, clean and dry. Ethelwyn went on talking to her, and praising her as if she had not only been the finest specimen of mortality in the world, but her own child to boot. She got her to take a few spoonfuls of milk and water, and then the little thing fell fast asleep.

She gave me the child, and going to a wardrobe in the room, brought out some night things and put them on her. I could not understand in the least why the sleeping darling must be endued with a little chemise and flannel and nightgown, and I do not know what all, requiring a world of nice care, and a hundred turnings to and fro, when it would have slept just as well (and I think much more comfortably) if laid in soft blankets and well covered over. I had never ventured to interfere with any of my own children, devoutly believing that there must be some hidden feminine wisdom in the whole process. But now that I had begun to question, I found that my opportunity had long gone by, if I had ever had one.

We went to bed again, and the forsaken child lay in Ethelwyn's bosom. So we had another child in the house, and nobody else knew anything about it. The household had never been disturbed by the going and coming. We had a good laugh over the whole matter, and then Ethelwyn fell to crying. "Pray for the poor thing, Harry," she sobbed.

I knelt down, and said, "O Lord our Father, this is as much Thy child and as certainly sent to us as if she had been born of us. Help us to keep the child for Thee. Take Thou care of Thy own, and teach us what to do with her, and how to order our ways toward her."

Then I said to Ethelwyn, "I dare say the little thing will sleep till morning, and I am sure I shall if she does. Good night, my love. You are a true mother."

"I am half asleep already, Harry. Good night," she returned.

I knew nothing more about anything till I woke in the morning, except that I had a dream. I found myself in a pleasant field full of daisies and white clover. The sun was setting. The wind was going one way and the shadows another. I saw a long, rather narrow stone lying a few yards from me. I wondered how it could have come there, for there were no mountains or rocks near—the field was part of a level country. I sat astride it and watched the setting of the sun. Somehow I fancied that its light was more sorrowful than the light of the setting sun should be, and I began to feel very heavy at heart. No sooner had the last brilliant spark of its light vanished, than I felt the stone under me begin to move. With the inactivity of a dreamer, however, I did not care to rise, but wondered only what would come next. My seat, after several strange tumbling motions, seemed to rise into the air a little way, and then I found that I was astride a gaunt, bony horse, a skeleton horse almost, only he had gray skin on him. He began, apparently with pain, as if his joints were all but too stiff to move, to go forward in the direction in which he found himself.

I kept my seat. Indeed, I never thought of dismounting—I was going on to meet what might come. Slowly, feebly, trembling at every step, the strange steed went; and as he went his joints seemed to become less stiff, and he went a little faster. The pleasant field vanished, and we were on the borders of a moor. Straight forward the horse carried me, and the moor grew very rough, and he went stumbling dreadfully, but always recovering himself. We reached a low, broken wall, over which he half walked, half fell into what was plainly a neglected ancient graveyard. The mounds were low and covered with rank grass. In some parts, hollows had taken the place of mounds. Gravestones lay in every position except the level or the upright, and broken masses of monuments were scattered about. My horse bore me into the midst of it, and there, slow and stiff as he had risen, he lay down again.

Once more I was astride a long narrow stone—an ancient gravestone (which I knew well) in a certain Sussex churchyard—the top of it carved into the rough resemblance of a human skeleton, that of a man, tradition said, who had been killed by a serpent that came out of a bottomless pool in the next field. How long I sat there I do not know, but at last the dawn grew against the horizon. But it was a wild dreary dawn, a blot of gray first, which then stretched into long lines of dreary yellow and gray, looking more like a blasted and withered sunset than a fresh sunrise. And well it suited that waste, wide, deserted churchyard—if churchyard I ought to call it where no church was to be seen, only a vast hideous square of graves.

I took special notice of one old grave, the flat stone of which had been broken in two and sunk in the middle. The crack in the middle closed, then widened again as the two halves of the stone were lifted up and flung outward, like the two halves of a folding door. From the grave rose a little child, smiling such perfect contentment as if he had just come from kissing his mother. His little arms had flung the stones apart, and they remained outspread for a moment as if blessing the sleeping people. Then he came toward me with the same smile and took my hand. I rose and he led me away over another broken wall toward the hill that lay before us. And as we went, the sun came nearer; the pale yellow bars flushed into orange and rosy red, till at length the edges of the clouds were swept with an agony of golden light which even my dreamy eyes could not endure, and I awoke weeping for joy.

This woke my wife who asked in some alarm, "What is the matter?"

So I told her my dream, and how in my sleep my gladness had overcome me.

"It was this little darling that set you dreaming so," she said, and turning, put the baby in my arms.

FOUR

THE NEW BABY

I will not attempt to describe the astonishment of the members of our household as the news of the child spread. Charlie was heard shouting across the stableyard to his brother, "Harry! Harry! Mamma has a new baby. Isn't it jolly?"

"Where did she get it?"

"In the parsley bed, I suppose," answered Charlie, and was nearer right than usual.

Every one of our family hugged her first, and then asked questions. (And that, I say, is the right way of receiving every good gift of God.)

The truth soon became known over the parish and then, strange to relate, we began to receive visits of condolence. How that baby was frowned upon, and how it had heads shaken over it, just because she was not Ethelwyn's baby!

"Of course, you'll give the information to the police," said one of my brethren who had the misfortune to be a magistrate as well.

"Why?" I asked.

"Why! That they may discover the parents, to be sure."

"Wouldn't it be as hard a matter to prove the parentage, as it would be easy to suspect it?" I asked. "And just think what it would be to give the baby to a woman who not only did not want her, but who was not her mother. If her own mother came to claim her now, I don't say I would refuse her, but I should think twice about giving her up, after the mother had abandoned her for a whole night in the open air. In fact, I don't want the parents."

"But you don't want the child."

"How do you know that?"

"Oh! Of course, if you want to have an orphan asylum of your own, no one has the right to interfere. But you ought to consider other people."

"That is just what I thought I was doing," I answered.

He went on without heeding my reply, "We shall all be having babies left at our doors, and some of us are not so fond of them as you are. Remember, you are your brother's keeper."

"And my sister's too," I answered. "And if the question lies between keeping a big burly brother like you, and a tiny, wee sister like that, I venture to choose for myself."

"She ought to go to the workhouse," said the magistrate—a friendly, good-natured enough man in ordinary—and rising, he took his hat and departed. (This man had no children, so he was not so much to blame.)

Some of Ethelwyn's friends were no less positive about their duty. I happened to go into the drawing room during the visit of Miss Bowdler.

"But my dear Mrs. Walton," she was saying, "soon all the tramps in England will be leaving babies at your door."

"The better for the babies," I interposed, laughing.

"Depend upon it, you'll repent it."

"I hope I shall never repent of anything but what is bad."

"It's not a thing to be made game of!"

"Certainly not. The baby shall be treated with the utmost respect in this house."

This lady was one of my oldest parishioners, and took liberties for which she had no justification, with an unhesitating belief in the superior rectitude of whatever came into her own head. When she was gone, my wife said, with a half-anxious and half-comic look, "But it *would* be rather alarming if this were to get abroad. We couldn't go out the door without being in danger of stepping on another abandoned baby."

"He who sent us this one can surely prevent any more from coming than He wants to come. If you believe that God sent this one, that is enough for the present. If He should send another, we should know that we had to take it in."

Before three months had passed, even Miss Bowdler had to admit that Theodora—for we turned the name of my youngest daughter upside down for her—"was a proper child." To none, however, did she seem to bring so much delight as to Constance. Oftener than not, when I went into Connie's room, I found the sleepy useless little thing lying beside her on the bed, and her staring at the baby with such loving eyes! How it began, I do not know, but it came at last to be called "Connie's Dora" or "Miss Connie's baby" all over the house, and nothing pleased Connie better. Not till she saw this did her old nurse take quite kindly to the infant. She had regarded her as an interloper who had no right to the tenderness which was lavished upon her. However, she had no sooner given in than the baby began to grow dear to her as well.

But before Theodora was three months old, anxious thoughts began to intrude into my mind, all centering round the question: in what manner was the child to be brought up?

FIVE

TALES OF TWO BOYS

During all this time Connie made no very perceptible recovery—of her bodily powers, I mean—for her heart and mind advanced remarkably. We continued to hold our Sunday evening assemblies in her room.

One evening I read to them the story of the Boy Jesus in the temple. I sought to make the story more real to them by dwelling a little on the growing fears of His parents as they went from group to group of their friends, tracing back the road toward Jerusalem, and asking every fresh company they knew if they had seen their Boy, till at length they were in great trouble when they could not find Him even in Jerusalem. Then came the delight of His mother when she did find Him at last, and His answer to what she said.

At that point Wynnie said, "That has always troubled me, Papa. I feel as if Jesus spoke unkindly to His mother when He said that to her."

I read again for them the words, "How is it that ye sought Me? Wist ye not that I must be about My Father's business?" And I sat silent for a while.

"Why don't you speak, Papa?" said Harry.

"I am sitting wondering at myself, Harry," I said. "I remember quite well that those words troubled me once as they now trouble you. But when I read them over now, they seemed to me so lovely that I could hardly read them aloud. I can hardly see now the hurt or offense the words gave me. I understand them now, and I did not understand them then. I once took them as uttered with a

30

tone of reproof; now I hear them as uttered with a tone of loving surprise."

"But how could He be surprised at anything?" said Connie. "If He was God, He must have known everything."

"He tells us Himself that He did not know everything. He said once that even He did not know one particular thing—only the Father knew it."

"But how could that be if He is God?"

"Since Jesus was a real man, and no mere appearance of a man, is it any wonder that, with a heart full to the brim of the love of God, He should be for a moment surprised—surprised that His mother should not have taken it as a matter of course that if He was not with her, He must be doing something His Father wanted Him to do? For His answer means just this: 'Why did you look for Me? Didn't you know that I must of course be doing something My Father had given Me to do?' A good many things had passed before then, which ought to have been sufficient to make Mary conclude that her missing Boy must be about God's business somewhere. If her heart had been as full of God and God's business as His was, she would not have been in the least uneasy about Him. And here is the lesson of His whole life: it was all His Father's business."

"But we have so many things to do that are not His business," said Wynnie, with a sigh of oppression.

"Not one, my darling. If anything is not His business, you not only do not have to do it, but you ought not to do it."

"I wish He would tell me something to do," said Charlie. "Wouldn't I do it!"

I made no reply, but waited for an opportunity which I was pretty sure was at hand, while I carried the matter a little further.

"But listen to this, Wynnie," I said. " 'And He went down with them, and came to Nazareth, and was subject unto them.' Was that not His Father's business too? Was it not also doing the business of His Father in heaven to honor His father and His mother, though He knew that His days would not be long in that land? But I am afraid I have wearied you children, and so, Charlie, my boy, perhaps you should go to bed."

But Charlie was very comfortable on the rug before the fire, and did not want to go. First one shoulder went up, and then the other, and the corners of his mouth went down, as if to keep the balance true, and he did not move to go. I gave him a few moments to recover himself, but, as the black frost still endured, I thought it was time to hold up a mirror to him. (When he was a very little boy, he was much in the habit of getting out of temper, and then as now, he made a face that was hideous to behold. To cure him of this, I used to make him carry a little mirror about his neck that it might be always at hand for showing him to himself—a sort of artificial conscience.)

"Charlie," I said, "a little while ago you were wishing that God would give you something to do. And now when He does, you refuse at once, without even thinking about it."

"How do you know that God wants me to go to bed?" said Charlie, with something of surly impertinence.

"I know that God wants you to do what I tell you, and to do it pleasantly. Do you think the Boy Jesus would have put on such a face as that—I wish I had the little mirror to show it to you—when His mother told Him it was time to go to bed?"

And now Charlie began to look ashamed. I left the truth to work in him, because I saw it was working. Had I not seen that, I should have compelled him to go at once, that he might learn the majesty of law. I went on talking to the others. In the space of not more than one minute, he rose and came to me, looking both good and ashamed, and held up his face to kiss me, saying, "Good night, Papa." I bade him good night, and kissed him more tenderly than usual, that he might know all was right between us. I required no formal apology, no begging of my pardon, as some parents think right. It seemed enough to me that his heart was turned. For it is a terrible thing to risk changing humility into humiliation.

SIX

THEODORA

On the following Monday morning I set out to visit one or two people whom the severity of the weather had kept from church on Sunday. The last severe frost of the season was possessing the earth. The sun was low in the wintry sky, and a very cold mist up in the air hid it from the earth. I was walking along a path in a field close by a hedge, and as I was getting over a stile, whom should I see in the next field along the footpath, but Miss Bowdler? I prepared myself to meet her in the strength of good humor.

"Good morning, Miss Bowdler," I said.

"Good morning, Mr. Walton," she returned. "I am afraid you thought me impertinent the other week—but you know by this time it is only my way."

"As such I take it," I answered, with a smile.

She did not seem quite satisfied that I did not defend her from her own accusation. But, as it was a just one, I could not do so. Therefore she went on to repeat the offense by way of justification.

"It was all for Mrs. Walton's sake. You ought to consider her, Mr. Walton. She has quite enough to do with that dear Connie, who is likely to be an invalid all her days—too much to take the trouble of a beggar's brat as well."

"Has Mrs. Walton been complaining to you about it, Miss Bowdler?" I asked.

"Oh, dear, no!" she answered. "She is far too good to complain

33

of anything. That's just why her friends must look after her a bit, Mr. Walton."

"Then I beg you won't speak disrespectfully of my little Theodora."

"Oh, dear me! No. Not at all. I don't speak disrespectfully of her."

"Even amongst the class of which she comes, 'a beggar's brat' would be regarded as bad language."

"I beg your pardon, I'm sure, Mr. Walton! If you will take offense. . . . "

"I do take offense. And you know there is One who has given especial warning against offending the little ones."

Miss Bowdler walked away in high displeasure—let me hope in conviction of sin as well. (She did not appear in church for the next two Sundays. Then she came again, but called very seldom at the Hall after this. I believe my wife was not sorry.)

Before I reached home I had at last a glimpse of the right way of bringing up Theodora. I found my wife in Connie's room and asked Ethelwyn to walk out with me.

"I can't just this moment," she answered, "for there is no one at liberty to stay with Connie."

"Oh, never mind me, Mamma," said Connie, cheerfully. "Theodora will take care of me." And she looked fondly at the child fast asleep at her side.

"There!" I said. And both looked up surprised, for neither knew what I meant. "I will tell you afterward," I said, laughing. "Come along."

Ethel put on her hooded cloak, and we went out together. I told her about Miss Bowdler, and what she had said. Ethelwyn was very angry at her impertinence.

"She seems to think," she said, "that she was sent into the world to keep other people right instead of herself. I am very glad you set her down."

"Oh, I don't think there's much harm in her," I returned, which was easy generosity, seeing my wife was taking my part. "Indeed, I am not sure that we are not both considerably indebted to her, for it was after I met her that a thought came into my head as to how we ought to raise Theodora."

"Still troubling yourself about that?"

"There's one thing we have both made up our minds about, that there is to be no concealment with the child. God's fact must be known by her. It would be cruel to keep the truth from her, even if it were not sure to come upon her with a terrible shock some day. She must know from the first that she came out of the shrubbery. That's settled, is it not?"

"Certainly."

"Now, are we bound to bring her up exactly as our own, or are we not?"

"We are bound to do as well for her as for our own."

"Assuredly. So here is my proposition: to bring up little Theodora as a servant to Constance."

My wife laughed. "Well," she said, "for one who says so much about not thinking of the morrow, you do look rather far forward."

"Not with any anxiety, however, if only I know that I am doing right."

"But just think—the child is only about three months old."

"Well, Connie will be none the worse that she is being trained for her. I don't say that she is to commence her duties at once."

"But Connie may be at the head of a house of her own long before that."

"The training won't be lost to the child though. But I fear that Connie will never be herself again, for Turner does not give much hope."

"Oh! Harry, Harry, don't say so. I can't bear it. To think of the darling child lying like that all her life!"

"It is sad, indeed, but no such awful misfortune, surely. Haven't you seen the growth of that child's nature since her accident? Ten times rather would I have her lying there, such as she is, than have her well and strong and silly."

"Yes, but she needn't have been like that. Wynnie never will."

"Well, God does all things not only well, but best, absolutely best. But just think what it would be in any circumstances to have a maid that had begun to wait upon her from the first days that she was able to toddle after something to fetch."

"Won't it be like making a slave of her?"

"Won't it be like giving her a divine freedom from the first? The lack of service is the ruin of humanity."

"But we can't train her then like one of our own."

"Why not? Could we not give her all the love and all the teaching?"

"Because it would not be fair to give her the education of a

35

lady, and then make a servant of her."

"You forget that the service would be part of her training from the first, and she would know no change of position in it. When we tell her that she was found in the shrubbery, we will add that we think God sent her to take care of Constance. You cannot have perfect service except from a lady. It is not education that unfits for service—it is the want of it. Connie loves the child; the child will love Connie and find delight in serving her like a little cherub. Train Theodora as a holy child-servant, and there will be no need to restrain any impulse of wise affection from pouring itself forth upon her. We would then love and honor her far more than if we made her just like one of our own."

"But what if she should turn out utterly unfit for it?"

"Ah! Then would come an obstacle. But it will not come till that discovery is made."

"But if we should be going wrong all the time?"

"Now there comes the kind of care that never troubles me. We ought always to act on the ideal—it is the only safe ground of action."

"Well, I will think about it, Harry. There is time enough."

"Plenty. And if a thing be good, the more you think about it, the better it will look. Its real nature will go on coming out and showing itself."

Only two days later my wife said to me, "I am more than reconciled to your plan, Harry. It seems to me delightful."

SEVEN

AN INVITATION

I have not mentioned Weir or my sister in connection with the accident, and for a very good reason—I had given them both a long holiday. Martha had been ill, and because there was some fear for her lungs, a winter in the south of France had been strongly recommended. They had decided to go (partly at my insistence), and had left in October, before the accident. My sister had grown almost quite well by the beginning of the following April, and I was not sorry to think that I should soon have a little more leisure for my small literary pursuits—to my own enrichment, and consequently, to the good of my parishioners and friends.

In the beginning of that same April, I received a letter from an old college friend of mine. His name was David Shepherd—a good name for a clergyman. As soon as I had read the letter, I went to find my wife.

"Here is Shepherd," I said to her, "with a clerical sore throat, and forced to give up his duty for at least a long summer. He asks me whether, as I have a good curate, it might not suit me to take my family to his place in his absence. He assures me I should like it, and that it would do us all good. His house, he says, is large enough to hold us, and he knows I should not like to be without duty wherever I was. And so on. Read the letter for yourself, and turn it over in your mind. Weir will come back so fresh and active that it will be no oppression to him to take the duty here. I will run and ask Turner whether it would be safe to move Connie, and whether the sea air would be good for her."

"One would think you were only twenty, Harry, you make up your mind so quickly and are in such a hurry."

The fact was, a vision of the sea had rushed in upon me. It was many years since I had seen the sea, and the thought of looking on it once more, in its most glorious show—the Atlantic itself, with nothing between us and America but the round of the ridgy water—had excited me so that my wife's reproof (if reproof it was) was quite necessary to bring me to my usually quiet and sober senses. I laughed, begged her pardon, and set off to see Turner.

"What do you think, Turner?" I said, and told him the case.

He looked rather grave. "When would you think of going?" he asked.

"About the beginning of June."

"Nearly two months," he said, thoughtfully. "And Miss Connie was not the worse for getting on the sofa yesterday? And no increase of pain since?"

"No. And no again."

He thought again. Although young, he was a careful man. "It is a long journey."

"She could make it by easy stages."

"It would certainly do her good to breathe the sea air and have such a thorough change in every way. I think, if you can get her up every day between now and then, we shall be justified in trying it at least. The sooner you get her out-of-doors the better too, but the weather is scarcely fit for that yet."

"Could you manage, supposing we make the experiment, to accompany us the first stage or two?"

"Very likely. I cannot tell beforehand."

I returned to my wife and found her in Connie's room. "Well, my dear," I said, "what do you think of it?"

"Of what?" she asked.

"Why, of Shepherd's letter, of course," I answered.

"I've been ordering the dinner since, Harry."

"The dinner!" I returned, with some show of contempt, for I knew my wife was only teasing me. "What's the dinner to the Atlantic?"

"What do you mean by the Atlantic, Papa?" said Connie, from whose roguish eyes I could see that her mother had told her all about it, and that she would get up, if only she could.

"The Atlantic, my dear, is the name given to that portion of the waters of the globe which divides Europe from America. I will fetch you the *Universal Gazetteer,* if you would like to consult it on the subject."

"O Papa!" laughed Connie. "You know what I mean."

"Yes, and you know what I mean too, you squirrel!"

"But you really do mean, Papa," she said, "that you will take me to the Atlantic?"

"If you will only oblige me by getting well enough to go as soon as possible."

The poor child half rose on her elbow, but sank back again with a moan, which I took for a cry of pain. I was beside her in a moment. "You have hurt yourself!"

"Oh, no, Papa. I felt for the moment as if I could get up if I liked. But I soon found that I hadn't any back or legs. Oh! What a plague I am to you!"

"On the contrary, you are the nicest doll in the world, Connie. One always knows where to find you."

She half laughed and half cried, and the two halves made a very bewitching whole.

"But," I went on, "I mean to try whether you won't bear moving. One thing is clear, I can't go without it. Do you think you could be got on the sofa today without hurting you?"

"I am sure I could, Papa. I feel better today. Mamma, do send for Susan, and get me up before dinner."

When I went in later, I found her lying on the couch, propped up with pillows, and looking out the window over the lawn at the back of the house. A smile hovered about her bloodless lips, and the blue-gray of her eyes looked sunny. Her white face showed the whiter because her dark brown hair was all about it.

"I have been trying to count the daisies on the lawn," she said.

"What a sharp sight you must have, child!"

"I see them all as clear as if they were enameled on that table before me."

I was not so anxious to get rid of the daisies as some people are. Neither did I keep the grass quite so close shaved.

"But," she went on, "I could not count them, for it gave me the fidgets in my feet. Isn't it wonderful?"

"Enough to go on my knees and thank God. I take it as a sign of the beginning of your recovery."

She lay very still. Only the tears rose slowly and lay shimmering in her eyes. "O Papa!" she said. "To think of ever walking out with you again, and feeling the wind on my face!"

"I think you might have half that pleasure at once," I answered.

I opened the window, let the spring air gently move her hair for one moment, and then shut it again. Connie breathed deep, and said after a little pause, "I had no idea how delightful it was. To think that I have been in the way of breathing that every moment for so many years, and have never thought about it!"

"I suspect we shall find someday that the loss of the human paradise consists chiefly in the closing of our eyes, that far more of it than people think remains about us still, only we are so filled with foolish desires and evil cares, that we cannot see or hear, cannot even smell or taste the pleasant things around us. Shall I tell you what such a breath of fresh air makes me think of?"

"It comes to me," said Connie, "like forgiveness when I was a little girl and was naughty. I used to feel just like that."

"Once when I was a young man, long before I saw your mamma, I had gone out for a long walk along some high downs. I had been working rather hard at Cambridge, and the life seemed to be all gone out of me. Though my holidays had come, they did not feel quite like the holidays. Even when walking along those downs, with the scents of sixteen grasses in my brain, with just enough of a wind to stir them up and set them in motion, I could not feel at all. I remembered something of what I had used to feel in such places, but instead of believing in that, I doubted now whether it had not been all a trick.

"I was walking along with the sea behind me. It was a warm, cloudy day—no sunshine. All at once I turned, and there lay the gray sea, but not as I had seen it last. Now it was dotted, spotted, and splashed all over with drops, pools, and lakes of light, of all shades of depth, from a light shimmer of tremulous gray through a translucent green half-light. There was no sun on me, but there were breaks in the clouds over the sea, and I could see the long lines of the sun rays descending on the waters like rain. I questioned the past no more. The present seized upon me, and I knew that the past was true, and that nature was more lovely, more awful in her loveliness, than I could grasp. It was a lonely place! I fell on my knees, and worshiped the God who made the glory and my soul."

While I spoke Connie's tears had been flowing quietly.

"And Mamma and I were making fun while you were seeing such things as those!" she said, pitifully.

"You didn't hurt them one bit, my darling—neither Mamma nor you. Your merriment only made me enjoy it more. And, Connie, I hope you will see the Atlantic before long."

"O Papa! Do you think we shall really go?"

"I do. I am going to write to Shepherd, my dear, that I will take his parish in hand. If I cannot go myself, I will find someone, so that he need not be anxious."

EIGHT

CONNIE'S DREAM

Dr. Turner, being a good mechanic as well as surgeon, proceeded to invent and construct a kind of litter. It could be placed in our carriage for Connie to lie on, and from that lifted and placed in the railway carriage. He had repeatedly laid Connie on it before he was satisfied that the arrangement was successful. But at length she declared it was perfect, and that she would not mind being carried across the Arabian Desert on a camel's back with that under her.

As the season advanced she continued to improve. I shall never forget the first time she was carried out on the lawn. If you can imagine an infant coming into the world capable of the observation and delight of a child of eight or ten, you will have some idea of how Connie received the new impressions of everything around her. They were almost too much for her at first, however. She who used to scamper about like a wild thing on her pony now found the delight of a breath of wind almost more than she could bear. There on the lawn she closed her eyes, and a smile flickered about her mouth, and two great tears crept softly out from under her eyelids and sank down her cheeks.

She lay so that she faced a rich tract of gently receding upland, plentifully wooded to the horizon's edge. Through the wood peeped the white and red houses of a little hamlet, with the square tower of its church rising above the trees. It was morning in early summer, when the leaves were not quite full-grown, and their shining green was as pure as the blue of the sky. The air was

42

warm, with no touch of bitterness, and it filled the lungs with the reviving as of a draught of cold water. A lark was scattering bright beads of ringing melody straight down upon our heads. A little stream scampered down the slope of the lawn from a well in the stableyard. White clouds floated in the majesty of silence across the blue deeps of the heavens.

We had fastened the carriage umbrella to Connie's sofa, so that it should shade her. "Papa," said Connie at length, and I was beside her in a moment. Her face looked almost glorified with delight: there was a hush of that awe upon it which is perhaps one of the deepest kinds of delight. She put out her thin white hand, took hold of a button of my coat, drew me down toward her, and said in a whisper, "Don't you think God is here, Papa?"

"Yes, I do, my darling," I answered.

"Doesn't He enjoy this?"

"Yes, my dear. He wouldn't make us enjoy it if He did not. It would be to deceive us to make us glad and blessed, if our Father did not care about it or how it came to us. At least it would amount to making us no longer His children."

"I am so glad you think so. I shall enjoy it so much more now." She could hardly finish her sentence, but burst out sobbing, so we left her to quiet herself. The emotion passed off in a summer shower, and soon her face was shining just like a wet landscape after the sun comes out. In a little while, she was merry—merrier than ever before.

"Look at that comical sparrow," she said. "Look how he cocks his head first on one side and then on the other. Does he want us to see him? Is he bumptious or what?"

"I hardly know, my dear. I think sparrows are like schoolboys, and I suspect that if we understood the one class thoroughly, we should understand the other. But I confess I do not yet understand either."

"Perhaps you will when Charlie and Harry are old enough to go to school," said Connie.

"It is my only chance of making any true acquaintance with the sparrows," I answered. "Look at them now!" I exclaimed, as a little crowd of them suddenly appeared and exploded in unintelligible excitement. After some fluttering of wings and pecking, they all vanished except two which walked about in a dignified manner, apparently trying to ignore each other.

"I think it was a political meeting of some sort," said Connie, as she laughed merrily.

"Well, they have this advantage over us," I answered, "that they get through their business with considerably greater expedition than we get through ours."

A short silence followed, during which Connie lay contemplating everything. "What do you think we girls are like, then, Papa?" she asked at length. "Don't say you don't know, now."

"I ought to know something more about you than I do about schoolboys. And I think I do know a little about girls, though they puzzle me a good deal sometimes. I know what a greathearted woman is, Connie."

"You can't help doing that, Papa," interrupted Connie, adding with her old roguishness, "but you mustn't pass yourself off for only knowing that. By the time Dora is grown up, your skill will be tried."

"I hope I shall understand her then, and you too, Connie."

A shadow, just like the shadow of one of those white clouds above us, passed over her face, and she said, trying to smile, "I shall never grow up, Papa. If I live, I shall only be a girl, at best— a creature you can't understand."

"On the contrary, Connie, I think I understand you almost as well as I do Mamma. But there isn't so much to understand yet as there will be."

Her merriment returned. "Tell me what girls are like, then, or I shall sulk all day because you say there isn't so much in me as in Mamma."

"Well, if boys are like sparrows, then girls are like swallows. Did you ever watch them before rain, Connie, skimming about over the lawn but never alighting? You never see them grubbing after worms. Nothing less than things with wings like themselves will satisfy them. They will be obliged to the earth only for a little mud to build themselves nests with. For the rest, they live in the air, and on the creatures of the air. And then, when they fancy the air begins to send little shoots of cold through their warm feathers, they vanish. They won't stand it. They're off to a warmer climate, and you never know till you find they're not there anymore. There, Connie!"

"I don't know, Papa, whether you are making game of us or not. If you are not, then I wish all you say were quite true of us. If you are, then I think it is quite like you to be satirical."

"I am no believer in satire, Connie. And I didn't mean any.

The swallows are lovely creatures, and there would be no harm if the girls were a little steadier than the swallows. Further satire than that I am innocent of."

"I don't mind that much, Papa. Only I'm steady enough—and no thanks to me for it," she added with a sigh.

"Connie," I said, "it's all for the sake of your wings that you're kept in your nest."

She did not stay out long this first day, but the next morning she was brighter and better, and longing to get up and go out again. When she was once more on the lawn, in the midst of the world of light, she said to me, "Papa, I had such a strange dream last night. It was dreadful at first, and delightful afterward. I dreamed I was lying quite still, without breathing even, with my hands straight down by my sides and my eyes closed. I knew that if I opened them I should see nothing but the inside of the lid of my coffin. I did not mind it much at first, for I was very quiet, and not uncomfortable. Everything was as silent as it should be, for I was ten feet under the surface of the earth in the churchyard. Old Rogers was not far from me on one side, and that was a comfort, only there was a thick wall of earth between. But as the time went on, I began to get uncomfortable. I could not help thinking how long I should have to wait for the resurrection. Somehow I had forgotten all that you teach us about that. Perhaps it was a punishment—the dream—for forgetting it."

"Silly child! Your dream is far better than your reflections."

"Well, I got very tired, and wanted to get up, oh, so much! I tried, but I could not move, and at last I burst out crying. I was ashamed of crying in my coffin, but I couldn't bear it any longer. I thought I was quite disgraced, for everybody was expected to be perfectly quiet and patient down there. But the moment I began to cry, I heard a sound—the sound of spades and pickaxes. And then—it was so strange—I was dreadfully frightened at the idea of the light and the wind, and of the people seeing me in my coffin and my nightdress. And I tried to persuade myself that it was somebody else they were digging for, or that they were only going to lay another coffin over mine. And I thought that if it was you, Papa, I shouldn't mind how long I lay there, for I shouldn't feel a bit lonely. But the sounds came on, nearer and nearer, and at last a pickaxe struck with a blow that jarred me through, upon the lid right over my head.

" 'Here she is, poor thing!' I heard a sweet voice say

" 'I am so glad we've found her,' said another voice.

" 'She couldn't bear it any longer,' said a third voice, more pitiful than the others. 'I heard her first,' it went on. 'I was away up in Orion, when I thought I heard a woman crying that oughtn't to be crying. And I stopped and listened. And I heard her again. Then I knew that it was one of the buried ones, and that she had been buried long enough, and was ready for the resurrection. So as any business can wait except that, I flew here and there till I fell in with the rest of you.'

"They cleared away the earth and stones from the top of my coffin. And I lay trembling and expecting every moment to be looked at, like a thing in a box as I was. But they lifted me, coffin and all, out of the grave, then they set it down, and I heard them taking the lid off. But after the lid was off, it did not seem to make much difference to me. I could not open my eyes, but I heard whispering about me. Then I felt warm, soft hands washing my face, and then I felt wafts of wind coming on my face, and thought they came from the waving of wings. And when they had washed my eyes, the air came on them, so sweet and cool! And I opened them, and I was lying here on this couch, with butterflies and bees flitting and buzzing about me, the brook singing somewhere near me, and a lark up in the sky. But there were no angels—only plenty of light and wind and living creatures. And I don't think I ever knew before what happiness meant. Wasn't it a resurrection, Papa, to come out of the grave into such a world as this?"

"Indeed it was, my darling, and a very beautiful and true dream. There is no need for me to moralize it to you. No dream of such delight can come up to the sense of fresh life and being that we shall have, when we put on the higher body, after this one is worn out and cast aside. The very ability of the mind to dream such things, whether of itself or by some inspiration of the Almighty, is proof of our capacity for them—a proof, I think, that for such things we were made. Here comes the chance for faith in God, the confidence in His being and perfection, that He would not have made us capable without meaning to fill that capacity. If He is able to make us capable, that is the harder half done already. The other He can easily do. And if He is love, He will do it. You should thank God for that dream, Connie."

"I was afraid to do that, Papa."

"That is to fear that there is one place to which you might flee, where God would not find you—the most terrible of all thoughts."

"Where do you mean, Papa?"

"Dreamland, my dear. If it is right to thank God for a beautiful thought—I mean a thought of strength and grace giving you fresh life and hope—then why should you be less bold to thank Him when such thoughts arise in the plainer shape of dreams?"

NINE

THE JOURNEY

For more than two months Charlie and Harry had been preparing for the journey. The moment they heard of it, they began to accumulate and pack stores both for the transit and the sojourn. First of all there was an extensive preparation of ginger beer, consisting (as I was informed in confidence) of brown sugar, ground ginger, and cold water. This store was exhausted and renewed about twelve times before the day of departure, when they remembered with dismay that they had drunk the last drop two days before, and there was none in stock.

Then there was a wonderful and more successful hoarding of marbles, carefully deposited in one of the many divisions of a huge old hair trunk, with its multiplicity of boxes and cupboards and drawers and trays and slides. In this same box was stowed also a quantity of hair—the gleanings of all the horse tails upon the premises. This was for making fishing tackle, with a vague notion on the part of Harry that it was to be employed in catching whales and crocodiles.

Then all their favorite books were stowed away in the same chest—including a packet of a dozen penny books from *Jack the Giant Killer* down to *Hop o' My Thumb*. Harry could not read these, and Charlie not very well, but they put confidence in them notwithstanding, in virtue of the red, blue, and yellow prints. Then there was a box of sawdust, a huge ball of string, a rabbit's skin, a Noah's ark, an American clock that refused to go—for all the variety of treatment they gave it—a box of lead soldiers, and twenty other things, amongst which was a huge gilt ball having an eagle of brass with outspread wings on the top of it.

Great was their consternation and dismay when they found that this trunk could not be taken with us to the station. Knowing well how little they would miss it, and with what shouts of discovery they would greet the forgotten treasure when they returned, I insisted on the lumbering article being left in peace. So that, as a man goes treasureless to his grave—whatever he may have accumulated before the fatal moment—they had to set off for the far country without chest or ginger beer—but not so desolate and unprovided for as they imagined. The abandoned treasure was forgotten the moment the few tears it had occasioned were wiped away.

It was the loveliest of mornings when we started our journey. The sun shone, the wind was quiet, and everything was glad. The swallows were twittering from the corbels of the dear old house.

"I'm sorry to leave the swallows behind," said Wynnie, as she stepped into the carriage after her mother. Connie was already there, eager and stronghearted for the journey.

We set off. Connie was delighted with everything, especially with all forms of animal life and enjoyment that we saw on the road. She seemed eager to enter into the spirit of the cows feeding in the meadows, of the donkeys eating by the roadside, of the horses we met trudging along the road with wagon or cart behind them. I sat by the coachman, so I could see Connie's face by the slightest turning of my head. A fleet of ducklings in a pool, paddling along under the convoy of the parent duck, attracted her.

"Look—look. Isn't that delicious?" she cried.

"I don't think I should like it though," said Wynnie. "To be in the water and not feel wet. Those feathers!"

"They feel it with their legs and their webby toes," said Connie. "And if you were a duck, you would feel the good of your feathers in winter, when you got into your cold morning bath."

We had to pass through the village to reach the railway station. Almost everyone was out to bid us good-by. I stopped the carriage to speak a word to one of my people, and the same instant there was a crowd of women about us. But Connie was the center of all their regards, for they hardly looked at the rest of us.

After we had again started, our ears were invaded with shouts from the post chaise behind us, in which Charlie and Harry were yelling in the exuberance of their gladness. Dora, more staid as became her years, was trying to act the matron with them in vain, and Old Nursey had too much to do with Miss Connie's baby to heed what the young gentlemen were about, so long as noise was all the mischief.

"Good-by, Marshmallows," they were shouting at the top of their voices, as if they had just been released from a prison where they had spent a wretched childhood. As it could hardly offend anybody's ears on the open country road, I allowed them to shout till they were tired, which condition fortunately arrived before we reached the station. I always sought to give them as much liberty as could be afforded them.

At the station we found Weir and my sister (looking well again) waiting to see us off. Turner was likewise there, and ready to accompany us a good part of the way. But beyond his valuable assistance in moving Connie, no occasion arose for the exercise of his professional skill. She bore the journey wonderfully, slept not infrequently, and only at the end showed herself wearied. We stopped three times on the way, first at Salisbury, where the streams running through the street delighted her. There we remained one whole day, but sent the children and Walter and the other servants (all but my wife's maid) on before us. This left us more at our ease, and at Exeter we stopped only for the night.

Here Turner left us. Connie looked a little out of spirits after his departure, but soon recovered. The next night we spent at a small town on the borders of Devonshire, which was the limit of our railway traveling. Here we remained for another whole day, for the remnant of the journey across part of Devonshire and Cornwall to the shore was a good five hours' work. We started about eleven o'clock. Connie was quite merry, for the air was thoroughly warm, and we had an open carriage with a hood. Wynnie sat opposite her mother, Dora and Eliza the maid in the rumble, and I by the coachman. The road being very hilly, we had four horses—and with four horses, sunshine, a gentle wind, hope, and thankfulness, who would not be happy?

I must have been the very happiest of the party myself. And ought I not to have been happy when all who were with me were happy? My Ethelwyn's face was bright with the brightness of a pale silvery moon that has done her harvest work and, a little weary, lifts herself again into the deeper heavens from stooping toward the earth. Wynnie's face was bright with the brightness of the morning star, ever growing pale and faint over the amber ocean that brightens at the sun's approach, for to Wynnie life looked severe and somewhat sad in its light. Connie's face was bright with the brightness of a lake in the rosy evening, content to be still and mirror the sunset.

We stopped once, and Connie begged to be carried into the parlor of the little inn, that she might see the china figures that were certain to be on the chimney piece, as indeed they were. She drank a whole tumbler of new milk before we lifted her to carry her back. Leaving, we came upon a wide high moorland country, the roads of which were lined with gorse in full golden bloom, while patches of heather all about were showing their bells, though not yet in their autumnal outburst of purple fire. Here I began to be reminded of Scotland, in which I had traveled a good deal in my younger years. The farther I went, the stronger I felt the resemblance to be. The look of the fields, the stone fences that divided them, the shape and color and materials of the houses, the aspect of the people, the feeling of the air and of the earth and sky generally, made me imagine myself in a milder and more favored Scotland. The west wind was fresh, but had none of that sharp edge which one can so often detect in otherwise warm winds blowing under a hot sun.

Though she had already traveled many miles, Connie brightened up within a few minutes after we reached this moor. And we had not gone much farther before a shout informed us that keen-eyed little Dora had discovered the Atlantic, blue and bright, through a dip in the high coast. We soon lost sight of it again, but in Connie's eyes it seemed to linger still. Their blue seemed to be the very reflection of the sea. Ethelwyn's eyes were full of it too, as she also expected the ocean. Down the winding of a gradual slope interrupted by steep descents, we approached this new chapter in our history.

We came again upon a few trees here and there, all with their tops cut off in a plane inclined upward away from the sea. For the sea winds, like a sweeping scythe, bend the trees toward the land, and keep their tops mown with their sharp rushing, keen with salt spray from the crests of the broken waves. Then we passed through some ancient villages, with streets narrow and steep and sharp-angled, that needed careful driving and the frequent pressure of the brake on the wheel.

At length we descended a sharp hill, reached the last level, drove over a bridge and down the line of the stream, over another

51

wooden drawbridge, and along the side of a canal in which lay half a dozen sloops and schooners. Then came a row of pretty cottages, then a gate and an ascent, and the sight of Charlie and Harry shouting and scampering along the top of a stone wall to meet us. A moment after, we drew up at a long porch, leading through the segment of a circle to the door of the rectory. The journey was over. We alighted in the little village of Kilkhaven, in the county of Cornwall.

TEN

KILKHAVEN

First of all, we carried Connie into her room, the best in the house, of course. She did seem tired now, and no wonder. After dinner, she fell fast asleep on the sofa, and Wynnie on the floor beside her. The drive and the sea air had had the same effect on both of them. What a wonderful satisfaction it may give to a father and mother to see this or that child asleep! When parents see their children asleep (especially if they have been suffering in any way) they breathe more freely. A load is lifted off their minds; their responsibility seems over; the children have gone back to their Father, and He alone is looking after them for a while.

Now, I had not been comfortable about Wynnie for some time. There was something amiss with her. She seemed constantly more or less dejected, as if she had something to think about that was too much for her, although I believe now that she had not quite enough to think about. She did not look quite happy, did not always meet a smile with a smile, looked almost reprovingly upon the frolics of her little brother imps. And though kindness itself when any real hurt or grief befell them, she had reverted to her old, somewhat dictatorial manner. She was service itself, only service without the smile which is the flame of the sacrifice and makes it holy. So Ethelwyn and I were both a little uneasy about her, for we did not understand her.

As I stood regarding my sleeping Wynnie, she suddenly opened her eyes and started to her feet, with the words, "I beg your pardon, Papa," looking almost guiltily round her, and putting up her hair hurriedly as if she had committed an impropriety in being caught untidy. This was a fresh sign of a condition of mind that was not healthy.

"My dear," I said, "what do you beg my pardon for? I was so pleased to see you asleep! And you look as if you thought I were going to scold you."

"O Papa," she said, laying her head on my shoulder, "I am afraid I must be very naughty. I so often feel now as if I were doing something wrong, or rather as if you would think I was doing something wrong. I am sure there must be something wicked in me somewhere, though I do not clearly know what it is. When I woke up now, I felt as if I had neglected something, and you had come to find fault with me. Is there anything, Papa?"

"Nothing whatever, my child. But you cannot be well if you feel like that."

"I am perfectly well, so far as I know. I was so cross to Dora today! Why shouldn't I feel happy when everybody else is? I must be wicked, Papa."

"My dear child," I said, "we must all pray to God for His Spirit, and then we shall feel as we ought to feel. It is not easy for anyone to tell himself how he ought to feel at any given moment, and still less to tell another how he ought to feel. Get your bonnet, Wynnie, and come out with me. We are going to explore a little of this desert island on which we have been cast."

When we left the door of the house, we went up the few steps of a stair leading to the downs. The ground underfoot was green and soft and springy, and sprinkled all over with the bright yellow flowers that live amidst the short grasses of the downs. I stood up, stretched out my arms, threw back my shoulders and my head, and filled my chest with a draught of the delicious wind. Wynnie stood apparently unmoved, thoughtful, and turning her eyes here and there.

"This makes me feel young again," I said.

"I wish it would make me feel old then," said Wynnie.

"What do you mean, my child?"

"Because then I should have a chance of knowing what it is like to feel young," she answered rather enigmatically.

I did not reply. We were walking up the brow which hid the sea from us. The smell of the down-turf was indescribable in its homely delicacy, and by the time we had reached the top, almost every sense was filled with its own delight. The top of the hill was the edge of the great shore-cliff, and the sun was hanging on the face of the mightier sky-cliff opposite. The sea stretched for visible miles and miles along the shore on either hand, its wide blue mantle fringed with lovely white wherever it met the land. The sense of space—of mighty room for life and growth—filled my soul, and I thanked God in my heart. I turned and looked at Wynnie, standing pleased but listless amidst that which lifted me into the heaven of the Presence.

"Don't you enjoy all this grandeur, Wynnie?"

"I told you I was very wicked, Papa."

"And I told you not to say so, Wynnie."

"You see I cannot enjoy it, Papa. I wonder why it is."

"I suspect it is because you haven't room, Wynnie. It is not because you are wicked, but because you do not know God well enough, and therefore your being, which can only live in Him, is 'cabined, cribbed, confined, bound in.' It is only in Him that the soul has room. The secret of your own heart you can never know, but you can know Him who knows its secret."

I paused to breathe the fragrant sea air. "Look up, my darling, see the heavens and the earth. You do not feel them, and I do not call upon you to feel them. It would be both useless and absurd to do so. But just let them look at you for a moment. Then tell me whether it must not be a blessed life that creates such a glory as this."

She stood silent for a moment, looked up at the sky, looked round on the earth, looked far across the sea to the setting sun, and then turned her eyes upon me. They were filled with tears, but whether from feeling or sorrow that she could not feel, I would not inquire. I made haste to speak again.

"Do not say it is too high for you. God made you in His own image, and therefore capable of understanding Him. For this He sent His Son, that They might come into you, and dwell with you. Till They do so, the temple of your soul is vacant. There is no light behind the veil, and no cloudy pillar over it, and the priests—your thoughts and feelings and loves and desires—moan and are troubled, for where is the work of the priests when God is not there? But do not think that I blame you, Wynnie, for feeling sad. I take it rather as the sign of large life in you—that you will not be satisfied with small things. I do not know when or how it may please God to give you the quiet of mind that you need, but it is to be had, and you must go on doing your work and trusting in God.

Tell Him to look at your sorrow. Ask Him to come and set it right, making the joy go up in your heart by His presence. Till He lays His hand on your head, you must be content to wash His feet with your tears."

Whatever the immediate occasion of her sadness, such was its only real cure. Nothing would do finally but God Himself.

We walked on together. Wynnie made me no reply, but clung to my arm. We walked a long way by the edge of the cliffs, beheld the sun go down, and then turned for home. When we reached the house, Wynnie left me, saying only, "Thank you, Papa. I think it is all true. I will try to be a better girl."

I went straight to Connie's room, where she was lying as I saw her last, looking out of her window.

"Connie," I said, "Wynnie and I have had such a treat—such a glorious sunset!"

"I've seen a little of the light of it on the waves in the bay there, but the high ground kept me from seeing the sunset itself. Did it set in the sea?"

"You do want the *General Gazetteer*, after all, Connie. Is that water the Atlantic, or is it not? And if it be, where on earth could the sun set but in it?"

"Of course, Papa. What a goose I am! But don't make game of me, *please*. I am too deliciously happy to be made game of tonight."

"I won't make game of you, my darling. I will tell you about the sunset, the colors of it, at least. This must be one of the best places in the whole world to see sunsets."

"But you had no tea, Papa. I thought you would come and have your tea with me. But you were so long that Mamma would not let me wait any longer."

"Oh, never mind the tea, my dear. But Wynnie has had none. You've a tea caddy of your own, haven't you?"

"Yes, and a teapot, and there's the kettle on the hob—for I can't do without a little fire in the evenings."

"Then I'll make some tea for Wynnie and myself, and tell you at the same time about the sunset. I never saw such colors— translucent green on the horizon, a broad band. Then came another broad band of pale rose, and above that the sky's own eternal blue. I never saw the green and blue divided and harmonized by the rose before. It was wonderful. If it is warm enough tomorrow, we will carry you out on the height, that you may see what the evening will bring."

"There are two things about sunsets," returned Connie, "that make me rather sad—about themselves, not about anything else. One thing is that we shall never, never, never see the same sunset again."

"That is true. But why should we? God does not care to do the same thing over again. When it is once done, it is done, and He goes on doing something new. For to all eternity, He never will have done showing Himself by new, fresh things. It would be a loss to do the same thing again."

"But that just brings me to my second trouble. The thing is lost. I forget it. Do what I can, I cannot remember sunsets. I try to fix them fast in my memory, but just as they fade out of the sky, so they fade out of my mind. Now, though I did not see this one, yet, after you have talked about it, I shall never forget it."

"They have their influence, and leave that far deeper than your memory—in your very being, Connie. But here comes Wynnie to see how you are. I've been making some tea for you, Wynnie, my love."

"Oh, thank you, Papa. I shall be so glad of some tea!" said Wynnie.

The same moment my wife came in. "Why didn't you send for me, Harry, to get your tea?"

"I did not deserve any, seeing I had disregarded proper times and seasons. And I knew you were busy."

"I have been superintending the arrangement of bedrooms, and the unpacking, and twenty different things," said Ethelwyn. "We shall be so comfortable! It is such a curious house! Have you had a nice walk?"

"Mamma, I never had such a walk in my life," returned Wynnie. "You would think the shore had been built for the sake of the show—just for a platform to see the sunsets. And the sea! But the cliffs will be rather dangerous for the children."

"I have just been telling Connie about the sunset. She could see something of the colors on the water, but not much more."

"O Connie, it will be so delightful to get you out! Everything is so big! And such room everywhere!" said Wynnie. "Even though," she continued thoughtfully, "it must be awfully windy in winter."

ELEVEN

MORE ABOUT KILKHAVEN

Our dining room was one story below the level at which we had entered the parsonage, for the house was built into the face of the cliff, just where it sunk nearly to the shores of the bay. At dinner, on the evening of our arrival, I kept looking from the window and saw first a little garden mostly in turf, and then a low stone wall. Beyond, over the top of the wall, was the blue water of the bay— then beyond the water, all alive with light and motion, the rocks and sand hills of the opposite side of the little bay. Not a quarter of a mile across, I could likewise see where the shore went sweeping out and away to the north, with rock after rock standing far into the water, as if gazing over the awful wild, where there was nothing to break the deathly waste between Cornwall and Newfoundland. If I moved my head a little to the right, I saw, over the top of the low wall, the slender yellow masts of a schooner. We must, I thought, be on the very harbor quay.

When I came down to breakfast in the same room the next morning, I stared. The blue had changed to yellow. The life of the water was gone. Nothing met my eyes but a wide expanse of dead sand across the bay to the hills opposite. From the look of the rocks, from the perpendicular cliffs on the coast, I had concluded that we were on the shore of a deep-water bay. It was high water then, and now I looked over a long reach of sands, on the far border of which the white fringe of the waves was visible. Beyond the fringe lay the low hill of the Atlantic. To add to my confusion, there was no schooner near the wall. I went out to look, and saw

58

in a moment how it was.

"Do you know, my dear," I said to my wife, "we are just at the mouth of that canal we saw as we came along? There are gates and a lock just outside there. The schooner that was under this window last night must have gone in with the tide. She is lying in the basin above now."

"Oh, yes, Papa," Charlie and Harry broke in together. "We saw it go up this morning. We've been out ever so long. It was so funny," Charlie went on—everything was funny with Charlie—"to see it rise up like a jack-in-the-box, and then slip into the quiet water through the other gates!"

After breakfast we had prayers as usual, and after a visit to Connie, I went out for a walk to explore the neighborhood and find the church. The day was glorious. I wandered along a green path in the opposite direction from our walk the evening before, with a fir-wood on my right hand and a belt of feathery tamarisks on my left. Behind lay gardens sloping steeply to a lower road, where a few pretty cottages stood.

Turning a corner, I came suddenly in sight of the church on the green down above me—a sheltered yet commanding situation. For, while the hill rose above it, protecting it from the east, it looked down the bay, and the Atlantic lay open before it. All the earth seemed to lie behind it, and all its gaze to be fixed on the symbol of the infinite. It stood as the church ought to stand, leading men up the mount of vision to the verge of the eternal, to send them back with their hearts full of the strength that springs from hope, by which alone the true work of the world can be done. And when I saw it, I rejoiced to think that once more I was favored with a church that had a history.

I looked about for some cottage where the sexton might live, and spied a slated roof nearly on a level with the road, a little distance in front of me. Before I reached it, however, an elderly woman came out and approached me. She was dressed in a white cap and dark-colored gown. On her face lay a certain repose which attracted me—she looked as if she had suffered but had consented to it, and therefore could smile. Her smile was near the surface, and a kind word would be enough to draw it up from the well where it lay shimmering—you could always see the smile there, whether it was born or not.

She drew near me, as if to pass me, and she would have done so had I not spoken. I think she came toward me to give me the opportunity of speaking if I wished, but she would not address me.

"Good morning," I said. "Can you tell me where to find Mr. Coombes, the sexton?"

"Well, Sir," she answered, with a gleam of the smile brightening beneath her old skin, "I be all the sexton you be likely to find this mornin'. My husband, he be gone out to see one o' Squire Tregarva's hounds as was took ill last night. So if you want to see the old church, Sir, you'll have to be content with an old woman to show you."

"I shall be quite content, I assure you," I answered.

"I have the key in my pocket, Sir, for I thought that would be what you'd be after. For mayhap, says I to myself, he be the gentleman as be come to take Mr. Shepherd's duty for him. Be ye now, Sir?"

All this was said in a slow, sweet, subdued tone, nearly of one pitch. She claimed the privilege of age with a kind of mournful gaiety, but was careful not to presume upon it, and was therefore as gentle as a young girl.

"Yes," I answered. "My name is Walton. I have come to take the place of my friend Shepherd and, of course, I want to see the church."

"Well, she be a bee-utiful old church. Some things, I think, grow more beautiful the older they grows. But it ain't us, Sir."

"I'm not so sure of that," I said. "What do you mean?"

"Well, Sir, there's my little grandson in the cottage there—he'll never be so beautiful again. Them children du be the loves. But we all grows uglier as we grows older. Churches don't seem to."

"I'm not so sure about all that," I said again.

"They did say, Sir, that I was a pretty girl once. I'm not much to look at now." And she smiled with gracious amusement. If there was any vanity left in this memory of her past loveliness, it was as sweet as the memory of old fragrance in the withered leaves of the roses.

"But it du not matter, du it, Sir? Beauty is only skin-deep."

"I don't believe that," I answered. "Beauty is as deep as the heart at least."

"Well, to be sure, my old husband du say I be as handsome in his eyes as ever I be. But I beg your pardon, Sir, for talkin' about myself. I believe it was the old church—she set us on to it."

"The old church didn't lead you into any harm then," I answered. "The beauty that is in the heart will shine out of the face again someday—be sure of that. After all, there is just the same kind of beauty in a good old face that there is in an old church. You can't say the church is so trim and neat as it was the day that the first blast of the organ filled it as with a living soul. The carving is not quite so sharp, the timbers are not quite so clean, and there is a good deal of mold and worm-eating and cobwebs about the old place. Yet both you and I think it more beautiful now than it was then. Well, it is the same with an old face. It is stained and weather-beaten and worn, but the wrinkles and the brownness can't spoil it. A light shines through it all—that of the indwelling Spirit. I wish we all grew old like the old churches."

She did not reply, but I saw in her face that she understood. We had been walking very slowly, had passed through the quaint lych-gate, and now the old woman had the key in the lock of the door, whose archway was figured and fashioned with a dozen curiously carved moldings.

TWELVE

THE OLD CHURCH

The awe that dwells in churches fell upon me as I crossed the threshold—an awe I never fail to feel, for the air of petition and of holy need seems to linger in the place. A flush of subdued glory invaded my eyes from the chancel—all the windows were of richly stained glass, and the roof of carved oak was lavishly gilded. There were carvings on the ends of the benches all along the aisle on both sides, and supporting arches of different fashion on the opposite sides. The pillars were of coarse country granite, each a single chiseled stone with chamfered sides.

Walking softly through the ancient house, I came at length into the tower, the basement of which was open and formed part of the body of the church. There hung many ropes through the holes in a ceiling above, as I would have expected, for bell-ringing was encouraged and indeed practiced by my friend Shepherd.

My guide was seated against the south wall of the tower, on a stool, I thought, or small table. While I was wandering about the church she had taken some socks and wires out of her pocket and was now knitting busily. How her needles did go! Her eyes never regarded them, however, but fixed on the slabs a yard or two from her feet, seemed to be gazing far out to sea. To try her, I took for the moment the position of an accuser.

"So you don't mind working in church?" I said.

She instantly rose. Her eyes turned from the far sea waves to my face, and light came out of them. With a smile she answered, "The church knows me, Sir."

"But what has that to do with it?"

"I don't think she minds it. We are told to be diligent in business, you know, Sir."

"Yes, but it does not say in church and out of church. You could be diligent somewhere else, couldn't you?"

As soon as I said this, I began to fear she would think I meant it. But she only smiled and said, "It won't hurt she, Sir, and my good man, who does all he can to keep her tidy, is out at toes and heels, and if I don't keep he warm he'll be laid up, and then the church won't be kep' nice till he's up again."

"But you could have sat down outside—there are some nice gravestones near—and waited till I came out."

"But what's the church for, Sir? The sun's werry hot today, and Mr. Shepherd, he say that the church is like the shadow of a great rock in a weary land. So you see, if I was to sit out in the sun, instead of comin' in here to the cool o' the shadow, I wouldn't be takin' the church at her word. It does my heart good to sit in the old church. There's a something do seem to come out o' the old walls and settle down like the cool o' the day upon my old heart that's nearly tired o' crying, and would fain keep its eyes dry for the rest o' the journey. My knitting won't hurt the church and, bein' a good deed, it's none the worse for the place. If He was to come by wi' the whip o' small cords, I wouldn't be afeard of His layin' it upo' my old back. Do you think He would, Sir?"

I made haste to reply, more delighted with the result of my experiment than I cared to let her know. "Indeed I do not. I was only talking and testing. It is only the selfish, cheating, or ill-done work that the church's Master drives away. All our work ought to be done in the shadow of the church."

"I thought you be only having a talk about it, Sir," she said, smiling her sweet old smile. "Nobody knows what this old church is to me."

"You have had a family?" I asked.

"Thirteen," she answered. "Six boys and seven maidens."

"Why, you are rich!" I returned. "And where are they all?"

"Four maidens be lying in the churchyard, Sir, and two be married, and one be down in the mill, there."

"And your boys?"

"One of them be lyin' beside his sisters—drownded afore my eyes, Sir. Three o' them be at sea, and two o' them in it."

At sea! I thought. What a wide *where*, and so vague to the

imagination! How a mother's thoughts must go roaming about the waste to find them!

"It be no wonder, be it, that I like to creep into the church with my knitting? Many's the stormy night, when my husband couldn't keep still, but would be out on the cliffs or on the breakwater, for no good in life, but just to hear the roar of the waves that he could only see by the white of them, with the balls o' foam flying in his face in the dark—many's the night I have left the house after he was gone, with this blessed key in my hand, and crept into the old church here, and sat down, and hearkened to the wind howling about the place. The church windows never rattle, Sir. Somehow, I feel safe in the church."

"But if you had sons at sea," said I, again wishing to draw her out, "it would not be of much good to you to feel safe yourself, so long as they were in danger."

"Oh! Yes it be, Sir. What's the good of feeling safe yourself but it let you know other people be safe too? It's when you don't feel safe yourself that you feel other people ben't safe."

"But," I said, "some of your sons *were* drowned, for all you say about their safety."

"Well, Sir," she answered with a sigh, "I trust they're none the less safe for that. It would be a strange thing for an old woman like me, well-nigh threescore and ten, to suppose that safety lay not in being drownded. Why, they might ha' been cast on a desert island, and wasted to skin and bone, and got home again wi' the loss of half the wits they set out with. Wouldn't that ha' been worse than being drownded right off? And that wouldn't ha' been the worst, either. The church she seemed to tell me all the time, that for all the roaring outside, there be really no danger after all. What matter if they go to the bottom? What is the bottom of the sea, Sir? You bein' a clergyman can tell that. I shouldn't ha' known it if I hadn't had boys o' my own at sea. But *you* can tell, though you ain't got none there."

She was putting her parson to his catechism. "The hollow of His hand," I said.

"I thought you would know it," she returned, with a little glow of triumph in her tone. "Well, then, that's just what the church tells me, when I come in here in the stormy night. I bring my knitting then too, for I can knit in the dark as well as in the light almost. And when they come home, if they do come home, they're none the worse that I went to the old church to pray for them.

There it goes roaring about them, poor dears, all out there—and their old mother sitting still as a stone almost in the quiet old church, a-caring for them. And then it do come across me, Sir, that God be a-sitting in His own house at home, hearing all the noise and all the roaring in which His children are tossed about in the world, watching it all, letting it drown some o' them and take them back to Him, and keeping it from going too far with others of them that are not quite ready for that same. I have my thoughts, you see, though I be an old woman, and not nice to look at."

I had come upon a genius. How nature laughs at our schools sometimes! For life is God's school, and they that will listen to the Master there will learn at God's speed. For one moment, I am ashamed to say, I was envious of Shepherd. And I repined that, now that old Rogers was gone, I had no such glorious old stained-glass window in my church to let in the eternal upon my light-thirsty soul.

"You are very nice to look at," I said. "You must not find fault with the work of God, because you would like better to be young and pretty than to be as you now are. Time and time's rents and furrows are all His making and His doing. God makes nothing ugly."

"Are you quite sure of that, Sir?"

I paused, and the thought of certain animals flashed into my mind, and I could not insist that God never made anything ugly.

"No, I am not sure," I answered. For any pretense of knowing more than I did know seemed repugnant to the spirit and mind of the Master. "But if He does," I went on to say, "it must be that we may see what it is like, and therefore not like it."

Then I turned the conversation to the sort of stool or bench on which my guide had been sitting. It was curiously carved in old oak, very much like the ends of the benches and bookboards.

"What is that you are sitting on?" I asked. "A chest?"

"It be here when we come to this place, and that be nigh fifty years agone. But what it be, you'll be better able to tell than I be, Sir."

"Perhaps a chest for holding the Communion plate in old time," I said. "But how should it then come to be banished to the tower?"

"No, Sir, it can't be that. It be some sort of ancient musical piano, I be thinking."

I stooped and saw that its lid was shaped like the cover of an organ. With some difficulty I opened it, and there was a row of huge keys, fit for the fingers of a Cyclops. I pressed upon them, one after another, but no sound followed. They were stiff to the touch, and once down, so they mostly remained until lifted again. There were a dozen little round holes in the fixed part of the top, which might afford some clue to the mystery of its former life. I glanced up at the holes in the ceiling through which the bell ropes went and spied two or three thick wires hanging through the same ceiling close to the wall, and right over the box with the keys. The vague suspicion of a discovery dawned upon me.

"Have you the key of the tower?" I asked.

"No, Sir. But I'll run home for it at once," she answered. And rising, she went out in haste.

"Run!" thought I, looking after her. "It is a word of the will and the feeling, not of the body." But I was mistaken. The dear old creature had no sooner got outside of the churchyard than she did run, and ran well too. I was on the point of starting after her, to prevent her from hurting herself, but reflected that her own judgment ought to be as good as mine.

I sat down on her seat, awaiting her reappearance, and gazed at the ceiling. There I either saw, or imagined I saw, signs of openings corresponding in number and position with those in the lid. In about three minutes the old woman returned; she was panting but not distressed, and she held a great crooked old key in her hand.

"You shouldn't run like that. I am in no hurry."

"Be you not, Sir? I thought, by the way you spoke, you be taken with a longing to get a-top o' the tower, and see all about you like. Fond as I be of the old church, I du feel sometimes as if she'd smother me, and then nothing will do but I must get at the top of the old tower. And then, what with the sun, if there be any sun, and what with the fresh air, which there always be up there, Sir— it du always be fresh up there, Sir," she repeated, "and I come back down again blessing the old church for its tower."

As she spoke she was toiling up the winding staircase after me, where there was just room enough for my shoulders to get through. As I ascended, I was thinking of what she had said. Strange to tell, the significance of the towers or spires of our churches had never been clear to me before. True, I was quite awake to their significance, at least to that of the spires, as fingers pointing ever upward to

... regions mild of calm and serene air,
Above the smoke and stir of this dim spot,
Which men call Earth.

Yet I had never thought of their symbolism as lifting one up above the church itself into a region where no church is wanted, because the Lord God Almighty and the Lamb are the temple of it. Happy church, indeed, if it destroys the need of itself by lifting men up into the eternal kingdom!

In the ascent I forgot all about the special object for which I had requested the key of the tower, and led the way myself up to the summit, and stepped out of a little door. And there, filling the west, lay the ocean beneath, with a dark curtain of storm hanging over part of its horizon. On the other side was the peaceful solid land, with its numberless shades of green, its heights and hollows, its farms and wooded vales, its scattered villages and country dwellings. Beyond lay the blue heights of Dartmoor. The old woman stood beside me, silently enjoying my enjoyment, with a smile that seemed to say, in kindly triumph, "Was I not right about the tower and the wind that dwells among its pinnacles?"

There were a good many trees in the churchyard, and as I looked down, their rich foliage hid all the graves directly below me, except a single flat stone looking up through an opening in the leaves, which seemed to have been just made for it to see the top of the tower. Upon the stone a child was playing with a few flowers, not once looking up to the tower. I turned to the eastern side, and looked over upon the church roof. It lay far below—looking very narrow and small but long, with the four ridges of four steep roofs stretching away to the eastern end.

When I turned to look down again, the little child was gone. Some butterfly fancy had seized her, and she was away. A little lamb was in her place, nibbling at the grass that grew on the side of the next mound.

Reentering by the angels' door to descend the narrow corkscrew stair, so dark and cool, I caught a glimpse of a tiny maidenhair fern growing out of the wall. I stopped and said, "I have a sick daughter at home, or I wouldn't rob your tower of this lovely little thing."

"Well, Sir, what eyes you have! I never saw the thing before. Do take it home to Miss. It'll do her good to see it. I be main sorry to hear you've got a sick maiden."

I succeeded with my knife in getting out all the roots without hurting them, and said, "She can't even sit up and must be carried everywhere."

"Poor dear! Everyone has their troubles, Sir. The sea's been mine."

She continued talking and asking kind questions about Connie as we went down the stair. Not till she opened a little door was I reminded of my first object in ascending the tower. For this door revealed a number of bells hanging in silent power in the brown twilight of the place. I entered carefully, for there were only some planks laid upon the joists to keep one's feet from going through the ceiling. My conjecture about the keys below was correct. The small iron rods I had seen hung down from this place. There were more of them hanging above, and there was yet enough mechanism remaining to prove that those keys (by means of the looped and cranked rods) had been in connection with hammers which struck the bells, so that a tune could be played upon them.

"A clever blacksmith, now," I said to myself, "could repair all this, and Shepherd could play a psalm tune to his parish when he pleased. I will see what can be done." I left the abode of the bells and descended to the church. Then I bade Mrs. Coombes good-morning (promising to visit her soon in her own house), and bore home to Connie the fern from the lofty wall.

THIRTEEN

CONNIE'S WATCHTOWER

Our "new" house was one of those that have grown, rather than being built after a straight-up-and-down model of uninteresting convenience. The builders must have had some plan—good, bad, or indifferent—but that plan they had left far behind. And now the fact that they have a history is plainly written on their aspect. These are the houses which fairies used to haunt, and hence perhaps the sense of soothing comfort which pervades us when we cross their thresholds. You do not know, the moment you have cast a glance about the hall, where the dining room, drawing room, and best bedroom are. You have it all to find out. It had formerly been a kind of manor house, though the germ cell of it was a cottage of the simplest sort. It had grown by the addition of other cells, till it had reached the development in which we found it.

The dining room was almost on the level of the shore—indeed, some of the flat stones that coped the low wall in front of it were thrown into the garden by the waves before the next winter. But Connie's room looked out on a little flower garden almost on the downs, sheltered only a little by the rise of a short grassy slope above it. This, however, left open the prospect from her window down the bay and out to sea.

To reach this room I had to go up but one simple cottage stair, for the door of the house entered on the first floor. The room had a large bay window, and in this window Connie was lying on her couch, with the lower sash wide open. There the breeze entered,

69

smelling of seaweed tempered with sweet grasses and the wall-flowers and stocks that were in the little plot under it. I thought I could see an improvement in her already. Certainly she looked very happy.

"O Papa!" she said. "Isn't it delightful?"

"What is, my dear?"

"Oh, everything. The wind, and the sky, and the sea, and the smell of the flowers. Do look at that seabird. His wings are like the barb of a terrible arrow. How he goes undulating, neck and body, up and down as he flies! I never felt before that a bird moves his wings. It always looked as if the wings flew with the bird. But I see the effort in him. He chooses and means to fly, and so he does it. It makes one almost reconciled to the idea of wings. Do angels have wings, Papa?"

"It is generally so represented, I think, in the Bible. But whether it is meant as a natural fact about them, is more than I take upon me to decide. But wings are very beautiful things, and I do not exactly see why you should need reconciling to them."

Connie gave a little shrug of her shoulders. "I don't like the notion of them growing out at my shoulder blades. And however would you get on your clothes? If you put them over your wings, they would be of no use, and would make you humpbacked besides. And if you did not, everything would have to be buttoned round their roots. You could not do it yourself, and even on Wynnie I don't think I could bear to touch the things—I don't mean the feathers, but the skinny, folding-up bits of them."

I laughed at her fastidious fancy.

"Papa," she said, "would you like to have wings?"

"I should like to fly like a bird, to swim like a fish, to gallop like a horse, and to creep like a serpent. But I suspect the good of all these is to be had without doing any of them. I mean by a perfect sympathy with the creatures that do these things. What it may please God to give to ourselves, we can quite comfortably leave to Him.

"Now, Connie, what would you think about getting out?"

"Think about it, Papa! I have been thinking about it ever since daylight."

"I will go and see what your mother is doing then, and if she is ready to go out with us."

In a few moments all was arranged. Walter and I lifted Connie and sofa and all out over the windowsill. We carried her high enough on the down for her to see the brilliant waters lying many feet below her, with the seabirds winging their undulating way between heaven and ocean. It is when first you have a chance of looking a bird in the face on the wing that you know what the marvel of flight is. There it hangs or rests, borne up, as far as any can witness, by its own will alone. One of those barb-winged birds rested over my head, regarding me from above, as if I might afford some claim to his theory of treasure trove.

Connie lay silent a long time. At length I spoke. "Are you longing to be running about amongst the rocks, my Connie?"

"No, Papa, not a bit. I don't know how it is, but I don't think I ever wished much for anything I knew I could not have. I am enjoying everything more than I can tell you. I wish Wynnie were as happy as I am."

"Why? Do you think she's not happy, my dear?"

"That doesn't want any thinking, Papa. You can see that."

"You're right, Connie. What do you think is the cause of it?"

"I think it is because she can't wait. She's always going out to meet things, and then when they're not there waiting for her, she thinks they're nowhere. But I always think her way is finer than mine. If everybody were like me, there wouldn't be much done in the world, would there, Papa?"

"At all events, my dear, your way is wise for you, and I am glad you do not judge your sister."

"Judge Wynnie, Papa! That would be cool impudence. She's worth ten of me.

"Don't you think, Papa," she added, after a pause, "that if Mary had said the smallest word against Martha, as Martha did against Mary, Jesus would have had a word to say on Martha's side next?"

"Indeed I do, my dear. And I think that Mary did not sit very long without asking Jesus if she mightn't go and help her sister. There is but one thing needful—that is, the will of God. When people love that above everything, they soon come to see that there are two sides to everything else, and that only the will of God gives fair play to both."

Another silence followed before Connie spoke. "Is it not strange, Papa, that the only thing here that makes me want to get up is nothing of all the grand things round about me? Do you see down there, away across the bay amongst the rocks at the other side, a man sitting sketching?"

I looked for some time before I could discover him.

"Your sight is good, Connie. I see the man, but I could not tell what he was doing."

"Don't you see him lifting his head every now and then for a moment, and then keeping it down for a longer while?"

"I cannot distinguish that. But then I am rather shortsighted, you know."

"Then I wonder how you see so many little things that nobody else seems to notice, Papa."

"That is because I have trained myself to observe. The power in the sight is of less consequence than the habit of seeing. But you have not yet told me what it is that makes you desirous of getting up."

"I want to look over his shoulder, and see what he is doing. Is it not strange that in the midst of all this beautiful plenty, I should want to rise to look at a few lines and scratches, or smears of color, upon a bit of paper?"

"No, it is not strange. There a new element of interest is introduced—the human."

"I think I understand you, Papa. But look a little farther off. Don't you see a lady's bonnet over the top of another rock? I do believe that's Wynnie. I know she took her box of watercolors out with her this morning, just before you came home. Dora went with her."

"Can't you tell by her ribbons, Connie? You seem sharpsighted enough to see her face if she would show it. I don't even see the bonnet. If I were like some people I know . . . but here comes Mamma at last."

Connie's face brightened as if she had not seen her mother for a fortnight. "Mamma, don't you think that's Wynnie's bonnet over that black rock there, just beyond where you see that man drawing?"

"You absurd child! How should I know Wynnie's bonnet at this distance?"

"Can't you see the little white feather you gave her out of your wardrobe just before we left? She put it in this morning before she went out."

"I think I do see something white. But I want you to look out there, toward what they call the Chapel Rock, at the other end of that long mound they call the breakwater. You will soon see a boat full of the coastguard. I saw them just as I left the house. Their officer came down with his sword, and each of the men had a cutlass. I wonder what it can mean."

We looked. But before the boat made its appearance, Connie cried out, "Look! That big boat rowing for the land, away northward there!"

I turned my eyes in the direction she indicated, and saw a long boat with some half-dozen oars, full of men rowing hard, apparently for some spot on the shore at a considerable distance to the north of our bay.

"Ah!" I said, "That boat has something to do with the coastguard and their cutlasses. You'll see that as soon as they get out of the bay, they will row in the same direction."

So it was. Our boat appeared presently, and made full speed after the other boat.

"Surely they can't be smugglers," I said. "I thought all that was over and done with."

In the course of another twenty minutes, both boats had disappeared behind the headland to the northward. I went to fetch Walter, and we carried Connie back. She had not been in the shadow of her own room five minutes before she was fast asleep.

It was nearly time for our early dinner. We always dined early when we could, that we might eat along with our children.

"Oh! We've seen such a nice gentleman!" said Dora, becoming lively under the influence of her soup.

"Have you, Dora? Where?"

"Sitting on the rocks, making a portrait of the sea."

"What makes you say he was a nice gentleman?"

"He had such beautiful boots!" answered Dora, at which there was a great laugh about the table.

"Oh! We must run and tell Connie that," said Harry. "It will make her laugh."

"What will you tell Connie, then, Harry?"

"Oh, what was it, Charlie? I've forgotten."

Another laugh followed at Harry's expense now, and we were all very merry when Dora, who sat opposite to the window, called out clapping her hands, "There's Niceboots again! There's Niceboots again!"

The same moment the head of a young man appeared over our wall by the entrance of the canal. I saw at once that he must be more than ordinarily tall to show his face, for he was not close to the wall. His was a dark countenance, with a long beard—a noble, handsome face, a little sad, with downbent eyes which, released from their more immediate duty toward nature, had now bent themselves upon the earth.

"He is a fine-looking fellow," said I, "and ought, with that face and head, to be able to paint good pictures."

"I should like to see what he has done," said Wynnie, "for, by the way we were sitting, I should think we were attempting the same thing."

"And what was that, Wynnie?" I asked.

"A rock," she answered, "that you could not see from where you were sitting. I saw you on the top of the cliff."

"Connie said it was you, by your bonnet. She too was wishing she could look over the shoulder of the artist at work beside you."

"Not beside me. There were yards and yards of solid rock between us."

"Space, you see, in removing things from the beholder, seems always to bring them nearer to each other, and the most differing things are classed under one name by the man who knows nothing about them. But what sort of rock were you trying to draw?"

"A strange looking, conical rock that stands alone in front of one of the ridges that project from the shore into the water. Three seabirds with long white wings were flying about it, and the little waves of the rising tide were beating themselves against it and breaking in white splashes. So the rock stood between the blue and white below and the blue and white above."

"Now, Dora," I said, "do you see why I want you to learn to draw? Look how Wynnie sees things. That is, in great measure, because she draws things, and has learned to watch in order to find out. It is a great thing to have your eyes open."

Dora's eyes were large, and she opened them to their full width, as if she would take in the universe at their little doors.

"Now let us go up to Connie, and tell her about the rock and everything else you have seen since you went out. We are all her messengers, sent out to discover things and bring back news of them."

After a little talk with Connie, I retired to the study, which was on the same floor as her room, completing, indeed, the whole of that part of the house. It had a roof of its own, and stood higher up the rock than the rest of the dwelling. Here I began to glance over Shepherd's books. To have the run of another man's library, especially if it has been gathered by himself, is like having a pass

key into the chambers of his thought. I found one thing plain
enough, that Shepherd had kept up that love for older English
literature which had been one of the cords to draw us together as
students long ago. I had taken down a last century edition of the
poems of the brothers Fletcher, and had begun to read a lovely
passage in "Christ's Victory and Triumph" when a knock came at
the door and Charlie entered, breathless with eagerness.

"There's the boat with the men with the swords in it, and
another boat behind them, twice as big."

I hurried out and there, close under our windows, were the two
boats we had seen in the morning, landing their crews on the little
beach. The second boat was full of weather-beaten men, in all
kinds of attire, some in blue jerseys, some in red shirts, some in
ragged coats. One man, who looked their superior, was dressed in
blue from head to foot.

"What's the matter?" I asked the officer.

"Vessel foundered, Sir," he answered. "Sprung a leak on Sunday morning. She was laden with iron, and in a heavy ground
swell it shifted and knocked a hole in her. The poor fellows are
worn out with the pump and rowing, upon little or nothing to
eat."

They were trooping past us by this time, looking rather dismal,
though not by any means abject.

"Where will they go now?"

"They'll be taken in by the people. We'll get up a little subscrip-
tion for them, but they all belong to the society the sailors have for
sending the shipwrecked to their homes, or where they want to
go."

"Well, here's something to help," I said, handing him a coin
from my pocket.

"Thank you, Sir. They'll be very glad of it. You are our new
clergyman, I believe."

"Not exactly that. Only for a little while, till my friend Mr.
Shepherd is able to come back to you."

"We don't want to lose Mr. Shepherd, Sir. He's what they call
high in these parts, but he's a great favorite with all the poor
people, because you see he understands them as if he was of the
same flesh and blood with themselves—as, for that matter, I suppose we all are."

"If we weren't, there would be nothing to say at all. Will any of
these men be at church tomorrow, do you suppose? I am afraid

sailors are not much in the way of going to church?"

"I am afraid not. You see they are all anxious to get home, and most likely they'll be traveling tomorrow. It's a pity. It would be a good chance for saying something to them. But I often think that sailors won't be judged exactly like other people. They're so knocked about, you see, Sir."

"Of course not. Nobody will be judged like any other body. To his own Master, who knows all about him, every man stands or falls. Depend upon it, God likes fair play far better than any sailor at all. But the question is this: shall we, who know what a blessed thing life is because we know what God is like, who can trust in Him with all our hearts because He is the Father of our Lord Jesus Christ, the friend of sinners, shall we not try all we can to let them know the blessedness of trusting in their Father in heaven? If we could only get them to say the Lord's Prayer, meaning it, think what that would be! Look here—this can't be called bribery, for they are in want of it, and it will show them I am friendly. Here's another sovereign. Give them my compliments, and say that if any of them happen to be in Kilkhaven tomorrow, I shall be quite pleased to welcome them to church. Tell them I will give them of my best there if they will come. Make the invitation merrily, you know. No long face and solemn speech. I will give them the solemn speech when they come to church. But even there I hope God will keep the long face from me. That is for fear and suffering, and the house of God holds the antidote against all fear and most suffering. But I am preaching my sermon on Saturday instead of Sunday, and keeping you from your ministration to your men."

"I will give them your message as near as I can," he said, and we shook hands and parted.

This was the first experience we had of the might and battle of the ocean. To our eyes it lay quiet as a baby asleep. On that Sunday morning there had been no commotion here. Yet now on the Saturday morning, home came the conquered and spoiled of the sea. As if with a mock, she takes all they have and flings them on shore again, with her weeds and her shells and her sand. There are few coasts on which the sea rages so wildly as this, where the whole force of the Atlantic breaks upon it. Even when all is still as a church on land, the storm which raves somewhere out upon the vast waste will drive the waves in upon the shore with such fury, that not even a lifeboat could make its way through the yawning hollows, and their fierce, shattered, and tumbling crests.

76

FOURTEEN

A SERMON FOR SAILORS

I hoped that some of the shipwrecked mariners might be present in church that bright Sunday—my first in this seaboard parish—with the sea outside the church flashing in the sunlight.

While I stood at the lectern, I could see little of my congregation, partly from my being on a level with them, partly from the necessity for keeping my eyes and thoughts upon that which I read. However, when I rose from prayer in the pulpit, I saw that one long bench in the middle of the church was full of sunburnt men in torn and worn garments, the very men in whom we had been so much interested. Not only were they behaving with perfect decorum, but their rough faces wore an aspect of solemnity which I do not suppose was their usual aspect.

I gave them no text. I had one myself, which was the necessary thing, and they should have it soon enough.

"Once upon a time," I said, "a man went up a mountain and stayed there till it was dark. Now, a man who finds himself on a mountain as the sun is going down, especially if he is alone, makes haste to get down before it is dark. But this man went up when the sun was going down and continued there for a good long while after it was dark. He went because he wished to be alone. He hadn't a house of his own. He hadn't even a room of his own into which he could go. True, he had kind friends who would give him a bed; but they were all poor people, and their houses were small, and very likely they had large families, and he could not always find a quiet place to go. And I daresay, if he had had a room, he would have been a little troubled with the children constantly coming to find him. For however much he loved them—and no man was ever so fond of children as he was—he needed to be left quiet sometimes. So, on this occasion, he went up the mountain just to be quiet.

"For he had been talking with men all day, which tires and sometimes confuses a man's thoughts, and now he wanted to talk with God, for that makes a man strong, and puts all the confusion in order again. So he went to the top of the hill. That was his secret chamber. It had no door, but that did not matter—no one could see him but God. It was so quiet up there! The people had all gone away to their homes, and perhaps next day would hardly think about him at all, as they were busy catching fish, or digging their gardens, or making things for their houses. But he knew that God would not forget him the next day any more than this day, and that God had sent him not to be the king that these people wanted him to be, but their servant. So, to make his heart strong, he went up into the mountain alone to have a talk with his Father. I need not tell you who this man was—it was the King of men, the Servant of men, the Lord Jesus Christ, the everlasting Son of our Father in heaven.

"Now this mountain had a small lake at the foot of it. He had sent His usual companions away in their boat across this water to the other side, where their homes and families were. You must remember that it was a little boat—and there are often tremendous storms upon these small lakes with great mountains about them. For the wind will come all at once, rushing down through the clefts in as sudden a squall as ever overtook a sailor at sea. He saw them worn out at the oar, toiling in rowing, for the wind was contrary to them. He went straight down. Could not His Father help them out without Him? Yes. But He wanted to do it Himself, that they might see that He did it. Otherwise they could only have thought that the wind fell of itself and the waves lay down without cause, never supposing for a moment that their Master or His Father had had anything to do with it. They would have done just as people do now—they would think that the help comes of itself. So when He reached the border of the lake, He found the waves breaking furiously upon the rocks. But that made no difference to Him."

The mariners had been staring at me up to this point, leaning forward on their benches, for sailors are nearly as fond of a good yarn as they are of tobacco. (I heard afterward that they had voted parson's yarn a good one.)

"The companions of our Lord had not been willing to go away and leave Him behind. Now, they wished more than ever that He had been with them—not that they thought He could do anything with a storm, only that somehow they would have been less afraid with His face to look at.

"At length, when they were nearly worn out, taking feebler and feebler strokes, sometimes missing the water altogether, at other times burying their oars in it up to the handles, one of them gave a cry, and they all stopped rowing and stared, leaning forward to peer through the darkness. And through the spray, they saw, perhaps a hundred yards or so from the boat, something standing up from the surface of the water. It was a shape like a man, and they all cried out with fear, for they thought it must be a ghost."

How the faces of the sailors strained toward me at this part of the story!

"But then, over the noise of the wind and the waters came the voice they knew so well—'It is I. Be not afraid.' In the first flush of his delight, Peter felt strong and full of courage. 'Lord, if it be Thou,' he said, 'bid me come unto Thee on the water.' Jesus just said, 'Come!' and Peter scrambled over the gunwale on to the sea. But when he let go of his hold on the boat and began to look around him, and when he saw how the wind was tearing the water, and how it tossed and raved between him and Jesus, he began to be afraid. And as soon as he began to be afraid he began to sink; but he had just sense enough to cry out, 'Lord, save me.' And Jesus put out His hand, and took hold of him, and lifted him out of the water, and said to him, 'O thou of little faith, wherefore didst thou doubt?' And then they got into the boat, and the wind fell all at once and altogether.

"Now, do not think that Peter was a coward. It wasn't that he hadn't courage, but that he hadn't enough of it. And why was it that he hadn't enough of it? Because he hadn't faith enough. You would have thought that once he found himself standing on the water, he need not be afraid of the wind and the waves that lay between him and Jesus. You would have thought that the greatest trial of his courage was over when he got out of the boat, and that there was comparatively little more ahead of him. Yet the sight of the waves and the blast of the boisterous wind were too much for him. When he got out of the boat, and found himself standing on

79

the water, he began to think much of himself for being able to do so, and fancy himself better and greater than his companions, and a special favorite of God. Now, there is nothing that kills faith sooner than pride. The two are directly against each other. The moment that Peter grew proud and began to think about himself instead of his Master, he began to lose his faith, and then he grew afraid, and then he began to sink, and that brought him to his senses. When he forgot himself and remembered his Master, the hand of the Lord caught him, and the voice of the Lord gently rebuked him for the smallness of his faith, asking, 'Wherefore didst thou doubt?'

"If the disciples had known that Jesus saw them from the top of the mountain and was watching them all the time, would they have been frightened at the storm? Suppose you were alone on the sea and expected your boat to be swamped any moment. If you saw that He was watching you from some lofty hilltop, would you be afraid? He might mean you to go to the bottom, you know. But would you mind going to the bottom with Him looking at you? I do not think I should mind it myself. But I must take care lest I be boastful like Peter.

"Why should we be afraid of anything with Him watching us? But we are afraid of Him instead, because we do not believe that He is what He says He is, the Saviour of men. We do not believe that what He offers us is salvation. We think it is slavery, and therefore we continue to be slaves. But, floating on the sea of your troubles, all kinds of fears and anxieties assailing you, is He not on the mountaintop? Sees He not the little boat of your fortunes tossed with the waves and the contrary wind? Do not think that the Lord sees and will not come. Down the mountain He will assuredly come, and you are now as safe in your troubles as the disciples were in theirs with Jesus looking on. They did not know it, but it was so—the Lord was watching them. And when you look back upon your past lives, cannot you see some instances of the same kind when you felt and acted as if the Lord had forgotten you, and you found afterward that He had been watching you all the time?

"You do not trust Him more because you obey Him so little. If you would only ask what God would have you to do, you would soon find your confidence growing. It is because you are proud and envious and greedy after gain, that you do not trust Him more. Ah! Trust Him to get rid of these evil things, and be clean and beautiful in heart.

"O sailors with me on the ocean of life, knowing that He is watching you from His mountaintop, will you do and say the things that hurt and wrong and disappoint Him? Sailors on the waters that surround this globe, He beholds you and cares for you and watches over you. Will you do that which is unpleasing, distressful to Him? Will you be irreverent, cruel, coarse? Will you say evil things, lie, and delight in vile stories and reports, with His eye on you, watching your ship on its watery ways, ever ready to come over the waves to help you? It is a fine thing, Sailors, to fear nothing. But it would be far finer to fear nothing because He is above all and over all and in you all. For His sake and for His love, give up everything bad, and take Him for your Captain. He will be both Captain and Pilot to you, and will steer you safe into the port of glory. Now to God the Father. . . . "

And so I preached that first Sunday morning, and followed it up with a short enforcement in the afternoon.

FIFTEEN

ANOTHER SUNDAY EVENING

In the evening we met in Connie's room, as usual, to have our talk.

The window was open, and the sun was brilliant in the west. We sat a little aside out of his radiance, and let him look full into the room. Only Wynnie sat back in a dark corner, as if she would get out of his way. Below him the sea lay bluer than belief—blue with a delicate yet deep silky blue, with the brilliant white lines of its lapping on the high coast to the north.

We had just sat down when Dora broke out, "I saw Niceboots at church. He did stare at you, Papa, as if he had never heard a sermon before."

"I dare say he never heard such a sermon before!" said Connie, with the perfect confidence of inexperience and partiality, not to say ignorance, seeing she had not heard the sermon herself.

Here Wynnie spoke from her dark corner, apparently forcing herself to speak, and thereby giving what seemed an unpleasant tone to what she said. "Well, Papa, I don't know what to think. You are always telling us to trust in Him, but how can we if we are not good?"

"The first good thing you can do is to look up to Him. That is faith and the beginning of trust in Him."

"But it's no use sometimes."

"How do you know that?"

"Because you—I mean I—can't feel good, or care about it at all."

"But is that any ground for saying that it is no use—that He does not heed you? Does He disregard the look cast up to Him? Will He not help you until your heart goes with your will? He made Himself strong to be the helper of the weak, and He pities most those who are most destitute. And who are so destitute as those who do not love what they want to love?"

Connie, as if partly to help her sister, followed on the same side. "I don't know exactly how to say what I mean, Papa, but I wish I could get this lovely afternoon, all full of sunshine and blue, into unity with all that you teach us about Jesus Christ. I wish this beautiful day came in with my thought of Him, like the frame—gold and red and blue—that you have around that picture of Him at home. Why doesn't it?"

"You do not know Him well enough yet. You do not yet believe that He means you all gladness, heartily, honestly, thoroughly."

"And no suffering, Papa?"

"I did not say that, my dear. There you are on your couch and can't move. But He does mean you gladness, nonetheless. What a chance you have, Connie, of believing in Him, of offering upon His altar!"

"But," said my wife, "are not these feelings in a great measure dependent on the state of one's health? I find it so different when the sunshine is inside me as well as outside me."

"No doubt, my dear. But that is only the more reason for rising above all that. From the way some people speak of physical difficulties, you would think that they were not merely inevitable, which they are, but insurmountable, which they are not. That they are physical and not spiritual is not only a great consolation, but also a strong argument for overcoming them. For all that is physical is put—or is in the process of being put—under the feet of the spiritual. Do not mistake me. I do not say you can make yourself merry or happy when you are in a physical condition which is contrary to such mental condition. But you can withdraw from it, not all at once, but by practice and effort you can learn to withdraw from it, refusing to allow your judgments and actions to be ruled by it. 'What does that matter?' you will learn to say. 'It is enough for me to know that the sun does shine, and that this is only a weary fog round me for the moment. I shall come out into the light beyond presently.' The most glorious instances of calmness in suffering are thus achieved—that the sufferers really do not suffer, for they have taken refuge in the inner chamber. Out of the spring of their life, a power goes forth that quenches the flames of the furnace of their suffering.

"Still less is physical difficulty to be used as an excuse for giving way to ill-temper and leaving ourselves to be tossed and shaken by every tremble of our nerves. That is as if a man should give himself into the hands and will and caprice of an organ-grinder to work on him, not with the music of the spheres but with the wretched growling of the streets."

"But Papa," said Wynnie, "you yourself excuse other people's ill-temper on the very ground that they are out of health. Indeed," she went on, "I have heard you do so for myself when you did not know that I was within hearing."

"Yes, my dear, most assuredly. A real difference lies between excusing ourselves and excusing others. No doubt the same excuse is just for ourselves that is just for other people. But we can do something to put ourselves right. Where we cannot work—that is, in the life of another—we have time to make all the excuse we can. Nay, more—it is only justice there. We are not bound to insist on our own rights, even of excuse; the wisest thing often is to forego them. We are bound by heaven, earth, and hell, to give them to other people. But it would be a sad thing to have to think that when we found ourselves in ungracious condition, from whatever the cause, we had only to submit to it saying, 'It is a law of nature.' It may be a law of nature, but it must yet bow before the Law of the Spirit of Life."

A little pause followed. That Wynnie, at least, was thinking, her next question made evident.

"What you say about a law of nature and a Law of the Spirit makes me think again how Jesus' walking on the water has always been a puzzle to me."

"It could hardly be other, seeing that we cannot possibly understand it," I answered.

"But I find it so hard to believe. Can't you say something, Papa, to help me believe it?"

"I think if you admit what goes before, you will find there is nothing against reason in the story. If all things were made by Jesus, the Word of God, would it be reasonable that the water that He had created should be able to drown Him?"

"It might drown His body."

"It would if He had not the power over it still, to prevent it from laying hold of Him. But just think for a moment. God is a

84

Spirit. Spirit is greater than matter. I suspect this miracle was wrought not through anything done to the water, but through the power of the Spirit over the body of Jesus. If we look at the history of our Lord, we shall find that true real human body as His was, it was yet used by His spirit after a fashion in which we cannot yet use our bodies."

"But then about Peter, Papa? What you have been saying will not apply to Peter's body, you know."

"I confess there is more difficulty there. But if you can suppose that such power were indwelling in Jesus, you cannot limit the sphere of its action. Peter's faith in Him brought even Peter's body within the sphere of the outgoing power of the Master. Do you suppose that because Peter ceased to be brave and trusting, therefore Jesus withdrew from him some sustaining power and allowed him to sink? I do not believe it. I believe Peter's sinking followed naturally. The pride of Peter had withdrawn him from the immediate spiritual influence of Christ, and had conquered his matter. Therefore, the Lord must come from His own height of safety above the sphere of the natural law, stretch out to Peter the arm of physical aid, lift him up, and lead him to the boat. The whole salvation of the human race is figured in this story. It is all Christ, my love. Does this help you to believe at all?"

"I think it does, Papa. But it wants thinking over a good deal."

"But there's one thing," said my wife, "that is more interesting to me than what you have been talking about. It is the other instances in the life of Peter in which you said he failed in a similar manner from pride or self-satisfaction."

"One, at least, seems to me very clear. You have often remarked to me, Ethelwyn, how little praise servants can stand—how almost invariably after you have commended the diligence or skill of any of your household, one of the first visible results was either a falling away in performance or an outbreak of self-conceit. Now you will see precisely the same kind of thing in Peter."

Here I opened my New Testament and read fragmentarily, " 'But whom say ye that I am? . . . Thou art the Christ, the Son of the living God . . . Blessed art thou, Simon . . . My Father hath revealed that unto thee. I will give unto thee the keys of the kingdom of heaven . . . I must suffer many things, and be killed, and be raised again the third day . . . Be it far from Thee, Lord. This shall not be unto Thee . . . Get thee behind Me, Satan. Thou art an offense unto Me.' Just contemplate the change here in the words of our Lord. 'Blessed art thou . . . Thou art an offense unto Me.' The Lord had praised Peter. Peter grew self-sufficient, even to the rebuking of Him whose praise had so uplifted him. But it is ever so. A man will gain a great moral victory; glad first, then uplifted, he will fall before a paltry temptation.

"I have sometimes wondered whether his denial of our Lord had anything to do with his satisfaction with himself for making that onslaught upon the high priest's servant. It was a brave and faithful act to draw a single sword against a multitude. Peter had justified his confident saying that he would not deny Him. He was not one to deny his Lord—who had been the first to confess Him! Yet ere the cock had crowed, ere the morning had dawned, the vulgar grandeur of the palace of the high priest and the accusation of a maid-servant were enough to make him quail. He was excited before, and now he was cold in the middle of the night, with Jesus gone from his sight a prisoner.

"Alas, that the courage which had led him to follow the Lord should have thus led him but into the denial of Him! Yet why should I say *alas?* If the denial of our Lord lay in his heart a possible thing, only prevented by his being kept in favorable circumstances for confessing Him, it was a thousand times better that he should deny Him, and thus know what a poor weak thing that heart of his was, trust it no more, and give it up to the Master to make it strong and pure and grand. For such an end, the Lord was willing to bear all the pain of Peter's denial."

Here I ceased and, a little overcome, rose and retired to my own room. There I could only fall on my knees and pray that the Lord Christ, who had died for me, might have His own way with me— that it might be worth His while to have done what He did and what He was doing now for me. To my Elder Brother, my Lord and my God, I gave myself yet again, confidently, because He cared to have me and because my very breath was His. I would be what He wanted, who knew all about it and had done everything that I might be a son of God—a living glory of gladness.

SIXTEEN

NICEBOOTS

The next morning the captain of the lost vessel called upon me early. He was a fine, honest-looking, burly fellow, dressed in blue from head to heel. I thought I had something to bring against him, and therefore I said to him, "They tell me, Captain, that your vessel was not seaworthy, and that you knew that."

"She was my own craft, Sir, and I judged her fit for several voyages more. If she had been A-1 she couldn't have been mine, and a man must do what he can for his family."

"But you were risking your life, you know."

"A few chances more or less don't much signify to a sailor, Sir. There ain't nothing to be done without risk. You'll find an old tub go voyage after voyage, and she beyond bail, and a clipper fresh off the stocks go down in the harbor. It's all in the luck, I assure you."

"Well, if it were your own life I should have nothing to say, seeing you have a family to look after. But what about the poor fellows who made the voyage with you—did they know what kind of vessel they were embarking in?"

"Wherever the captain's ready to go he'll always find men ready to follow him. Bless you, Sir, they never ask no questions. If a sailor was always to be thinking of the chances, he'd never set his foot offshore."

"Still I don't think it's right they shouldn't know."

"I daresay they knowed all about the brig as well as I did myself. You gets to know all about the craft just as you do about

87

her captain. She's got a character of her own, and she can't hide it long, anymore than you can hide yours, Sir, begging your pardon."

"I daresay that's all correct, but still I shouldn't like anyone to say to me, 'You ought to have told me, Captain.' Therefore, I'm telling you, Captain, and now I'm clear. A glass of wine before you go?" I concluded, ringing the bell.

"Thank you, Sir. I'll turn over what you've been saying, and anyhow I take it kind of you."

So we parted. I have never seen him since and shall not, most likely, in this world. But he looked like a man who could understand why and wherefore I spoke as I did.

All the next week, I wandered about my parish, making acquaintance with different people in an outside sort of way, only now and then finding an opportunity of seeing into their souls. But I enjoyed endlessly the aspects of the country. It was not picturesque except in parts. There was a little wood and there were no hills, only undulations, though many of them were steep enough from a pedestrian's point of view. Neither were there any plains except high moorland tracts. But the impression of the whole country was large, airy, sunshiny, and it was clasped in the arms of the infinite, awful yet bountiful sea. The sea and the sky dwarfed the earth, made it of small account beside them, but who could complain of such an influence?

My children bathed in this sea every day, and gathered strength and knowledge from it. It was, as I have indicated, a dangerous coast to bathe on. The sweep of the tides varied with the sands that were cast up. There was sometimes a strong undertow, a reflux of the inflowing waters, quite sufficient to carry out into the great deep all those who could not swim well. But there was a fine, strong Cornish woman to take charge of the ladies and the little boys, and she, watching the ways of the wild monster, knew the when and the where and all about it.

Connie got out on the downs every day, and the weather continued superb. What rain there was fell at night, just enough for nature to wash her face with, and so look quite fresh in the morning. We contrived a dinner on the sands on the other side of the bay, for the Friday of this same week.

That morning rose gloriously. Harry and Charlie were turning the house upside down, to judge by their noise, long before I was in the humor to get up, for I had been reading late the night before. I never made much objection to mere noise, knowing that I could stop it the moment I pleased, and knowing too that so far from there being anything wrong in making a noise, the sea would make noise enough in our ears before we left Kilkhaven. But the moment that I heard a thread of whining or a burst of anger in the noise, I would interfere—treating these as things that must be dismissed at once.

So, far from seeking to put an end to the noise—I knew Connie did not mind it—I listened to it with a kind of reverence, as the outcome of a gladness which the God of joy had kindled in their hearts. Soon after, however, I heard certain dim growls of expostulation from Harry, and having ground for believing that the elder was tyrannizing the younger, I sent Charlie to find out where the tide would be between one and two o'clock, and Harry to run to the top of the hill, to find out the direction of the wind. Before I was dressed, Charlie was knocking at my door with the news that it would be half tide about one. Harry speedily followed with the discovery that the wind was northeast by southwest, which determined that the sun would shine all day.

As the dinner hour drew near, the servants went over, with Walter at their head, to choose a rock convenient for a table under the shelter of the rocks on the sands across the bay. And there, when Walter returned, we bore Connie, carrying her litter close by the edge of the retreating tide, which sometimes broke in a ripple of music under her, wetting our feet with an innocuous rush. The child's delight was extreme, as she thus skimmed the edge of the ocean, with the little ones gamboling about her, and her mamma and Wynnie walking quietly on the landward side, for she wished to have no one between her and the sea.

After scrambling with difficulty over some rocky ledges, and stopping, at Connie's request, to let her look into a deep pool in the sand, which somehow or other retained the water after the rest had retreated, we set her down near the mouth of a cave in the shadow of a rock. And there was our dinner nicely laid for us on a flat rock in front of the cave. The cliffs rose behind us, with curiously carved and variously angled strata. The sun in full splendor threw dark shadows on the brilliant yellow sand, more and more of which appeared as the bright blue water withdrew itself, now rippling over it as if to hide it all up again, now uncovering more as it withdrew for another rush. Before we had finished our dinner, the foremost wavelets appeared so far away over the plain of the sand, that it seemed a long walk to the edge that had been almost at our feet a little while ago. Between us and it lay a lovely desert of glittering sand.

When even Charlie and Harry had concluded that it was time to stop eating, we left the shadow and went out into the sun, carrying Connie and laying her down in the midst of "the ribbed sea sand," which was very ribby today. On a shawl a little way off from her lay the baby, crowing and kicking with the same jollity that had possessed the boys ever since the morning. I wandered about with Wynnie on the sands, picking up, amongst other things, strange creatures in thin shells ending in vegetablelike tufts. My wife sat on the end of Connie's litter, and Dora and the boys (a little way off) were trying how far the full force of three wooden spades could, in digging a hole in the sand, keep ahead of the water tumbling in. Behind, the servants were busy washing the plates in a pool and burying the fragments of the feast, for I made it a rule wherever we went that the fair face of nature was not to be defiled.

In our roaming, Wynnie and I approached a long low ridge of rock, rising toward the sea into which it ran. Crossing this, we came suddenly upon the painter whom Dora had called Niceboots, sitting with a small easel before him. We were right above him, and he had his back toward us, so that we saw at once what he was painting.

"O Papa!" cried Wynnie involuntarily, and the painter looked around.

"I beg your pardon," I said. "We came over from the other side and did not see you before. I hope we have not disturbed you much."

"Not in the least," he answered courteously, and rose as he spoke.

I saw that the subject on his easel suggested that of which Wynnie had been making a sketch, on the day when Connie first lay on the top of the opposite cliff. But he was not even looking in the same direction now.

"Do you mind having your work seen before it is finished?"

"Not in the least, if the spectators will remember that most processes have a seemingly chaotic stage," answered he.

I was struck with the mode and tone of the remark. "Here is no common man," I said to myself.

"I wish we could always keep that in mind with regard to

90

human beings themselves, as well as their works," I said aloud.

The painter looked at me, and I looked at him.

"We speak each from the experience of his own profession, I presume," he said.

"But," I returned, glancing at his little picture in oils, "this must have long ago passed the chaotic stage."

"It is nearly as much finished as I care to make it," he returned. "I hardly count this work at all. I am chiefly amusing, or rather pleasing, my own fancy at present."

"Apparently," I remarked, "you had the conical rock outside the bay for your model, and now you are finishing it with your back turned toward it. How is that?"

"I will soon explain," he answered. "The moment I saw this rock it reminded me of Dante's Purgatory."

"Ah, you are a reader of Dante?" I asked. "In the original, I hope."

"Yes. A painter friend of mine, an Italian, set me going with that—and once going with Dante, nobody could well stop."

"That is quite my own feeling. Now, to return to your picture."

"Without departing at all from natural forms, I thought to make it suggest that Purgatorio to any who remembered the description given of the place. Of course, that thing there is a mere rock, yet it has certain mountain forms about it. I have put it at a much greater distance, you see, and have sought to make it look a solitary mountain in the midst of a great water. The circles of Purgatory are suggested without any artificial structure, and there are occasional hints at figures, which you cannot definitely detach from the rocks—which, you remember, were in one part full of sculptures. I have kept the mountain near enough to indicate the great expanse of wild flowers on the top, which the Lady of the Sacred Forest was so busy gathering. I want to indicate too the wind up there in the terrestrial paradise, ever and always blowing one way. You remember, Mr. Walton?

> An air of sweetness, changeless in its flow,
> With no more strength than in a soft wind lies,
> Smote peacefully against me on the brow.
> By which the leaves all trembling, levelwise,
> Did every one bend thitherward to where
> The high mount throws its shadow at sunrise.
> (*Purgatorio*, Canto XXVIII)

"I thought you said you did not use translations?"

"I thought it possible that—Miss Walton—might not follow the Italian so easily."

"She won't lag far behind, I flatter myself," I returned. "Whose translation do you quote?"

He hesitated a moment, then said carelessly, "I have cobbled a few passages after that fashion myself."

"It has the merit of being near the original at least," I returned, "and that seems to me one of the chief merits a translation can possess."

"Then," the painter resumed, rather hastily, as if to avoid any further remark upon his verses, "you see those white things in the air above?" Here he turned to Wynnie. "Miss Walton will remember—I think she was making a drawing of the rock at the same time I was—how the seagulls or some such birds kept flitting about the top of it?"

"I remember quite well," answered Wynnie, with a look of appeal to me.

"Yes," I interposed, "my daughter spoke especially of the birds over the rock. She said the white lapping of the waves looked like the spirits trying to get loose, and the white birds like the foam that had broken its chains and risen in triumph into the air."

Here Mr. Niceboots (for as yet I did not know what else to call him) looked at Wynnie almost with a start. "How wonderfully that falls in with my fancy about the rock!" he said. "Purgatory indeed! With imprisoned souls lapping at its foot, and the free souls winging their way aloft in ether. Well, this world is a kind of purgatory anyhow, is it not, Mr. Walton?"

"Certainly it is. We are here tried as by fire, to see what our work is, whether wood, hay, stubble, or gold and silver and precious stones."

"You see," resumed the painter, "if anybody only glanced at my little picture, he would take those for seabirds. But if he looked into it and began to suspect me, he would find they were Dante and Beatrice on their way to the sphere of the moon."

"What is there in the world, that the spiritual man will not see merely the things of nature but the things of the spirit?"

"I am no theologian," said the painter, turning away somewhat coldly, I thought.

I could see that Wynnie was greatly interested in him. Perhaps she thought that here was some enlightenment of the riddle of the world for her, if she could but get at what he was thinking. She was used to my way of it; here might be something new.

"If I can be of any service to Miss Walton with her drawing, I shall be happy to do so," he said.

But his last gesture had made me a little distrustful of him, and I received his advances on this point with a coldness which I did not wish to make more marked than his own toward my last observation.

"You are very kind," I said, "but Miss Walton does not presume to be an artist."

I saw a slight shade pass over Wynnie's countenance. When I turned to Mr. Niceboots, a shade of a different sort was on his. Surely I had said something wrong to cast a gloom on two young faces. I made haste to make amends. "We are just going to have some coffee," I said. "Will you come and allow me to introduce you to Mrs. Walton?"

"With much pleasure," he answered. He was a finely built, black-bearded, sunburnt fellow, with clear gray eyes, a rather Roman nose, and good features generally. But there was an air of oppression, if not sadness, about him.

"But," I said, "how am I to effect an introduction, seeing I do not yet know your name?"

I had had to keep a sharp lookout on myself lest I should call him Mr. Niceboots. He smiled very graciously, and replied, "My name is Percivale—Charles Percivale."

"A descendant of Sir Percivale of King Arthur's Round Table?"

"I cannot count quite so far back as that," he answered, "I do come of a fighting race, but I cannot claim Sir Percivale."

We were now walking along the edge of the still retreating waves toward the group upon the sands, Mr. Percivale and I foremost, and Wynnie lingering behind.

"Oh, look, Papa!" she cried, from some little distance.

We turned and saw her gazing at something on the sand at her feet. Hastening back, we found it to be a little narrow line of foam bubbles, which the water had left behind on the sand, slowly breaking and passing out of sight. Why there should be foam bubbles there then, and not always, I do not know. But there they were—and such colors! Deep rose and grassy green and ultramarine blue and above all, one dark, yet brilliant and intensely burnished, metallic gold. All of them were of a solid-looking burnished color, like opaque body color laid on behind translucent crystal.

Those little ocean bubbles were well worth turning to see, and so I said to Wynnie. But, as we gazed, they went on vanishing, one by one. Every moment a heavenly glory of hue burst, and was gone.

We walked away again toward the rest of our party.

"Don't you think those bubbles more beautiful than any precious stones you ever saw, Papa?"

"Yes, my love, I think they are, except the opal. In the opal, God seems to have fixed the evanescent and made the vanishing eternal."

"And flowers are more beautiful than jewels?" she asked.

"Many—perhaps most flowers are," I granted.

"And did you ever see such curves and delicate textures anywhere else as in the clouds, Papa?"

"I think not. But what are you putting me to my catechism for in this way, my child?"

"O Papa, I could go on a long time with that catechism, but I will end with one question more, which you will perhaps find a little harder to answer. Only, I daresay you have had an answer for years, lest one of us should ask you someday."

"No, my love. I never got an answer ready for anything lest one of my children should ask me. But it is not surprising either that children should be puzzled about the things that have puzzled their father, or that by the time they are able to put the questions, he should have some sort of an answer to most of them. Go on with your catechism, Wynnie."

"It's not a funny question, Papa—it's a very serious one. I can't think why the unchanging God should have made all the most beautiful things wither and grow ugly, or burst and vanish, or die somehow and be no more. Mamma is not so beautiful as she once was, is she?"

"In one way no, but in another and better way much more so. But we will not talk about her kind of beauty just now: we will keep to the more material loveliness of which you have been speaking—though, in truth, no loveliness can be only material. I think it is because God loves beauty so much that He makes all beautiful things vanish quickly."

"I do not understand you, Papa."

"I will explain, if Mr. Percivale will excuse me."

"On the contrary, I am greatly interested, both in the question and the answer."

"Well, Wynnie, if the flowers were not perishable, we should cease to contemplate their beauty, for they should become commonplace and therefore dull. To compare great things with small, the flowers wither, the bubbles break, the clouds and sunsets pass, for the very same holy reason. Therefore, that we may always have them, and ever learn to love their beauty and yet more their truth, God sends the beneficent winter that we may think about what we have lost, and welcome them when they come again."

"I told you, Papa, you would have an answer ready, didn't I?"

"Yes, my child—but with this difference: I found the answer to meet my own necessities, not yours."

"And so you had it ready for me when I wanted it."

"Just so. That is the only certainty you have in regard to what you give away. No one who has not tasted it and found it good has a right to offer any spiritual dish to his neighbor."

Mr. Percivale took no part in our conversation. The moment I had presented him to Mrs. Walton and Connie, and he had paid his respects by a somewhat stately old-world obeisance, he merged the salutation into a farewell, and either forgetting my offer of coffee, or having changed his mind, he withdrew.

He was scarcely beyond hearing when Dora came up to me from her digging with an eager look on her sunny face.

"Hasn't he got nice boots, Papa?"

"Indeed, my dear, I am unable to support you in that assertion, for I never saw his boots."

"I did then," returned the child, "and I never saw such nice boots."

"I accept the statement willingly," I replied, and we heard no more of the boots, for his name was now substituted for his nickname. Nor did I see him again for some days, not till the next Sunday—though why he should come to church at all was something of a puzzle to me, especially when I knew him better.

SEVENTEEN

THE BLACKSMITH

The next day I set out after breakfast to inquire about a blacksmith. It was not any blacksmith that would do. There was one in the village, but I found him an ordinary man who could shoe a horse and avoid the quick, but from whom any greater delicacy of touch was not to be expected. Inquiring further, I heard of a young smith in a hamlet a couple of miles distant, but still within the parish. In the afternoon I set out to find him. To my surprise he was a pale-faced, thoughtful-looking man, with a huge frame which appeared worn rather than naturally thin, and large eyes that looked at the anvil as if it were the horizon of the world. He had a horseshoe in his tongs when I entered. Notwithstanding the fire that glowed on the hearth, and the sparks that flew like a nimbus in eruption about his person, the place seemed very dark and cool to me, entering from the glorious blaze of the almost noontide sun. I could see the smith by the glow of his horseshoe, but all between me and the shoe was dark.

"Good morning," I said. "It is good to find a man by his work. I heard you half a mile off or so, and now I see you, but only by the glow of your work. It is a grand thing to work in fire."

He lifted his hammered hand to his forehead courteously, and as lightly as if the hammer had been the butt end of a whip. "I don't know if you would say the same if you had to work at it in weather like this," he answered.

"If I did not," I returned, "that would be the fault of my weakness."

"Well, you may be right," he rejoined with a sigh. Throwing the horseshoe on the ground, he let the hammer drop beside the anvil, and leaning against it, held his head for a moment between his hands and regarded the floor. "It does not much matter to me," he went on, "if I only get through my work and have done with it. No man shall say I shirked what I'd got to do. And then when it's over there won't be a word to say agen me, or—"

He did not finish the sentence.

"I hope you are not ill," I said.

He made no answer, but taking up his tongs caught with it from a beam one of a number of roughly finished horseshoes which hung there, and put it on the fire. While he turned it in the fire, and blew the bellows, I stood regarding him. "This man will do for my work," I said to myself, "though I should not wonder from the look of him if it was the last piece of work he ever did under the New Jerusalem."

The smith's words broke in on my meditations. "When I was a little boy," he said, "I once wanted to stay home from school. I had a little headache but nothing worth minding. I told my mother that I had a headache and she kept me, and I helped her at her spinning, which was what I liked best of anything. But in the afternoon the Methodist preacher came to see my mother. He asked what was the matter with me, and my mother answered that I had a bad head. He looked at me, and as my head was quite well by this time, I could not help feeling guilty. And he saw my look, I suppose, for I can't account for what he said any other way. He turned to me and said, solemnlike, 'Is your head bad enough to send you to the Lord Jesus to make you whole?' I could not speak a word, partly from bashfulness, I suppose, for I was but ten years old. So he followed it up, 'Then you ought to be at school.' I said nothing, because I couldn't. But never since then have I given in as long as I could stand. And I can stand now, and lift my hammer too," he said, as he took the horseshoe from the forge, laid it on the anvil, and again made a nimbus of coruscating iron.

"You are just the man I want," I said. "I've got a job for you, down to Kilkhaven."

"What is it, Sir? I should ha' thought the Church was all spic and span by this time."

"I see you know who I am," I said.

"Of course I do," he answered. "I don't go to Church myself, being brought up a Methodist, but anything that happens in the parish is known the next day all over it."

"You won't mind doing my job though you are a Methodist, will you?" I asked.

"Not I, Sir. If I've read right, it's the fault of the Church that we don't pull alongside. You turned us out, Sir, we didn't go out of ourselves. At least, if all they say is true, which I can't be sure of you know, in this world."

"You are quite right there," I answered. "And in doing so, the Church had the worst of it, as all that judge and punish their neighbors have. But you have been the worse for it too, all of which is to be laid to the charge of the Church. For there is not one clergyman I know—mind, I say that I know—who would have made such a cruel speech to a boy as that the Methodist parson made to you."

"But it did me good, Sir."

"Are you sure of that? I am not. Are you sure, first of all, that it did not make you proud? Are you sure it has not made you work beyond your strength—I don't mean your strength of arm, for clearly that is all that could be wished—but of your chest, your lungs? Is there not some danger of your leaving someone who is dependent on you too soon unprovided for? Is there not some danger of your having worked as if God were a hard master? Of your having worked fiercely, indignantly, as if He wronged you by not caring for you, not understanding you?"

He returned me no answer, but hammered momentarily on his anvil. I thought it best to conclude the interview with business. "I have a delicate little job that wants nice handling, and I fancy you are just the man to do it to my mind," I said.

"What is it, Sir?" he asked, in a friendly enough manner.

"I would rather show it to you than talk about it," I returned.

"As you please, Sir. When do you want me?"

"The first hour you can come."

"Tomorrow morning?"

"If you feel inclined."

"For that matter, I'd rather go to bed."

"Come to me instead: it's light work."

"I will, Sir, at ten o'clock."

"If you please."

And so it was arranged.

EIGHTEEN
THE LIFEBOAT

After breakfast and prayers the next day, I left for the church to await the arrival of the smith. In order to obtain entrance, I had to go to the cottage of the sexton. To reach the door, I crossed a hollow by a bridge built over what had once been the course of a rivulet from the heights above. Now it was a kind of little glen, grown with grass and wild flowers and ferns, and some of them rare and fine. The roof of the cottage came down to the road, but the ground behind fell suddenly away and left a bank against which the cottage was built.

Crossing a tiny garden by a flag-paved path, I entered the building and found myself in a waste-looking space that seemed to have forgotten the use for which it had been built. There was a sort of loft along one side of it, and it was heaped with indescribable lumber-looking stuff, with here and there a hint at possible machinery. (The place had been a mill for grinding corn, and its wheel had been driven by the stream which had run for ages in the hollow. But when the canal was built, the stream was turned aside to feed the canal, so that the mill fell into disuse and decay.) Crossing this floor, I entered another door, and turning sharp to the left, went down a few steps of a ladder stair, and after knocking my hat against a beam, emerged in a comfortable quaint little cottage kitchen.

The ceiling, which consisted only of the joists and the floorboards of the bedroom above, was so low that necessity, if not politeness, compelled me to take off my already bruised hat. Some of these joists were made further useful by supporting each a shelf, before which hung a little curtain of printed cotton, concealing the few stores and postponed eatables of the house, forming, in fact, both storeroom and larder of the family. On the walls hung several colored prints, and within a deep glazed frame the figure of a ship in full dress, carved in rather high relief in sycamore.

As I entered, Mrs. Coombes rose from a high-backed settle near the fire, and bade me good-morning with a curtsy.

"What a lovely day it is, Mrs. Coombes! It is so bright over the sea," I said, going on to the one little window which looked out on the great Atlantic, "that one almost expects a great merchant navy to come sailing into Kilkhaven, sunk to the water's edge with silks and ivory and spices and apes and peacocks, like the ships of Solomon that we read about."

"I know, Sir. When I was as young as you, I thought like that about the sea myself. Everything comes from the sea. For my boy Willie he du bring me home the beautifullest parrot and the talkingest you ever see, and a red shawl all worked over with flowers. He made that ship you see in the frame there, all with his own knife, out of a bit of wood that he got at the Marishes, as they calls it—a bit of an island somewheres in the great sea. And I thought like that till my third boy fell asleep in the wide water—for it du call it falling asleep, don't it, Sir?"

"The Bible certainly does," I answered.

"It's the Bible I be meaning, of course," she returned. "Well, after that I did begin to think about the sea as something that took away things and didn't bring them no more. And somehow or other she never looked so blue after that, and she gave me the shivers. But now she always looks to me like one o' the shining ones that come to fetch the pilgrims. You've heard tell of the *Pilgrim's Progress,* I daresay, among the poor people. They do say it was written by a tinker, though there be a power o' good things in it that I think the gentle folk would like if they knowed it."

"I do know the book—nearly as well as I know the Bible," I answered, "and the shining ones are very beautiful in it. I am glad you can think of the sea that way."

"It's looking in at the window all day as I go about the house," she answered, "and all night too when I'm asleep, and if I hadn't learned to think of it that way, it would have driven me mad, I du believe. I was forced to think that way about it, or not think at all. And that wouldn't be easy, with the sound of it in my ears the last thing at night and the first thing in the morning."

"The truth of things is indeed the only refuge from the look of things," I replied. "But I came for the key to the church, if you will trust me with it, for I have something to do there this morning. And the key of the tower as well, if you please."

With her old smile, ripened only by age, she reached the ponderous keys from the nail where they hung, and gave them into my hand. I left her in the shadow of her dwelling, and stepped forth into the sunlight.

The blacksmith was waiting for me at the church door. He was plainly far from well. There was a flush on his thin cheek, and his eyes had something of the far country in them—"the light that never was on the sea or shore." But his speech was cheerful, for he had been walking in the light of this world, and that had done something to make the light within him shine a little more freely.

"How do you find yourself today?" I asked.

"Quite well, Sir, thank you," he answered. "A day like this does a man good. But," he added, and his countenance fell, "the heart knoweth its own bitterness."

"It may know it too much," I returned, "just because it refuses to let a stranger meddle therein."

He made no reply. I turned the key in the great lock, and the iron-studded oak opened and let us into the solemn gloom.

It did not require many minutes to make the man understand what I wanted of him. "We must begin at the bells and work down," he said.

So we went up into the tower where, with the help of a candle, he made a good many measurements; found that carpenter's work was necessary; undertook the management of the whole; and in the course of an hour and a half went home to do what had to be done, assuring me that he had no doubt of bringing the job to a satisfactory conclusion.

"In a fortnight, I hope you will be able to play a tune to the parish, Sir," he added as he took his leave.

I resolved to know more of the man and find out his trouble, for I was certain there was a deep cause for his gloom.

As I left the churchyard, the sound of voices reached my ear. There, down below me, at the foot of the high bank on which I stood, lay a gorgeous shining thing upon the bosom of the canal, full of men and surrounded by men, women, and children delighting in its beauty. It was the lifeboat, but in its gorgeous colors

101

red and white and green—it looked more like the galley that bore Cleopatra to Actium. Nor, floating so light on the top of the water, and broad in the beam, curved upward and ornamented, did it look at all formed to battle the elements. A pleasure boat it seemed, fit to be drawn by swans. Ten men sat on the thwarts, and one in the stern by the yet useless rudder, while men and boys drew the showy thing by a rope to the lockgates. The men in the boat wore blue jerseys, but you could see little of the color for the strange unshapely things that they wore above them, like armor cut out of a row of organ pipes. They were their cork jackets, for every man had to be made into a lifeboat himself.

They towed the shining thing through the upper gate of the lock, and slowly she sank from my sight, and for some moments was no more to be seen. All at once there she was beyond the lockhead, abroad and free, fleeting from the strokes of ten swift oars over the still waters of the bay toward the waves that roared farther out where the ground swell was broken by the rise of the sandy coast. There was no vessel in danger now; they were going out for exercise and show. It seemed all child's play for a time, but when they got among the broken waves, then it looked quite another thing. The motion of the waters laid hold upon her, and soon tossed her fearfully, now revealing the whole of her capacity on the near side of one of their slopes, now hiding her whole bulk in one of the hollows beyond. She, careless as a child in the troubles of the world, floated about with what appeared too much buoyancy for the promise of a safe return. Again and again she was driven from her course toward the low rocks on the other side of the bay, and again and again returned to disport herself like a sea animal, upon the backs of the wild bursting billows.

"Can she go no farther?" I asked of the captain of the coast-guard, a man named Roxton, who was standing by my side.

"Not without some danger," he answered.

"What, then, must it be in a storm!"

"Then, of course," he returned, "they must take their chances. But there is no good in running risks for nothing. That swell is quite enough for exercise."

"But is it enough to accustom them to face the danger that will come?" I asked.

"With danger comes courage," said the old sailor.

While we spoke I saw on the pierhead the tall figure of Percivale looking earnestly at the boat. (He had been, I learned soon after, a crack oarsman at Oxford and had belonged to the University boat.)

In a little while the boat sped swiftly back, entered the lock, was lifted above the level of the storm-heaved ocean, and floated calmly up the smooth canal to the pretty little Tudor-fashioned house in which she lay.

All this time I had the keys in my hand, and now went back to the cottage to restore them to their place. When I entered, there was a young woman of sweet and interesting countenance talking to Mrs. Coombes. I had never yet seen the daughter who lived with her, and thought this was she.

"I've found your daughter at last then?" I said, approaching them.

"Not yet, Sir. She goes out to work, and her hands be pretty full at present. But this be almost my daughter," she added. "This is my next daughter, Mary Trehern, from the south. She's got a place nearby, to be near her mother that is to be, that's me."

Mary was hanging her head and blushing as the old woman spoke.

"I understand," I said. "And when are you going to get your new mother, Mary? Soon, I hope."

But she gave me no reply, only hung her head lower and blushed deeper.

Mrs. Coombes spoke for her. "She's shy, but if she was to speak her mind, she would ask you whether you wouldn't marry her and Willie when he comes home from his next voyage."

Mary's hands were trembling now, and she turned half away.

"With all my heart," I said.

The girl tried to turn toward me, but could not. I looked at her face a little more closely. Through all its tremor, there was a look of constancy that greatly pleased me. I tried to make her speak. "When do you expect Willie home?" I said.

She lifted a pair of soft brown eyes with one glance and a smile, and then sank them again.

"He'll be home in about a month," answered the mother. "She's a good ship he's aboard of, and makes good voyages."

"It is time then to think about the banns. Just come to me when you think it proper, and I will attend to it."

I thought I could hear a murmured "Thank you, Sir," from the girl, but I could not be certain. I shook hands with them, and went for a stroll on the other side of the bay.

NINETEEN

MR. PERCIVALE

I returned home and found my whole family about Connie's couch. With them was Mr. Percivale, who was showing her some sketches. Wynnie stood behind Connie, looking over her shoulder at the drawing in her hand.

My two daughters were talking away with the young man as if they had known him for years, and my wife was seated at the foot of the couch, apparently taking no exception to the suddenness of the intimacy.

"I think, though," Connie was saying, "it is only fair that Mr. Percivale should see *your* work, Wynnie."

"Then I will fetch my portfolio, if Mr. Percivale will promise to remember that I have no opinion of it. At the same time, if I could do what I wanted to do, I think I should not be ashamed of showing my drawings even to him." As Wynnie spoke, she turned and went back into the house to fetch some of her work. Now, had she been going on a message for me, she would have gone like the wind, but on this occasion she stepped along in a stately manner. And I could not help noting that Mr. Percivale's eyes also followed her. She was not long in returning, and came back with the same dignified motion.

"There is nothing really worth either showing or concealing," she said to Mr. Percivale, as she handed him the portfolio—to help himself, as it were. She then turned away, as if a little feeling of shyness had come over her, and began to look for something to do about Connie. I could see that, although she had hitherto been almost indifferent about the merit of her drawings, she had a newborn wish that they might not appear altogether contemptible in the eyes of Mr. Percivale. And Connie hastened to her sister's rescue.

"Give me your hand, Wynnie," said Connie, "and help me to move one inch farther on my side. I may move just that much on my side, mayn't I, Papa?"

"I think you had better not, my dear, if you can do without it," I answered, for the doctor's injunctions had been strong.

"Very well, Papa, but I feel as if it would do me good."

"Mr. Turner will be here next week, and you must try to stick to his rules till he comes to see you. Perhaps he will let you relax a little."

Connie smiled very sweetly and lay still, while Wynnie stood holding her hand.

Meantime Mr. Percivale, having received the drawings, had walked away with them toward what they called the storm tower—a small building standing square to the points of the compass, with little windows from which the coastguard could see along the coast on both sides and far out to sea with their telescopes. This tower stood on the very edge of the cliff, but behind it was a steep descent, where he went round the tower and disappeared. He evidently wanted to make a leisurely examination of the drawings—somewhat formidable for Wynnie. It impressed me favorably that he was not inclined to pay a set of stupid and untrue compliments the instant the portfolio was opened, but, in order to speak what was real about them, would take the trouble to make himself acquainted with them.

I therefore strolled after him, seeing no harm in taking a peep at him while he was taking a peep at my daughter's mind. I went round the tower to the other side, and there saw him at a little distance below me, but farther out on a great rock that overhung the sea, connected with the cliff by a long narrow isthmus, a few yards lower than the cliff itself, and only just broad enough for a footpath along its top, and on one side going sheer down with a smooth hard rock face to the sands below. The other side was less steep, and had some grass on it. But the path was too narrow, and the precipice too steep for me. So I stood and saw him from the mainland—saw his head bent over the drawings; saw how slowly he turned from one to the other; saw how, after having gone over them once, he turned to the beginning and went over them again, even more slowly than before; saw how he turned back the third time. Then I went back to the group on the down, caught sight of Charlie and Harry turning heels over head down the slope, and found that my wife had gone home. Only Connie and Wynnie were left. The sun had disappeared under a cloud, the sea had turned a little slaty, and the wind had just the suspicion of an edge in it. And Wynnie's face looked a little cloudy too, I thought, and I feared that it was my fault.

"Run, Wynnie, and ask Mr. Percivale, with my compliments, to come and lunch with us," I said, more to let her see I was not displeased, however I might have looked, than for any other reason. She went, sedately as before.

Almost as soon as she was gone, I saw that I had put her in a difficulty. For I had discovered, very soon after coming to these parts, that her head was no more steady than mine upon high places. But if she could not cross that narrow and really dangerous isthmus, still less could she call across the chasm to a man she had seen but once. I therefore set off after her, leaving Connie lying in loneliness between the sea and the sky.

But when I got to the other side of the tower, instead of finding Wynnie standing hesitating on the brink of action, there she was on the rock beyond. Mr. Percivale had risen, and the next moment they turned to come back.

I stood trembling almost to see her cross the knife-back of that ledge. In the middle of the path—up to which point she had been walking with perfect steadiness and composure—she lifted her eyes, saw me, looked as if she saw a ghost, half lifted her arms, swayed as if she would fall, and indeed, was falling over the precipice, when Mr. Percivale caught her in his arms, almost too late for both of them. So nearly down was she already, that her weight bent him over the rocky side till it seemed as if he must yield, or his body snap. For he bent from the waist, and his feet kept hold on the ground. It was all over in a moment, and in another moment they were at my side—she with a wan, terrified smile, he in ruddy alarm. I was unable to speak and could only, with trembling steps, lead the way from the dreadful spot. Without a word they followed me.

Before we reached Connie, I recovered myself sufficiently to say, "Not a word to Connie," and they understood me. I told Wynnie to run to the house and send Walter to help me carry Connie home. Until Walter came, I talked to Mr. Percivale as if nothing had happened. He did not do as some young men, wishing to ingratiate themselves, would have done—he did not offer to help me carry Connie home. I saw that the offer rose in his mind, and that he repressed it. He understood that I must consider such a permission as a privilege not to be accorded to the acquaintance of a day, that I must know him better before I could again allow the weight of my child to rest upon his strength. But he responded to my invitation to lunch with us, and walked by my side as Walter and I bore the precious burden home.

During our meal, he made himself quite agreeable; he talked well on the topics of the day—not altogether as a man who had made up his mind, but as one who had thought about them and did not find it easy to come to a conclusion. His behavior was entirely that of a gentleman, and his education was good. But what I did not like was, that as often as the conversation made a bend in the direction of religious matters, he was sure to bend it away in some other direction. This, however, might have various reasons to account for it, and I would wait.

After lunch, as we rose from the table, he took Wynnie's portfolio from the side table where he had laid it, and with no more than a bow and thanks returned it to her. I thought she looked a little disappointed, though she said as lightly as she could, "I am afraid you have not found anything worthy of criticism in my poor attempts, Mr. Percivale."

"On the contrary, I shall be most happy to tell you what I think of them."

"I shall be greatly obliged to you," she said, "for I have had no help since I left school, except Mr. Ruskin's book called *Modern Painters*. Do you know the author, Mr. Percivale?"

"I wish I did. He has given me much help. I have such a respect for him that I always feel as if he must be right, whether he seems to me to be right or not. And if he is severe, it is with the severity of love that will speak only the truth."

This last speech fell on my ear like the tone of a church bell. "I've been waiting for that, my friend," I thought, but I said nothing to interrupt.

He opened the portfolio on the side table, and placed a chair in front of it for my daughter. Then, seating himself by her side, but without the least approach to familiarity, he began to talk to her at length about her drawings, generally praising the feeling, but finding fault with the want of nicety in the execution.

107

"But," said my daughter, "it seems to me that if you get the feeling right, that is the main thing."

"So much the main thing," returned Mr. Percivale, "that any imperfection or coarseness or untruth which interferes with it becomes of the greatest consequence."

"But can it really interfere with the feeling?"

"Perhaps not with most people, simply because most people observe so badly that their recollections of nature are all blurred and blotted and indistinct, and therefore the imperfections do not affect them. But with the more cultivated, it is otherwise. It is for them you ought to work, for you do not thereby lose the others. Besides, the feeling is always intensified by the finish, for that belongs to the feeling too, and must have some influence even where it is not noted."

"But is it not a hopeless thing to attempt the finish of nature?"

"Not at all—to the degree, that is, in which you can represent anything else of nature. But in this drawing now you have nothing to hint at or recall the feeling of the exquisiteness of nature's finish. Why should you not at least have drawn a true horizon line there? Has the absolute truth of the meeting of sea and sky nothing to do with the feeling which such a landscape produces? I should have thought you would have learned that, if anything, from Mr. Ruskin."

Mr. Percivale spoke earnestly. Wynnie, either from disappointment or despair, probably from a mixture of both, apparently felt as if he was scolding her, and got cross. This was anything but dignified, especially with a stranger, and one who was doing his best to help her. Her face was flushed, and tears came in her eyes, and she rose, saying with a little choke in her voice, "I see it's no use in trying. I won't intrude anymore into things I am incapable of. I am much obliged to you, Mr. Percivale, for showing me how presumptuous I have been."

The painter rose as she rose, looking greatly concerned, but he did not attempt to answer her. Indeed, she gave him no time. He could only spring after her to open the door for her. A more than respectable bow as she left the room was his only adieu.

But when he turned his face again toward me, it expressed consternation. "I fear," he said, "I have been rude to Miss Walton, but nothing was farther—"

"I heard all you were saying, and you were not rude in the least. On the contrary, I consider you very kind to take the trouble with her you did. Allow me to make the apology for my daughter. She will recover from the disappointment of finding unexpected obstacles in the way of her favorite pursuit. She is only too ready to lose heart, and she paid too little attention to your approbation and too much to your criticism. She lost her temper, but more with herself and her poor attempts, I assure you, than with your remarks."

"But I must have been to blame if I caused any such feeling with regard to those drawings, for I assure you they contain great promise."

"I am glad you think so. That I should myself be of the same opinion can be of no consequence."

"Miss Walton at least sees what ought to be represented. All she needs is greater severity in the quality of representation. And that would have grown without any remarks from onlookers, but a friendly criticism opens the eyes a little sooner than they would have opened themselves. And time," he added, "is half the battle in this world. It is over so soon."

"No sooner than it ought to be," I rejoined.

"So it may appear to you," he returned. "Here I am nearly thirty, and have made no mark on the world yet."

"I don't know that that is of so much consequence," I said. "I have never hoped for more than to rub out a few of the marks already made."

"Perhaps you are right," he returned. "Every man has something he can do, and more, I suppose, that he can't do. But I have no right to turn a visit into a visitation. Will you please tell Miss Walton that I am very sorry I presumed on the privileges of a drawing master, and gave her pain. It was so far from my intention that it will be a lesson to me for the future."

With these words he took his leave, and I could not help being greatly pleased. He was clearly anything but a common man.

TWENTY

THE SHADOW OF DEATH

When Wynnie appeared at dinner she looked ashamed of herself, and her face betrayed that she had been crying. But I said nothing, for I had confidence that all she needed was time to come to herself, that the voice that speaks louder than any thunder might make its stillness heard. And when I came home from my walk the next morning, I found Mr. Percivale once more in the group about Connie, and evidently on the best possible terms with all. The same afternoon Wynnie went out sketching with Dora. I had no doubt that she had made some sort of apology to Mr. Percivale, but I did not make the slightest attempt to discover what had passed between them. For though it is of all things desirable that children should be quite open with their parents, I was most anxious to lay upon them no burden of obligation. Therefore I trusted my child. And when I saw that she looked at me a little shyly when we next met, I only sought to show her the more tenderness and confidence, telling her all about my plans with the bells and my talks with the smith and Mrs. Coombes. She listened with interest, asking questions, and making remarks, but I still felt that there was the thread of a little uneasiness through the web of our talk. Yet it was for Wynnie to bring it out, not me.

And she did not leave it long. For as she bade me good-night in my study, she said suddenly, yet with hesitating openness, "Papa, I told Mr. Percivale that I was sorry I had behaved so badly about the drawings."

"You did right, my child," I replied. "And what did

110

Mr.Percivale say?"

"He took the blame all on himself, Papa."

"Like a gentleman."

"But I could not leave it so, you know, Papa, because that was not the truth."

"Well?"

"I told him that I had lost my temper from disappointment—that I had thought I did not care for my drawings because I was so far from satisfied with them. But when he made me feel that they were worth nothing, then I found from the vexation I felt that I had cared for them. But I think, Papa, I was more ashamed of having shown them, and vexed with myself, than cross with him. I was very silly."

"Well, and what did he say?"

"He began to praise them then. But you know I could not take much of that, for what could he do?"

"You might give him credit for a little honesty, at least."

"Yes, but things may be true in a way, you know, and not mean much."

"He seems to have succeeded in reconciling you to the prosecution of your efforts, however, for I saw you go out with your sketching apparatus this afternoon."

"Yes," she answered, shyly. "He was so kind, that somehow I got heart to try again. He's very nice, isn't he?"

My answer was not quite ready.

"Don't you like him, Papa?"

"Well—I like him—yes. But we must not be in haste with our judgments, you know. I have had very little opportunity of seeing into him. There is much in him that I like, but—"

"But what, please, Papa?"

"I can speak my mind to you, my child; he has a certain shyness of approaching the subject of religion. I have my fears lest he should belong to some school of a fragmentary philosophy which acknowledges no source of truth but the testimony of the senses and the deductions made therefrom by the intellect."

"But is not that a hasty conclusion, Papa?"

"That is a hasty question, my dear. I have come to no conclusion. I was only speaking confidentially about my fears."

"Perhaps, Papa, it's only that he's not sure enough and is afraid of appearing to profess more than he believes. I'm sure, if that's it, I have the greatest sympathy with him."

I looked at her, and saw the tears gathering fast in her eyes.

"Pray to God on the chance of His hearing you, my darling, and go to sleep," I said. "I will not think hardly of you because you cannot be so sure as I am. How could you be? You have not had my experience. Perhaps you are right about Mr. Percivale too. But it would be an awkward thing to get intimate with him, you know, and then find out that we did not like him after all. You couldn't like a man much, could you, who did not believe in anything greater than himself, anything marvelous, grand, beyond our understanding, who thought that he had come out of the dirt and was going back to the dirt?"

"I could, Papa, if he tried to do his duty notwithstanding, for I am sure *I* couldn't. I should cry myself to death."

"You are right, my child. I should honor him too. But I should be very sorry for him, for he would be so disappointed in himself." I do not know whether this was the best answer to make, but I had little time to think.

"But you don't know that he's like that."

"I do not, my dear. And more, I will not associate the idea with him till I know for certain. We will leave it to ignorant old people who lay claim to an instinct for theology to jump at conclusions, and reserve ours till we have sufficient facts from which to draw them. Now go to bed, my child."

"Good night then, dear Papa," she said, and left me with a kiss.

I was not altogether comfortable. I had tried to be fair to the young man both in word and thought, but I could not relish the idea of my daughter falling in love with him—which looked likely enough—before I knew more about him, and found that more hope-giving. There was but one rational thing left to do, and that was to cast my care on Him that careth for us, on the Father who loved my child more than I even could love her, and loved the young man too, and regarded my anxiety, and would take its cause upon Himself. After I had lifted up my heart to Him and was at ease, I read a canto of Dante's *Paradisio* and then went to bed.

As I went out for my walk the next morning, I caught sight of the sexton busily trimming some of the newer graves in the churchyard. I turned in through the nearer gate.

"Good morning, Coombes," I said.

He turned up a wizened, humorous, old face, the very type of a gravedigger; and with one hand leaning on the edge of the green mound where he had been cropping the too long and too thin grass, he touched his cap with the other and bade me a cheerful good-morning in return.

"You're making things tidy," I said.

"It take time to make them all comfortable, you see, Sir," he returned, taking up his shears again, and clipping away at the top and sides of the mound.

"You mean the dead, Coombes?"

"Yes, Sir, to be sure."

"You don't think it makes much difference to their comfort, do you, whether the grass is one length or another upon their graves?"

"Well, no, I don't suppose it makes much difference to them. But it look more comfortable, you know. And I like things to look comfortable. Don't you, Sir?"

"To be sure I do, Coombes. And you are quite right. The resting-place of the body, although the person it belonged to be far away, should be respected."

"That's what I think, though I don't get no credit for it. I do my best to make the poor things comfortable."

He seemed unable to rid his mind of the idea that the comfort of the departed was dependent upon his ministrations.

"The trouble I have with them sometimes! There's now this same one as lies here, old Jonathan Giles. He have the gout so bad! And just as I come within a couple o' inches o' the right depth, out come the edge of a great stone in the near corner at the foot of the bed. Thinks I, he'll never lie comfortable with that under his gouty toe. But the trouble I had to get out that stone! I du assure you, Sir, it took me nigh half the day. But this be one of the nicest places to lie in, all up and down the coast—a nice gravelly soil, dry, and warm, and comfortable. Them poor things as comes out of the sea must quite enjoy the change."

It was a grotesque and curious way for the humanity that was in him to find expression, but I did not like to let him go on thus. It was so much opposed to all that I believed and felt about the change from this world to the next!

"But, Coombes," I said, "why will you go on talking as if it made an atom of difference to the dead bodies where they were buried? They care no more about it than your old coat would care where it was thrown after you had done with it."

He turned and regarded his coat where it hung beside him on

113

the headstone, shaking his head with a smile that seemed to doubt whether the said old coat would be altogether so indifferent to such treatment. Then he began to approach me from another angle—and I confess he had the better of me before I was aware of what he was about.

"The church of Boscastle stands high on the cliff. You've been to Boscastle, Sir?"

"Not yet, but I hope to go before the summer is over."

"Ah, you should see Boscastle, Sir. That's where I was born. And when I was a boy that church was haunted. It's a damp place, and the wind in it awful. I du believe it stand higher than any church in the country, and have got more wind in it of a stormy night than any church whatsomever. Well, they said it was haunted, and every now and then there was a knocking heard down below. And this always took place of a stormy night, as if there was some poor thing down in the low wouts," (for so he pronounced *vaults*) "and he wasn't comfortable and wanted to get out. Well, one fearful night the sexton went and took the blacksmith and a ship's carpenter, and they go together and they open one of the old family wouts that belongs to the Penhaligans, and they go down with a light. Now the wind was a-blowing all as usual, only worse than common. And there to be sure what do they see but the wout half full of seawater, and nows and thens a great spout coming in through a hole in the rock, for it was high water and a wind off the sea, as I tell you. And there was a coffin afloat on the water, and every time the spout come through, it set it knocking agen the side o' the wout, and that was the ghost."

"What a horrible idea!" I said, with a half-shudder at the unrest of the dead.

The old man uttered a queer long-drawn sound, neither a chuckle, a crow, nor a laugh, but a mixture of all three, and said, "I thought you would like to be comfortable then as well as other people, Sir."

I could not help laughing to see how the cunning old fellow had caught me. I have not yet been able to find out how much truth was in his story. From the twinkle of his eye I cannot help suspecting that if he did not invent the tale, he embellished it. Neither could I help thinking with pleasure, as I turned away, how the merry little old man would enjoy telling his companions how he had posed the old parson. Very unwelcome was he to his laugh, for my part.

I gladly left the churchyard, with its sunshine above and its darkness below. I had to look up to the glittering vanes on the four pinnacles of the church tower, dwelling aloft in the clean sunny air, to get the feeling of the dark vault and the floating coffin and the knocking in the windy church out of my brain. But the thing that did free me was the reflection with what supreme disregard the disincarcerated spirit would look upon any possible vicissitudes of its abandoned vault. For the body of man's revelation becomes a vault, a prison, from which it must be freedom to escape at length. The house we like best would be a prison of awful sort if the doors and windows were all built up. Man's abode, as age begins to draw nigh, fares thus. Age is the mason that builds up the doors and the windows, and death is the angel that breaks the prison-house and lets the captives free. Thus I got something out of the sexton's horrible story.

But before the week was over, death came near indeed. I had retired to my study after lunch and was dozing in my chair, for the day was hot, when Charlie rushed into the room with the cry, "Papa, Papa, there's a man drowning!"

I hurried down to the drawing room which looked out over the bay. I could see nothing but people running about on the edge of the quiet waves. No sign of human being was on the water, but one boat was coming out from the lock of the canal, and Roxton of the coastguard was running down from the tower on the cliff with ropes in his hand. He would not stop the boat even for the moment it would need to take him on board, but threw them in and urged them to haste.

I stood at the window and watched. Every now and then I fancied I saw something white heaved up on the swell of a wave, and as often was satisfied that I had but fancied it. The boat seemed to be floating about lazily, if not idly. The eagerness to help made it appear as if nothing was going on. Could it, after all, have been a false alarm? I watched, and still the boat kept moving from place to place, so far out that I could see nothing distinctly of the motions of its crew. At length a long white thing rose from the water slowly, and was drawn into the boat which was rowed swiftly to the shore. There was but one place fit to land upon—a little patch of sand under the window at which I stood, and immediately under our garden wall. There stood Roxton, earnest and sad, waiting to use—though without much immediate hope—every appliance so well known to him.

I will not linger over the sad details of the vain endeavor. The honored head of a family had departed, and left a good name behind him. But even in the midst of my poor attentions to the quiet, speechless pale-faced wife who sat at the head of the corpse, I could not help feeling anxious about the effect on Connie, for it was impossible to keep the matter concealed from her. The undoubted concern on the faces of the two boys was enough to reveal that something serious and painful had occurred, while my wife and Wynnie, and indeed the whole household, were busy in attending to every remotest suggestion of aid that reached them from the little crowd gathered about the body. The body was borne away, and I led the poor lady to her lodging, and remained there with her till she lay on the sofa and slept.

I left her with her son and her daughter, and returned to my own family. Had they only heard of the occurrence, it would have had little effect, but death had appeared to them. Everyone but Connie had seen the dead lying there, and before the day was over, I wished she had too. For I found from what she said at intervals, and from the shudder that now and then passed through her, that her imagination was at work, showing the horrors that belong to death, without the enfolding peace that accompanies the sight of the dead.

And now I became more grateful than ever for the gift of Theodora, for I felt no anxiety about Connie so long as she was with her. The presence even of her mother could not relieve her, for Ethelwyn and Wynnie were both clouded with the same awe, and its reflex in Connie was distorted by her fancy. But the sweet ignorance of the baby healed, for she appeared in her sweet merry ways—to the mood in which they all were—like a little sunny window in a cathedral crypt, telling of a whole universe of sunshine and motion beyond those oppressed pillars and low-groined arches.

But my wife suffered nearly as much as Connie. As long as she was going about the house or attending to the wants of her family, she was free. But no sooner did she lay her head on the pillow than in rushed the cry of the sea—fierce, unkind, craving like a wild beast. Again and again she spoke of it to me, for it came to her mingled with the voice of the tempter, saying, "Cruel chance," over and over again. For although the two words contradict each other when put together thus, each in its turn would assert itself.

"It is all fancy, my dear," I said to her. "There is nothing more terrible in this than in any other death. On the contrary, I can hardly imagine a less fearful one. A big wave falls on the man's head and stuns him, and without further suffering he floats gently out on the sea of the unknown."

But though she always seemed satisfied after any conversation of the sort, yet every night she would call out once and again, "Oh, that sea out there!" I was very glad indeed when Turner, who had arranged to spend a short holiday with us, arrived.

He was concerned at the news I gave him and counseled an immediate change, that time might, in the absence of surrounding associations, obliterate something of the impression that had been made. So we resolved to remove our household, for a short time, to some place not too far off to permit of my attending to my duties at Kilkhaven, but out of the sight and sound of the sea. It was Thursday when Mr. Turner arrived, and he spent the next two days in finding a suitable spot for us.

On the Saturday, the blacksmith was busy in the church tower, and I went to see how he was getting on.

"You had a sad business here last week," he said, after we had done talking about the repairs.

"A very sad business, indeed."

"It was a warning to us all."

"We may take it so," I returned. "But it seems to me that we are too ready to think of such remarkable things only by themselves, instead of being roused by them to regard everything, common and uncommon, as ordered by the same care and wisdom."

"One of our local preachers made a grand use of it."

I made no reply, so he resumed. "They tell me you took no notice of it last Sunday."

"I made no immediate allusion to it, certainly, but I preached under the influence of it. And I thought it better that those who could reflect on the matter should be thus led to think for themselves, than that they should be subjected to the reception of my thoughts and feelings about it. For in the main, it is life and not death that we have to preach."

"I don't quite understand you, Sir. But then you don't care much for preaching in your churches."

"Anyone who can preach what you call rousing sermons is considered a grand preacher amongst you Methodists, and there is a great danger of him being led thereby to talk more nonsense than sense. And then when the excitement goes off, there is no seed left in the soil to grow in peace, and they are always craving after more excitement."

"Well, there is the preacher to rouse them up again."

"And so they continue like children—the good ones, I mean—and have hardly a chance of making a calm, deliberate choice of that which is good. And those who have been only excited, and nothing more, are hardened and seared by the recurrence of such feeling as is neither aroused by truth nor followed by action."

"You'd daren't talk like that if you knew the kind of people in this country that the Methodists, as you call them, have got a hold of. They tell me it was like hell itself down in those mines before Wesley come among them."

"I should be a fool or a bigot to doubt that the Wesleyans have done incalculable good in the country. And that not alone to the people who never went to church. The whole Church of England is under obligation to Methodism such as no words can overstate."

"I wonder you can say such things against them then."

"I confess I do not know much about your clergy, for I have not had the opportunity. But I do know this, that some of the best and most liberal people I have ever known have belonged to your community."

"They do gather a deal of money for good purposes."

"Yes. But that is not what I meant by 'liberal.' It is far easier to give money than to be generous in judgment. I meant, by 'liberal,' able to see the good and true in people that differ from you, glad to be roused to the reception of truth in God's name from whatever quarter it may come, and not readily finding offense. But I see that I ought to be more careful, for I have made you misunderstand me."

"I beg your pardon, Sir. I was hasty. But I do think I am more ready to lose my temper since—"

Here he stopped. A fit of coughing came on, and was followed by what could only be the result of a rupture in the lungs. I insisted on his dropping his work and coming home with me, where I made him rest the remainder of the day and all Sunday, sending word to his mother that I could not let him go home.

When we left on the Monday morning, we took him with us in the carriage hired for the journey, and set him down at his mother's, apparently no worse than usual.

TWENTY-ONE
THE KEEVE

Leaving the younger members of the family at home with the servants, we set out for a farmhouse, some twenty miles off, which Turner had discovered for us. Through deep lanes with many cottages and here and there a very ugly little chapel, over steep hills (up which Turner and Wynnie and I walked), and along sterile moors we drove. We stopped often at roadside inns, to raise Connie and let her look about upon the extended prospect. On the way Turner warned us that we were not to expect a beautiful country, although the place was within reach of much that was remarkable. Therefore we were not surprised when we drew up at the door of a bare-looking house, with scarcely a tree in sight, and a stretch of undulating fields on every side.

"A dreary place in winter, Turner," I said. We had seen Connie comfortably deposited in the nice white-curtained parlor, smelling of dried roses even in the height of the fresh ones, and had strolled out while our tea-dinner was being got ready for us.

"No doubt of it, but just the place I wanted for Miss Connie," he replied. "We are high above the sea, and the air is very bracing and not too cold now. A month later I should not on any account have brought her here."

We all went to bed early and, for the first time for many nights, my wife said nothing about the crying of the sea. The following day Turner and I set out to explore the neighborhood. The rest remained quietly at home.

It was, as I have said, a high bare country. The fields lay side by side, parted from each other chiefly—as so often in Scotland—by walls of thin stone plates laid on their edges. In the middle of the fields came here and there patches of yet unreclaimed moorland.

Now in a region like this, beauty must be looked for below the surface. There is a probability of finding hollows of repose, sunken spots of loveliness hidden away—existent because they are below the surface, and not laid bare to the sweep of the cold winds that roam above.

When Turner and I set out that morning to explore, I expected to light upon some mine or other in which nature had hidden away rare jewels, but I was not prepared to find such as we did find. With our hearts full of a glad secret we returned home, but we said nothing about it, in order that Ethelwyn and Wynnie might enjoy the discovery even as we had.

There was another grand fact with regard to the neighborhood about which we judged it better to be silent for a few days. We were considerably nearer the ocean than my wife and daughters supposed, for we had made a great round in order to arrive from the landside. We were, however, out of the sound of its waves, which broke along the shore at the foot of tremendous cliffs. What cliffs they were, they would soon find.

"Now, Wynnie!" I said, after prayers the next morning, "you must come out for a walk as soon as ever you can get your bonnet on."

"But we can't leave Connie, Papa," objected Wynnie.

"Oh, yes, you can, quite well. There's Nursie to look after her. What do you say, Connie?"

"I am entirely independent of help from my family," returned Connie, grandiloquently. "I am a woman of independent means," she added. "If you say another word, I will rise and leave the room."

Then, her mood changing, she added, as if to suppress the tears gathering in her eyes, "I am the queen of luxury and self-will, and I won't have anybody come near me till dinnertime. I mean to enjoy myself."

So the matter was settled and we went out for our walk. Ethelwyn was not such a good walker as she had been; but even if she retained the strength of her youth, we should not have got on much the better for it, so often did she and Wynnie stop to grub ferns out of the chinks and roots of the stone walls.

At length, partly by the inducement I held out to them of a much greater variety of ferns where we were bound, I succeeded in getting them over two miles in little more than two hours. After passing from the lanes into the fields, we reached a very steep large slope with a delightful southern exposure, and covered with the sweetest down-grasses. It was just the place to lie in, as on the edge of the earth, and look abroad upon the universe of air and floating worlds.

"Let us have a rest here, Ethelwyn," I said. "I am sure this is much more delightful than uprooting ferns."

"What's that in the grass?" cried Wynnie.

I looked where she had indicated, and saw a slowworm, or blindworm, basking in the sun. I rose and went toward it.

"Here's your stick," said Turner.

"What for?" I asked. "Why should I kill it? It is perfectly harmless and, to my mind, beautiful."

I took it in my hands and brought it to my wife. She gave an involuntary shudder as it came near her.

"I assure you it is harmless," I said, "though it has a forked tongue." And I opened its mouth as I spoke. "I do not think the serpent form is essentially ugly."

"It makes me feel ugly," said Wynnie.

"I allow I do not quite understand the mystery of it," I said. "But you never saw lovelier ornamentation than these silvery scales, with all the neatness of what you ladies call a set pattern. And you never saw lovelier curves than this little patient creature makes with its long thin body."

"I wonder how it can look after its tail, it is so far off," said Wynnie.

"It does though, better than you ladies look after your long dresses. I wonder whether it is descended from creatures that once had feet, but did not make a good use of them. Perhaps they had wings, even, and would not use them at all, and so lost them. Its ancestors may have had poison fangs, but it is innocent enough. But it is a terrible thing to be all feet, is it not? There is an awful significance in the condemnation of the serpent—'On thy belly shalt thou go, and eat dust.' But it is better to talk of beautiful things. Let us go on."

They did not seem willing to rise. But the glen drew me, and I rose first, and on we went.

We turned down the valley in the direction of the sea. It was but a narrow cleft, and narrowed much toward a deeper cleft in which we now saw the tops of trees, and from which we heard the rush of water. Nor had we gone far in this direction before we came upon a gate in a stone wall, which led into what seemed a neglected garden. We entered and found a path turning and winding among small trees and luxuriant ferns. There were great stones, and fragments of ruins down toward the bottom of the chasm. The noise of falling water increased as we went on, and at length, after some scrambling and several sharp turns, we found ourselves with a nearly precipitous wall on each side, clothed with shrubs and ivy and creeping things of the vegetable world. Up this cleft there was no advance. The head of it was a precipice down which shot the stream from the vale above, pouring out of a deep slit it had itself cut in the rock as with a knife. Halfway down, it tumbled into a great basin of hollowed stone, and flowing from a chasm in its side (which left part of the lip of the basin standing like the arch of a vanished bridge) it fell into a black pool below, whence it crept as if stunned or weary down the gentle decline of the ravine. It was a little gem of nature, complete and perfect in effect, and the ladies were full of pleasure. Wynnie, forgetting her usual reserve, broke out in exclamations of delight.

We stood for a while regarding the ceaseless pour of the water down the precipice, full of force and purpose, here falling in great curls of green and gray, there rejoicing the next moment to find itself brought up boiling and bubbling in the basin to issue in the gathered hope of experience. Then we turned down the stream a little way, crossed it by a plank, and stood again to regard it from the opposite side. The whole affair was small—not more than about a hundred and fifty feet in height—but full of variety. I was contemplating it fixedly, when a little stifled cry from Wynnie made me start and look round. Her face was flushed, yet she was trying to look unconcerned.

"I thought we were quite alone, Papa," she said, "but I see a gentleman sketching."

I looked whither she indicated. A little way down, the bed of the ravine widened considerably, and was no doubt filled with water in rainy weather. Now it was swampy, full of reeds and willow bushes. But on the opposite side of the stream, with a little canal going all around it, lay a great flat rectangular stone, not more than a foot above the level of the water. On a campstool in the center of this stone sat a gentleman sketching. Wynnie recognized him at once. And I was annoyed, and indeed, angry, to think that Mr. Percivale had followed us here. But while I regarded him, he looked up, rose very quietly and, with his pencil in his hand, came toward us. With no nearer approach to familiarity than a bow, and no expression of either much pleasure or any surprise, he said, "I have seen your party for some time, Mr. Walton—since you crossed the stream—but I would not break your enjoyment with the surprise of my presence."

I answered with a bow, for I could not say with truth that I was glad to see him. He resumed, doubtless penetrating my suspicion, "I have been here almost a week. I certainly had no expectation of the pleasure of seeing you."

This he said lightly, though no doubt with the object of clearing himself. And I was, if not reassured, yet disarmed, by his statement, for I could not believe, from what I knew of him, that he would be guilty of such a white lie as many a gentleman would have thought justifiable on the occasion. Still, I suppose he found me a little stiff, for presently he said, "If you will excuse me, I will return to my work."

Then I felt as if I must say something, for I had shown him no courtesy during the interview. "It must be a great pleasure to carry away such talismans with you—capable of bringing the place back to your mental vision at any moment."

"To tell the truth," he answered, "I am a little ashamed of being found sketching here. Such bits of scenery are not my favorite studies. But it is a change."

"It is very beautiful here," I said.

"It is very pretty," he answered, "very lovely, if you will—not very beautiful, I think. I would keep that word for things of larger regard. Beauty requires width and here is none."

"Why, then, do you sketch such a place?"

"A very fair question," he returned, with a smile. "Just because it is soothing from the very absence of beauty. I would rather, however, if I were only following my taste, take the barest bit of the moor above, with a streak of the cold sky over it. That gives room."

"You would like to put a skylark in it, wouldn't you?"

"That I would, if I knew how. I see you know what I mean. But the mere romantic I never had much taste for, and I am not working now. I am only playing."

"With a view to working better afterward, I have no doubt."

"You are right there, I hope," was his quiet reply, as he turned and walked back to the island.

He had not made a step toward joining us, and had only taken his hat off to the ladies. He was gaining ground upon me rapidly.

"Have you quarreled with our new friend, Harry?" said my wife, as I came up to her. She was sitting on a stone. Turner and Wynnie were farther off toward the foot of the fall.

"Not in the least," I answered, slightly outraged by the question. "He is only gone to his work, which is a duty belonging both to the first and second tables of the Law."

"I hope you have asked him to come home to our early dinner, then," she rejoined.

"I have not. That remains for you to do. Come, I will take you to him."

Ethelwyn rose at once, put her hand in mine, and with a little help, soon reached the table rock. Percivale rose, and when she came near enough, held out his hand, and she was beside him in a moment. After the usual greetings, which on her part, although very quiet—like every motion and word of hers—were yet cordial and kind, she said, "When you get back to London, Mr. Percivale, might some friends of mine call at your studio to see your paintings?"

"With all my heart," answered Percivale. "I must warn you, however, that I have not much they will care to see. They will perhaps go away less happy than they entered. Not many people care to see my pictures twice."

"I would not send you anyone I thought unworthy of the honor," answered my wife.

Percivale bowed one of his stately, old-world bows, which I greatly liked.

"Any friend of yours—that is guarantee sufficient," he answered.

There was this peculiarity about any compliment Percivale paid, that you had not a doubt of its being genuine.

"Will you come and take an early dinner with us?" said my wife. "My invalid daughter will be very pleased to see you."

"I will with pleasure," he answered, but in a tone of some hesitation, as he glanced from Ethelwyn to me.

"My wife speaks for us all," I said. "It will give us all pleasure."

"We're not quite ready to go yet," said my wife, loath to leave the lovely spot. "What a curious flat stone this is!" she added.

"It is," said Percivale. "The man to whom the place belongs, a worthy yeoman of the old school, says that this wider part of the channel must have been the fishpond, and that the portly monks stood on this stone and fished in the pond."

"There was a monastery here?" I asked.

"Certainly. The ruins of the chapel are on the top, just above the fall—rather a fearful place to look down from. They say it had a silver bell in the days of its glory, which now lies in a deep hole under the basin, halfway between the top and the bottom of the fall. But the old man says that nothing will make him look, or let anyone else lift the huge stone. For he is much better pleased to believe that it may be there, than he would be to know it was not there. Certainly, if it were found, it would not be left there long."

As he spoke, he had turned toward his easel and hastily bundled up his things. He now led our party up to the chapel ruins, and thence down a few yards to the edge of the chasm, where the water fell headlong. I turned away with that fear of high places which is one of my many weaknesses, and when I turned again toward the spot, there was Wynnie on the very edge, looking over into the flash and tumult of the water below, but with a nervous grasp of the hand of Percivale, who stood a little farther back.

In going home, the painter led us by an easier way out of the valley, left his little easel and other things at a cottage, and then walked on in front between my wife and daughter, while Turner and I followed. He seemed quite at his ease with them, and plenty of talk and laughter rose on the way. I, however, was chiefly occupied with finding out Turner's impression of Connie's condition.

"She is certainly better," he said. "The pain is nearly gone from her spine, and she can move herself a good deal more than when she left. I do think she might be allowed a little more change of posture now."

"Then you have some hope of her final recovery?"

"I have hope, most certainly. But what is hope in me, you must not allow to become certainty in you. I am nearly sure, though, that she can never be other than an invalid."

"I am thankful for the hope," I answered. "For all true hope, even as hope, man has to be unspeakably thankful."

TWENTY-TWO

THE RUINS OF TINTAGEL

I was able to arrange a young visiting clergyman to take my duty for me the next Sunday in Kilkhaven. Turner and Wynnie and I walked together the two miles to the church nearest the farmhouse. It was a lovely morning, with just a tint of autumn in the air. But even that tint, though all else was of the summer, brought a shadow to Wynnie's face, and it was with a tremor that she spoke.

"I never know, Papa, what people mean by talking about childhood in the fond way they do. I never seem to have been a bit younger and more innocent than I am."

"Don't you remember a time, Wynnie, when the things about you—the sky and the earth, say—seemed to you much grander than they seem now? You are old enough to have lost something."

She thought for a little while before she answered. "My dreams were, I know. I cannot say so of anything else."

"Then you must make good use of your dreams, my child."

"Why, Papa?"

"Because they are the only memories of childhood you have left."

"How am I to make a good use of them? I don't know what to do with my silly old dreams." But she gave a sigh as she spoke that testified her silly old dreams had a charm for her still.

"If your dreams, my child, have ever testified to you of a condition of things beyond that which you see around you; if they have been to you the hints of a wonder and glory beyond what visits you now, you must not call them silly, for they are the scents of paradise. If you have had no childhood, permit your old father to say that it is this childhood after which you are blindly longing, without which you find that life is hardly to be endured. Thank God for your dreams, my child. In Him you will find that the essence of those dreams is fulfilled. We are saved by hope. Never man hoped too much, or repented that he had hoped. The plague is that we don't hope in God half enough."

We reached the church, where, if I found the sermon neither healing nor inspiring, I found the prayers full of hope and consolation. They at least are safe beyond human caprice, conceit, or incapacity. But I did think they were too long for any individual Christian soul to sympathize with or respond to from beginning to end. It is one thing to read prayers and another to respond, and I had very few opportunities of being in the position of the latter duty. I had had suspicions before—and now they were confirmed—that the present crowding of services was most inexpedient. And as I pondered on the matter, instead of trying to go on praying after I had already uttered my soul, I thought how our Lord had given us such a short prayer to pray, and I began to wonder when or how the services came to be so heaped the one on the back of the other as they now were. No doubt many people defended them; no doubt many people could sit them out, but how many people could pray from beginning to end of them? On this point we had some talk as we went home. Wynnie was opposed to any change of the present use on the ground that we should only have the longer sermons.

"Still," I said, "I do not think even that so great an evil. A sensitive conscience will not reproach itself so much for not listening to the whole of a sermon, as for kneeling in prayer and not praying. I think that after prayers are over, each man should be at liberty to go out and leave the sermon unheard, if he pleases. I think the result would be in the end a good one both for parson and people. It would break through the deadness of the custom. Many a young mind is turned for life against churchgoing, just by the feeling that he *must* do so and so, that he *must* go through a certain round of duty. It is willing service that the Lord wants. No forced devotions are either acceptable to Him, or other than injurious to the worshiper, if such we can call him."

After attending to my duties each of the two following Sundays at Kilkhaven, I returned on the Monday or Tuesday to the farmhouse. Turner left us in the middle of the second week, and we missed him much. It was some days before Connie was quite as cheerful again as usual. I do not mean that she was in the least gloomy—she was only a little less merry. Certainly she appeared to us to have made considerable progress. One evening, while we were still at the farm, she startled us by calling out suddenly, "Papa, Papa! I moved my big toe! I did indeed!"

We were all about her in a moment. But I saw that she was excited, and I said, as calmly as I could, "But, my dear, you are possessed of two big toes; which of them are we to congratulate on this first stride in the march of improvement?"

She broke out in the merriest laugh, and then looked puzzled. All at once she said, "Papa, it is very odd, but I can't tell which of them," and burst into tears. I was afraid that I had done her more harm than good.

"It is not of the slightest consequence, my child," I said. "You have had so little communication of late with the twins, that it is no wonder you should not be able to tell the one from the other."

She smiled again, but was silent, yet with shining face, for the rest of the evening. Our hopes took a fresh start, but we heard no more from her of her power over her big toe. As often as I inquired she said she was afraid she had made a mistake, for she had not had another hint of its existence. Still I thought it could not have been fancy, and I would cleave to my belief in the good sign.

Percivale called to see us several times, but always appeared anxious not to intrude more of his society upon us than might be agreeable. He grew in my regard, however, and at length I asked him if he would assist me in another surprise which I had meditated for my companions, and this time for Connie as well, and which I hoped would prevent the painful influences of the sea from returning upon them when they went back to Kilkhaven—they must see the sea from a quite different shore first. An early day was fixed for carrying out our project, and I proceeded to get everything ready.

On the morning of a glorious day of blue and gold, we set out for the little village of Trevenna. Connie had been out every day since she came, now in one part of the fields, now in another, enjoying the expanse of earth and sky, but she had had no drive, and consequently had seen no variety of scenery. Therefore, believing she was now thoroughly able to bear it, I quite reckoned of the good she would get from the inevitable excitement. We resolved, however, after finding how much she enjoyed the few miles' drive, that we would not demand more of her strength that day, and therefore put up at the little inn, where after ordering dinner, Percivale and I left the ladies, and sallied forth to reconnoiter.

We walked through the village and down the valley beyond, sloping steeply between hills toward the sea. But when we reached the mouth of the valley, we found that we were not yet on the shore, for a precipice lay between us and the little beach below. On the left a great peninsula of rock stood out into the sea, upon which rose the ruins of the keep of Tintagel; while behind on the mainland stood the ruins of the castle itself, connected with the other only by a narrow isthmus. We had read that this peninsula had once been an island, and that the two parts of the castle were formerly connected by a drawbridge.

Looking up at the great gap which now divided the two portions, it seemed at first impossible to believe that they had ever been thus united; but a little reflection cleared up the mystery. The fact was that the isthmus, of half the height of the two parts connected by it, had been formed entirely by the fall of portions of the rock and soil on each side into the narrow dividing space, through which the waters of the Atlantic had been wont to sweep. And now the fragments of walls stood on the very verge of the precipice, and showed that large portions of the castle itself had fallen into the gulf between.

We turned to the left along the edge of the rock, and so by a narrow path reached and crossed to the other side of the isthmus. We then found that the path led to the foot of the rock (the former island) of the keep, and thence in a zigzag up the face of it to the top. We followed it, and after a great climb reached a door in a modern battlement. Entering, we found ourselves on grass amidst ruins haggard with age. We turned and surveyed the path by which we had come. It was steep and somewhat difficult, but the outlook was glorious. It was indeed one of God's mounts of vision upon which we stood. The thought, "Oh that Connie could see this!" was swelling in my heart, when Percivale broke the silence— not with any remark on the glory around us, but with the commonplace question—"You haven't got your man with you, I think, Mr. Walton?"

"No," I answered, "we thought it better to leave him to look after the boys."

He was silent for a few minutes, while I gazed in delight.

"Don't you think," he said, "it would be possible to bring Miss

Constance up here? It would delight her all the rest of her life."

"It would, indeed. But it is impossible."

"I do not think so, if you would allow me the honor to assist you. I think we could do it perfectly between us."

I was again silent for a while. Looking down on the way we had come, it seemed an almost dreadful undertaking. Percivale added, "As we shall come here tomorrow, we need not explore the place now. Shall we go down at once and observe the whole path with a view to carrying her up?"

"There can be no objection to that," I answered, as a little hope, and courage with it, began to dawn in my heart. "But you must allow it does not look very practical."

"Perhaps it would seem more so to you, if you had come up with the idea in your head all the way, as I did. Any path seems more difficult in looking back, than at the time when the difficulties themselves have to be met and overcome."

"Yes, but then you must remember that we have to take the way back whether or no, if we once take the way forward."

"True. And now I will go down with the descent in my head as well."

"Well, there can be no harm in reconnoitering it at least. Let us go."

"We can rest as often as we please," said Percivale, and turned to lead the way.

It certainly was steep, and required care even in our own descent; but for a man who had climbed mountains, as I had done in my youth, it could hardly be called difficult even in middle age. By the time we had got again into the valley road, I was all but convinced of the practicality of the proposal. I was a little vexed, however, that a stranger should have thought of giving such pleasure to Connie, when the bare wish that she might have enjoyed it had alone arisen in my mind. I reflected that this was one of the ways in which we were to be weaned from the world and knit the faster to our fellows. For even the middle-aged, in the decay of their daring, must look to the youth which follow at their heels for fresh thought and fresh impulse.

By the time we reached home we had agreed to make the attempt. As soon as we had arrived at this conclusion, I felt so happy in the prospect that I grew quite merry, especially after we had further agreed that, both for the sake of her nerves and for the sake of the lordly surprise, we should bind Connie's eyes so that she should see nothing till we had placed her high in the castle ruins.

"What mischief have you two been about?" said my wife, as we entered our room in the inn, where the cloth was already laid for dinner. "You look just like two schoolboys who have been laying some plot and can hardly hold their tongues about it."

"We have been enjoying our little walk amazingly," I answered. "So much so, that we mean to set out for another the moment dinner is over."

"I hope you will take Wynnie with you, then."

"Or you, my love," I returned.

"No. I will stay with Connie."

"Very well. You and Connie too, shall go out tomorrow, for we have found a place we want to take you to."

When dinner was over—and a very good dinner it was—Wynnie and Percivale and I set out again. For as Percivale and I came back in the morning, we had seen the church standing far aloft and aloof on the other side of the little valley, and we wanted to go to it. It was rather a steep climb, and Wynnie accepted Percivale's offered arm. I led the way, therefore, and left them to follow—not so far in the rear, however, but that I could take a share in the conversation. It was some little time before any arose, and it was Wynnie who led the way into it.

"What kinds of things do you like best to paint, Mr. Percivale?" she asked.

He hesitated. "I would rather you should see some of my pictures. I should prefer that to answering your question."

"But I have seen some of your pictures," she returned.

"Pardon me. Indeed you have not, Miss Walton."

"At least I have seen some of your sketches and studies."

"Some of my sketches. None of my studies."

"But you make use of your sketches for your pictures, do you not?"

"Never of such as you have seen. They are only a slight antidote to my pictures. But I would rather, I repeat, say nothing about my pictures till you see some of them."

"But how am I to have that pleasure, then?"

"You go to London, sometimes, do you not?"

"Very rarely. More rarely still when the Royal Academy is open."

"That does not much matter. My pictures are seldom to be

found there."

"Do you not care to send them there?"

"I send one at least every year. But they are rarely accepted."

"Why?"

This was a very improper question, I thought, but if Wynnie had thought so she would not have put it.

He hesitated a little before he replied. "It is hardly for me to say why, but I cannot wonder much at it, considering the subjects I choose."

He said no more. And till we reached the church, nothing more of significance passed between them.

What a waste, bare churchyard that was! It had two or three lych-gates, but they had no roofs. Not a tree stood in that churchyard. Rank grass was the sole covering of the soil heaved up with the dead beneath. The ancient church stood in the midst, with its low, strong, square tower, and its long narrow nave, the ridge bowed with age, like the back of a horse worn out in the service of man, and its little homely chancel, like a small cottage that had leaned up against its end for shelter from the western blasts. It was locked, and we could not enter. But of all world-worn, sad-looking churches, that one was the dreariest I had ever beheld. Surely it needed the Gospel of the resurrection fervently preached therein, to keep it from sinking to the dust with dismay and weariness. Near it was one huge mound of grass-grown rubbish, looking like the grave where some former church had been buried, when it could stand erect no longer before the onsets of Atlantic winds. I walked round and round it, gathering its architecture, and peeping in at every window I could reach. Suddenly I was aware that I was alone.

Returning to the other side, I found Percivale seated on the churchyard wall, next to the sea. It would have been less dismal had it stood immediately on the cliffs, but they were at some little distance beyond the bare downs and rough stone walls. He was sketching the place, and Wynnie stood beside him, looking over his shoulder. I did not interrupt him, but walked among the graves, reading the poor memorials of the dead and wondering how many of the words of laudation that were inscribed on their tombs were spoken of them while they were yet alive. I was yet wandering around and reading, and stumbling over the mounds, when my companions joined me, and without a word, we walked out of the churchyard. We were nearly home before one of us spoke.

"That church is oppressive," said Percivale. "It looks like a great sepulchre, a place built only for the dead—The Church of the Dead."

"It is only that it partakes with the living," I returned, "suffers with them the buffetings of life, outlasts them, but shows, like the shield of the Red-Cross Knight, the 'old dints of deep wounds.' "

"Still, is it not a dreary place to choose for a church to stand in?"

"The church must stand everywhere. There is no region into which it must not, ought not, enter. If it refuses any earthly spot, it is shrinking from its calling. This one stands high-uplifted, looking out over the waters as a sign of the haven from all storms, the rest in God. And down beneath lie the bodies of men—you saw the graves of some of them on the other side—flung ashore from the gulfing sea." Then I told them the conversation I had had with the sexton at Kilkhaven. "But," I went on, "these fancies are only the ghostly mists that hang about the eastern hills before the sun rises. We shall look down on all that with a smile, for the Lord tells us that if we believe in Him we shall never die."

By this time we were back once more with the others, and gave Connie an account of all we had seen.

TWENTY-THREE

THE SURPRISE

The next day I awoke very early, full of anticipation for the attempt. I got up at once, found the weather most promising. After breakfast I went to Connie's room and told her that Mr. Percivale and I had devised a treat for her. Her face shone at once.

"But we want to do it our own way."

"Of course, Papa," she answered.

"Will you let us tie your eyes up?"

"Yes—and my ears and my hands too. It would be no good tying my feet, when I don't know one big toe from the other." And she laughed merrily.

"We'll try to keep up the talk all the way, so that you shan't weary of the journey."

"You're going to carry me somewhere with my eyes tied up. Oh! How jolly! And then I shall see something all at once! Jolly! Jolly!" she repeated. "Even the wind on my face would be pleasure enough for half a day. I shan't get tired so soon as you will—you dear, kind Papa! I am afraid I shall be dreadfully heavy. But I shan't jerk your arms much. I will lie so still!"

"And you won't mind letting Mr. Percivale help me carry you?"

"No. Why should I, if he doesn't mind it? He looks strong enough."

"Very well, then. I will send Mamma and Wynnie to dress you at once, and we shall set out as soon as you are ready."

She clapped her hands with delight, then caught me round the neck and gave me one of her best kisses, and began to call as loud as she could for her mamma and Wynnie to come and dress her.

It was indeed a glorious morning. The wind came in little wafts, like veins of cool, white, silver amid the great warm, yellow-gold of the sunshine. The sea lay before us, a mound of blue closing up the end of the valley, and the hills lay like great green sheep, basking in the blissful heat. The gleam from the waters came up the pass and the grand castle crowned the lefthand steep, seeming to warm its old bones, like the ruins of some awful megatherium in the lighted air.

And of all this we talked to Connie as we went, and every now and then she would clap her hands gently in the fullness of her delight, although she beheld the splendor only as with her ears, or from the kisses of the wind on her cheeks. But, since her accident, she seemed to have approached the condition which Milton represents Samson as longing for in his blindness, wherein

the sight should be through all the parts diffused,
That she might look at will through every pore.
(*Samson Agonistes*)

I arranged with the rest of the company that the moment we reached the cliff over the shore and turned to cross the isthmus, they should no longer converse about the things around us, and that no exclamation of surprise or delight should break from them before Connie's eyes were uncovered. I said nothing about the difficulties of the way, that, seeing us take them as ordinary things, they might so take them too, and not be uneasy.

We never stopped till we reached the foot of the keep. There we set Connie down, to take breath and ease our arms before we began the arduous way.

"Now, now!" said Connie, eagerly, lifting her hands to her eyes.

"No, no, my love, not yet," I said, and she lay still again, only more eager than before.

"I am afraid I have tired out you and Mr. Percivale, Papa," she said.

Percivale laughed so amusedly, that she rejoined roguishly, "Oh, yes! I know every gentleman is a Hercules—at least he chooses to be considered one! But, notwithstanding my firm faith in the fact, I have a little womanly conscience left that is hard to hoodwink."

There was a speech for wee Connie to make! The best answer and the best revenge was to lift her and go on. This we did, trying to prevent the difference of level between us from tilting the litter too much for her comfort.

"Where are you going, Papa?" she said once, but without fear in her voice, as a little slip I made lowered my end of the litter suddenly. "You must be going up a steep place. Don't hurt yourself, dear Papa."

We had changed our positions and were now carrying her, head foremost, up the hill. Percivale led and I followed. Now I could see every change on her lovely face, and it made me strong to endure—for I did find it hard work, I confess, to get to the top. Percivale strode on as if he bore a feather behind him. I did wish we were at the top, for my arms began to feel like iron cables, stiff and stark. I was afraid of my fingers giving way, and my heart was beating uncomfortably too. But Percivale strode on unconcernedly, turning every corner of the zigzag where I expected to halt, and striding on again. But I held out, strengthened by the play on my daughter's face, delicate as the play on an opal—one that inclines more to the milk than the fire.

When at length we turned in through the gothic door in the battlement wall, and set our lovely burden down upon the grass, I said, "Percivale," forgetting the proprieties in the affected humor of being angry with him, so glad was I that we had her at length on the mount of glory, "why did you go on walking like a castle, and pay no heed to me?"

"You didn't speak, did you, Mr. Walton?" he returned, with just a shadow of solicitude in the question.

"No. Of course not," I rejoined.

"Oh, then," he returned, in a tone of relief, "how could I stop? You were my captain: how could I give in so long as you were holding on?"

I am afraid the "Percivale"—without the "Mister"—came again and again after this, though I pulled myself up for it as often as I caught myself.

"Now, Papa!" said Connie from the grass.

"Not yet, my dear. Wait till your mamma and Wynnie come. Let us go and meet them, Percivale."

"Oh, yes, do, Papa. Leave me alone here without knowing where I am or what kind of place I am in. I should like to know how it feels. I have never been alone in all my life."

"Very well, my dear," I said, and Percivale and I left her alone in the ruins.

We found Ethelwyn toiling up with Wynnie helping her.

"Dear Harry," she said, "how could you think of bringing Connie up such an awful place? I wonder you dared to do it."

"It's done, you see, Wife," I answered, "thanks to Mr. Percivale, who has nearly torn the breath out of me. But now we must get you up, and you will say that to see Connie's delight, not to mention your own, is quite wages for the labor."

"Isn't she afraid to find herself so high up?"

"She knows nothing about it yet."

"You do not mean you have left the child there with her eyes tied up!"

"We could not uncover them before you came. It would spoil half the pleasure."

"Do let us make haste then. It is surely dangerous to leave her so."

"Not in the least—but she must be getting tired of the darkness. Take my arm now."

"Don't you think Mrs. Walton had better take my arm?" said Percivale. "Then you can put your hand on her back, and help her a little that way."

We tried the plan and found it a good one, and soon reached the top. The moment our eyes fell on Connie, we could see that she had found the place neither fearful nor lonely. The sweetest ghost of a smile hovered on her pale face, which shone in the shadow of the old gateway of the keep with light from her own sunny soul. She lay in still expectation, as if she had just fallen asleep after receiving an answer to prayer.

But she heard our steps, and her face awoke. "Has Mamma come?"

"Yes, my darling. I am here," said her mother. "How do you feel?"

"Perfectly well, Mamma, thank you. Now, Papa!"

"One moment more, my love. Percivale?"

We carried her to the spot we had agreed on, and while we held her a little inclined that she might see the better, her mother undid the bandage from her head.

"Hold your hands over her eyes, a little way from them," I said to her as she untied the handkerchief, "that the light may reach them by degrees and not blind her."

Ethelwyn did so for a few moments, then removed them. Still, for a moment or two more, it was plain from Connie's look of utter bewilderment, that all was a confused mass of light and color. Then she gave a little cry, and to my astonishment, half rose to a sitting posture. One moment more, and she laid herself gently back, and tears glistened in her eyes and down each cheek.

And now I may tell of the glory that made her weep.

Through the gothic-arched door in the battlemented wall, Connie saw a great gulf at her feet, full to the brim of a splendor of light and color. Before her rose the great ruins of rock and castle: rough stone below, clear green grass above, even to the verge of the abrupt and awful precipice. At the foot of the rocks, hundreds of feet below, the blue waters broke white upon the dark gray sands, and all was full of the gladness of the sun overflowing in speechless delight. But the main marvel was the look sheer below into the abyss full of light and air and color, its sides lined with rock and grass, and its bottom lined with blue ripples and sand.

"O Lord God!" I said, almost involuntarily, "Thou art very rich. Thou art the one Poet, the one Maker. We worship Thee. Make our souls as full of glory in Thy sight as this chasm is to our eyes, glorious with the forms which Thou hast cloven and carved out of nothingness, and we shall be worthy to worship Thee, O Lord, our God." For I was carried beyond myself with delight, and with sympathy with Connie's delight and with the calm worship of gladness in my wife's countenance.

But when my eye fell on Wynnie, I saw trouble mingled with her admiration, a self-accusation, I think, that she did not and could not enjoy it more—and when I turned from her, there were the eyes of Percivale fixed on me in wonderment. For the moment I felt as David must have felt, when, in his dance of undignified delight that he had got the ark home again, he saw the contemptuous eyes of Michal fixed on him in the window. But I could not leave it so. I said to him, coldly, I daresay, "Excuse me, Mr. Percivale. I forgot for the moment that I was not amongst my own family."

Percivale took his hat off. "Forgive my seeming rudeness, Mr. Walton. I was half envying and half wondering. You would not be surprised at my unconscious behavior if you had seen as much of the wrong side of life as I have seen in London."

I had some idea what he meant, but this was no time to enter upon a discussion. I could only say, "My heart was full, Mr.

Percivale, and I let it overflow."

"Let me at least share in its overflow," he rejoined, and nothing more passed on the subject.

For the next ten minutes we stood in absolute silence. We had set Connie down on the grass again, but propped up so that she could see through the doorway. And she lay in still ecstasy. But there was more to be seen ere we descended. There was the rest of the little islet with its crop of down-grass, on which the horses of all the knights of King Arthur's Round Table might have fed for a week—yes, a fortnight. There were the ruins of the castle so built of plates of the laminated stone of the rocks on which they stood, and so woven in with the outstanding rock themselves, that in some parts I found it impossible to tell which was building and which was rock—the walls seeming like a growth out of the island itself. But the walls were in some parts so thin that one wondered how they could have stood so long. They must have been built before the time of any formidable artillery—enough only for defense from arrows. But then the island was nowhere commanded, and its own steep cliffs would be more easily defended than any edifices on it. Clearly the intention was that no enemy should thereon find rest for the sole of his foot, for if he was able to land, farewell to the notion of any further defense.

Outside the walls there was the little chapel—such a tiny chapel! Little more than the foundation remained, with the ruins of the altar still standing, and outside the chancel, nestling by its wall, a coffin hollowed in the rock. The churchyard a little way off was full of graves which, I presume, would have vanished long ago were it not that the very graves were founded on the rock. There still stood old wornout headstones of thin slate, but no memorials were left. Then there was the fragment of an arched underground passage laid open to the air in the center of the islet; and last, and grandest of all, the awful edges of the rock, broken by time, and carved by the winds and the waters into grotesque shapes and threatening forms.

Over all the surface of the islet we carried Connie, and from three sides of this sea-fortress she looked abroad over "the Atlantic's level powers." Over the edge she gazed at the strange fantastic needle-rock, and round the corner she peeped to see Wynnie and her mother seated in what they call Arthur's Chair—a canopied hollow wrought in the plated rock by the mightiest of all solvents, air and water. At length it was time to leave, so we issued by the gothic door and wound away down the dangerous path to the safe ground below.

"I think we had better tie up your eyes again, Connie," I said.

"Why?" she asked, in wonderment. "There's nothing higher yet, is there?"

"No, my love. If there were, you would hardly be able for it today. It is only to keep you from being frightened at the precipice as you go down."

"But I shan't be frightened, Papa."

"How do you know that?"

"Because you are going to carry me."

"But what if I should slip? I might, you know."

"I don't mind. I shan't mind being tumbled over the precipice, if you do it. I shan't be to blame, and I'm sure you won't, Papa." Then she drew my head down and whispered in my ear, "If I get as much more by being killed, as I have got by having my poor back hurt, I'm sure it will be well worth it."

I tried to smile a reply, for I could not speak one. We took her just as she was and—with some tremor on my part, but not a single slip—we bore her down the winding path, her face showing all the time that, instead of being afraid, she was in a state of ecstatic delight. My wife, I could see, was nervous, and she breathed a sigh of relief when we were once more at the foot.

"Well, I'm glad that's over," she said.

"So am I," I returned as we set down the litter.

"Poor Papa! I've pulled his arms to pieces! And Mr. Percivale's too!"

Meantime, Wynnie had scrambled down to the shore and came running back to us out of breath with the news, "Papa! Mr. Percivale! There's such a grand cave down there! It goes right through under the island."

Connie looked so eager, that Percivale and I glanced at each other, and without a word, lifted her, and followed Wynnie. It was a little way, but very broken and difficult, but at length we stood in the cavern. What a contrast to the vision overhead—nothing to be seen but the cool, dark vault of the cave, long and winding, with the fresh seaweed lying on its pebbly floor, and its walls wet with the last tide. The forms of huge outlying rocks looked in at the farther end where the roof rose like a grand cathedral arch. Gleaming veins, rich with copper, dashed and streaked the darkness. The floor of heaped-up pebbles rose and rose within to meet the descending roof. It was like going down from paradise into the grave—but a cool, friendly, brown-lighted grave. Even in its darkest recesses there was a witness to the wind of God outside—an occasional ripple of shadowed light, from the play of the sun on the waves, that wandered across the jagged roof. But we dared not keep Connie long in the damp coolness, and we soon returned.

My family had now beheld the sea in such a different aspect that I no longer feared to go back to Kilkhaven. There we went three days after, and at my invitation, Percivale took Turner's place in the carriage.

TWENTY-FOUR

JOE AND HIS TROUBLE

How bright the yellow shores of Kilkhaven looked after the dark sands of Tintagel! But how low and tame its highest cliffs, after the mighty rampart of rocks facing the sea! It was pleasant to settle down again, after a boisterous welcome by Dora and the boys. Connie's baby crowed aloud and stretched forth her chubby arms at the sight of her. And the dread vision of the shore receded far into the past.

I called at the blacksmith's house, and found that he was so far better as to be working at his forge again. His mother said he was used to such attacks and soon got over them, but I feared that they indicated an approaching breakdown.

"Indeed, Sir," she said, "Joe might be well enough if he liked. It's all his own fault."

"What do you mean?" I asked. "I cannot believe that your son is in any way guilty of his own illness."

"He's a well-behaved lad, my Joe," she answered, "but he hasn't learned what I had to learn long ago."

"What is that?" I asked.

"To make up his mind and to stick to it. To do one thing or the other."

She was a woman with a long upper lip and a judicial face, and as she spoke, her lip grew longer and longer. When she closed her mouth in resolution, that lip seemed to occupy two-thirds of all her face under her nose.

"And what is it he won't do?"

142

"I don't mind whether he does it or not, if he would only *make up his mind and stick to it!*"

"What is it you want him to do, then?"

"I don't want him to do it, I'm sure. It's no good to me—and wouldn't be much good to him, that I'll be bound. Howsomever, he must please himself."

I thought it not very wondrous that he looked gloomy, if there was no more sunshine for him at home than his mother's face indicated. I made no further attempt to question her.

In passing Joe's workshop, I stopped for a moment and made an arrangement to meet him at the church. Harry Cobb, his carpenter cousin, was to come with him.

The two soon arrived, and a small consultation followed. They had done a good deal in our absence, and little remained except to get the keys put to rights, and the rods attached to the cranks in the box.

The cousin was a bright-eyed, cherub-cheeked little man, with a ready smile and white teeth. I thought he might help me understand what was amiss in Joe's affairs, but I would not make the attempt except openly. I therefore said (half in a jocular fashion) as the gloomy smith was fitting one loop into another in two of his iron rods, "I wish we could get this cousin of yours to look a little more cheerful. You would think he had quarreled with the sunshine."

The carpenter showed his white teeth between his rosy lips. "Well, Sir, if you'll excuse me, you see my cousin Joe is not like the rest of us. He's a religious man, is Joe."

"But I don't see how that should make him miserable. It hasn't made me miserable."

"Ah, well," returned the carpenter, in a thoughtful tone, as he worked away gently to get the inside out of the oak chest without hurting it, "I don't say it's the religion, for I don't know, but perhaps it's the way he takes it up. He don't look after hisself enough. He's always thinking about other people, and if you don't look after yourself, why, who is to look after you? That's common sense, I think."

"But," I said, "if everybody would take Joe's way of it, there would then be no occasion for taking care of yourself."

"I don't see why."

"Why, because everybody would take care of everybody else."

"Not so well, I doubt."

143

"Yes, and a great deal better."

"At any rate, that's a long way off, and meantime, who's to take care of the odd man like Joe there, that don't look after hisself?"

"Why, God, of course."

"Well, there's just where I'm out. I don't know nothing about that branch, Sir."

I saw a grateful light mount up in Joe's gloomy eyes as I spoke thus upon his side of the question. He said nothing, however, and as his cousin volunteered no further information, I did not push the advantage.

At noon I made them leave their work and come home with me to have their dinner, for they hoped to finish the job before dusk. Harry Cobb and I dropped behind, and Joe walked on in front, apparently sunk in meditation.

Scarcely were we out of the churchyard, and on the road leading to the rectory, when I saw the sexton's daughter Agnes before us. She had almost come up to Joe before he saw her, for his gaze was bent on the ground, and he started. They shook hands in what seemed to me an odd and constrained, yet familiar fashion, and then stood as if they wanted to talk, but without speaking. Harry and I passed, both with a nod of recognition to the young woman. When we reached the turning that would hide them from our view, I looked back and there they were still standing. But before we reached the door of the rectory, Joe caught up with us.

There was something remarkable in the appearance of Agnes Coombes. She was about six and twenty, the youngest of the family, with a sallow, rather sickly complexion, somewhat sorrowful eyes, a rare and sweet smile, a fine figure, tall and slender, and a graceful gait. I now saw further into the smith's affairs.

After dinner, the men went back to the church and I went straight to the sexton's cottage. I found the old man seated at the window, with his pot of beer on the sill, and an empty plate beside it.

"Come in, Sir," he said, rising as I put my head in at the door. "The mis'ess ben't in, but she'll be here in a few minutes."

"Oh, it's of no consequence," I said. "Are they all well?"

"All comfortable, Sir. It be fine dry weather for them. It be in winter it be worst for them. There ben't much snow in these parts—but when it du come, that be very bad for them, poor things!"

Could it be that he was harping on the old theme again?

"But at least this cottage keeps out the wet," I said. "If not, we must have it seen to."

"This cottage du well enough. It'll last my time, anyhow."

"Then why are you pitying your family for having to live in it?"

"Bless your heart, Sir! It's not them. They du well enough. It's my people out yonder. You've got the souls to look after, and I've got the bodies, to be sure!"

The last exclamation was uttered in a tone of impatient surprise at my stupidity in giving all my thoughts and sympathies to the living, and none to the dead. (I pursued the subject no further, but as I lay in bed later that night, it began to dawn upon me as a lovable kind of hallucination in which the man indulged. He too had an office in the church of God, and he would magnify that office. He could not bear that there should be no further outcome of his labor—that the burying of the dead out of sight should be "the be-all and the end-all." When all others had forsaken the dead, he remained their friend, caring for what little comfort yet remained possible to them. It was his way of keeping up the relation between the living and the dead.) Finding I made no reply, he took up the word again.

"You've got your part, Sir, and I've got mine. You up in the pulpit, and I down in the grave. But it'll be all the same by and by."

"I hope it will," I answered. "But when you do go down into your own grave, you'll know a good deal less about it than you do now. You'll find you've got other things to think about. But here comes your wife. She'll talk about the living rather than the dead."

"That's natural, Sir. She brought 'em to life, and I buried 'em— at least the best part of 'em. If only I had the other two safe down with the rest!" He regarded his drowned boys as still tossed about in the weary wet cold ocean, and would have gladly laid them to rest in the warm dry churchyard.

He wiped a tear from the corner of his eye with the back of his hand, and saying, "Well, I must be off to my gardening," left me to his wife. I saw then that, humorist as the old man might be, his humor lay close about the wells of weeping.

"The old man seems a little out of sorts," I said to his wife.

"Well, Sir," she answered, with her usual gentleness, "this be the day he buried our Nancy, this day two years ago, and today

145

Agnes be come home from her work poorly. The two things together, they've upset him a bit."

"I met Agnes coming this way. Where is she?"

"I believe she be in the churchyard. I've been to the doctor about her."

"I hope it's nothing serious."

"I hope not, Sir, but you see—four on 'em!"

"Well, she's in God's hands, you know."

"That she be, Sir."

"I want to ask you about something, Mrs. Coombes."

"What be that? If I can tell, I will, you may be sure."

"I want to know what's the matter with Joe Harper, the blacksmith."

"They du say it be consumption, Sir."

"But what has he got on his mind?"

"He's got nothing on his mind, Sir. He be as good a boy as ever, I assure you."

"There is something on his mind. He's not the man to be unhappy because he's ill. A man like him would not be miserable because he was going to die. It might make him look sad sometimes, but not gloomy."

"Well, Sir, I believe you to be right, and perhaps I know summat. I believe my Agnes and Joe Harper are as fond upon one another as any two in the county."

"Are they not going to be married then?"

"There be the pint, Sir. I don't believe Joe ever said a word o' the sort to Aggy. She never could ha' kep it from me."

"Why doesn't he then?"

"That's the pint again, Sir. All as knows him says it's because he be in such bad health, and he thinks he oughtn't to go marrying with one foot in the grave."

"What does your daughter think?"

"The same. And so they go on talking to each other, quiet-like, like old married folks, not like lovers at all. But I can't help fancying it have something to do with my Aggy's pale face."

"And something to do with Joe's pale face too, Mrs. Coombes," I said. "Thank you. You've told me more than I expected. It explains everything. I must have it out with Joe now."

"Oh, deary me! Sir, don't go and tell him I said anything, as if I wanted him to marry my daughter."

"Don't you be afraid. I'll take good care of that. And don't fancy I'm fond of meddling with other people's affairs. But this is a case in which I ought to do something. Joe's a fine fellow."

"That he be, Sir. I couldn't wish a better for a son-in-law."

I put my hat on and went straight to the church. There were the two men working away in the shadowy tower, and there was Agnes beside, knitting like her mother, quiet and solemn, as if she were a long-married wife hovering about her husband at his work. Harry was saying something to her as I went in, but when they saw me they were silent, and Agnes left the church.

"Do you think you will get through tonight?" I asked.

"Sure of it, Sir," answered Harry.

And Joe responded, "You shouldn't be sure of anything, Harry. We are told in the New Testament that we ought to say 'If the Lord will.' "

"Now, Joe, you're too hard on Harry," I said. "You don't think that the Bible means to pull a man up every time like that, till he's afraid to speak a word? It was about a long journey and a year's residence that the Apostle James was speaking."

"But the principle's the same. Harry can no more be sure of finishing his work before it be dark, than those people could of their long journey."

"That is perfectly true. But you are taking the letter for the spirit. Religion does not lie in not being sure about anything, but in a loving desire that the will of God in the matter, whatever it may be, may be done. And if Harry has not learned yet to care about the will of God, what is the good of coming down upon him that way, as if that would teach him in the least. When he loves God, then, and not till then, will he care about His will. Nor does religion lie in saying, 'if the Lord will' every time anything is to be done. It is a most dangerous thing to use sacred words often, for it makes them so common. Our hearts ought to ever be in the spirit of those words, but our lips ought to utter them rarely. Besides, there are some things a man might be pretty sure the Lord wills."

"It sounds fine, Sir, but I'm not sure I understand you. It sounds to me like a darkening of wisdom."

I saw I had irritated him, and so had in some measure lost ground. But Harry struck in, "How can you say that now, Joe? I know what the parson means well enough, and everybody knows I ain't got half the brains you've got."

"The reason is, Harry, that he's got something in his head that stands in the way."

"And there's nothing in my head to stand in the way!" returned Harry, laughing.

I laughed too, and even Joe could not help a sympathetic grin. By this time it was getting dark.

"I'm afraid, Harry, after all, you won't get through tonight."

"I think so too. And there's Joe saying, 'I told you so,' over and over to himself, though he won't say it out like a man."

Joe answered only with another grin.

"Harry," I said, "you must come again on Monday. And on your way home just look in and tell Joe's mother that I have kept him over tomorrow. The change will do him good."

"No, Sir, that can't be. I haven't got a clean shirt."

"You can have a shirt of mine," I said. "But I'm afraid you'll want your Sunday clothes."

"I'll bring them for you, Joe, before you're up," interposed Harry. "And then you can go to church with Agnes."

Here was just what I wanted.

"Hold your tongue, Harry," said Joe angrily. "You're talking of what you don't know anything about."

"Well, Joe, I ben't a fool, even if I ben't so religious as you be. You ben't a bad fellow, though you be a Methodist, and I ben't a fool, though I be Harry Cobb. Nobody could help seeing the eyes you and Aggy make at each other, and why you don't port your helm and board her—I won't say it's more than I know, but I du say it be more than I think fair to the young woman."

"Hold your tongue, Harry."

"I've answered you, so no more at present. But I'll be over with your clothes afore you're up in the morning."

As Harry spoke he was busy gathering his tools. "They won't be in the way, will they?" he said, as he heaped them together in that farthest corner of the tower.

"Not in the least," I returned. "If I had my way, all the tools used in building the church should be carved on the posts and pillars of it to indicate the sacredness of labor. For a necessity of God is laid upon every workman as well as on the Apostle Paul. Only Paul saw it, and every workman doesn't, Harry."

"I like that way of it. I almost think I could be a little bit religious after your way of it, Sir."

"Almost, Harry?" growled Joe, not unkindly.

"Now you hold your tongue, Joe," I said. "Leave Harry to me. You may take him, if you like, after I've done with him."

Laughing merrily, but making no other reply than a hearty good-night, Harry strode away out of the church, and Joe and I went home together. When he had had his tea, I asked him to go out with me for a walk.

The sun was shining aslant upon the downs from over the sea. As we rose out of the shadowy hollow to the sunlit brow, I was a little in advance of Joe. Happening to turn, I saw the light full on his head and face, while the rest of his body had not yet emerged from the shadow.

"Stop, Joe," I said. "I want to see you so for a moment."

He stood—a little surprised.

"You look just like a man rising from the dead, Joe," I said. "Your head and face are full of sunlight, but the rest of your body is still buried in the shadow. Look—I will stand where you are now, and you come here. You will see what I mean."

We changed places. Joe stared for a moment, and then his face brightened. "I see what you mean," he said.

I stood up in the sunlight, so that my eyes caught only about half the sun's disc. Then I bent my face toward the earth.

"What part of me is the light shining on now, Joe?"

"Just the top of your head," answered he.

"There, then," I returned, "that is just what you are like—a man with the light on his head, but not on his face. And why not on your face? Because you hold your head down. To be frank with you, Joe, I do not see that light in your face. Therefore I think something must be wrong with you. Remember a good man is not necessarily in the right. Peter was a good man, yet our Lord called him Satan and meant it, of course, for He never said what He did not mean."

"How can I be wrong when all my trouble comes from doing my duty—nothing else, as far as I know?"

"Then," I replied, a sudden light breaking in on my mind, "I doubt whether what you suppose to be your duty can be your duty. If it were, I do not think it would make you so miserable."

"What is a man to go by, then? If he thinks a thing is his duty, is he not to do it?"

"Most assuredly, until he knows better. The supposed duty may· be the will of God, or the invention of one's own fancy or mistaken judgment. A real duty is always something right in itself. The duty a man makes his for the time, by supposing it to be a duty, may be something quite wrong in itself. The duty of a Hindu widow is to burn herself on the body of her husband, but that duty lasts only till she sees that, not being the will of God, it is not her duty. It was the duty of the early hermits to encourage the growth of vermin upon their bodies, for they supposed that was pleasing to God—but they could not fare so well as if they had seen that the will of God was cleanliness. And there may be far more serious things done by Christian people against the will of God, in the fancy of doing their duty, than such a trifle as swarming with worms. In a word, thinking a thing is your duty makes it your duty only till you know better. And the prime duty of every man is to seek and find, that he may do the will of God."

"But how are you to know the will of God in every case?" asked Joe.

"By looking at the general laws of life, and obeying them—unless there be anything special in a particular case to bring it under a higher law."

"Ah! But that be just what there is here."

"Well, my dear fellow, that may be; but the special conduct may not be right for the special case. But it is of no use talking generals. Let us come to particulars. If you can trust me, tell me all about it, and we may be able to let some light in."

"I will turn it over in my mind, Sir, and if I can bring myself to talk about it, I will. I would rather tell you than anyone else."

I said no more. We watched a glorious sunset—there never was a grander place for sunsets—and went home.

TWENTY-FIVE

A SMALL ADVENTURE

The next morning Harry came with the clothes, but Joe did not go to church. Neither did Agnes make an appearance that morning. They were, however, both present at the evening service.

When we came out of church, the sky was dark, covered with one cloud, and not a star cracked through. The wind was *gurly*, blowing cold from the sea. (I once heard that word in Scotland, and never forgot it.)

I have always had a certain peculiar pleasure in the surly aspects of nature. When I was a young man, this took form in opposition and defiance, but since I had begun to grow old, the form had changed into a sense of safety. So, after supper, I put on my greatcoat and traveling cap, and went out into the ill-tempered night.

I meant to stroll down to the breakwater. At the farther end of it, always covered at high water, was an outlying cluster of low rocks, in the heart of which the lord of the manor (a noble-hearted Christian gentleman of the old school) had constructed a bath of graduated depth—an open-air swimming pool, the only really safe place for men who were not swimmers to bathe. I was in the habit of bathing with my two little men there every morning.

The nearest way to the breakwater was, strangely, through Connie's room. By the side of her window was a narrow door communicating with a narrow, curving, wood-built passage, leading into a little wooden hut, the walls of which were formed of outside planks with the bark still on them. From this hut one or two little windows looked seaward, and a door led out on the bit of sward in which lay the flower bed under Connie's window. Then a door in the low wall and thick hedge led out on the downs, where a path wound along the cliffs that formed the side of the bay till, descending under the storm tower, it came out upon the root of the breakwater.

When I went into Connie's room, I found her lying in bed, a very picture of peace. But my entrance destroyed the picture.

"Papa," she said, "why have you got your coat on? Surely you are not going out tonight. The wind is blowing dreadfully."

"Not very dreadfully, Connie. It blew much worse the night we found your baby."

"But it is very dark."

"I allow that, but there is a glimmer from the sea. I am only going on the breakwater for a few minutes. You know I like a stormy night as much as a fine one."

"I shall be miserable till you come home, Papa."

"Nonsense, Connie. You don't think your father hasn't sense to take care of himself? Or rather, Connie, for I grant that is poor ground of comfort, you don't think I can go anywhere without my Father to take care of me?"

"But there is no occasion, is there, Papa?"

"Do you think I should be better pleased with my boys if they shrunk from everything involving the least possibility of danger because there was no occasion for it? That is just the way to make cowards. There is positively no ground for apprehension, and I hope you won't spoil my walk by the thought that my foolish little girl is frightened."

"I will be good—indeed I will, Papa," she said, holding up her mouth to kiss me.

I left through the wooden passage. The wind roared about the bark hut, shook it, and pawed it, and sang and whistled in the chinks of the planks. I went out and shut the door. That moment the wind seized upon me, and I had to fight with it. When I reached the path leading along the edge of the downs, I felt something lighter than any feather fly in my face. When I put up my hand, I found my cheek wet. They were flakes of foam, bubbles worked up into little masses of adhering thousands, which the wind blew off the waters and across the downs, carrying some of them miles inland.

Now and then a little rush of water from a higher wave swept over the top of the broad breakwater, as with head bowed side-ways against the wind, I struggled along toward the rock at its end. But I said to myself, "The tide is falling fast, and salt water hurts nobody." And I struggled on over the huge rough stones of the mighty heap, outside which the waves were white with wrath, inside which they had fallen asleep, only heaving with the memory of their late unrest. I reached the tall rock at length, climbed the rude stair leading up to the flagstaff, and looked abroad into the thick dark. But the wind blew so strong on the top that I was glad to descend. The deathly waves rolled between me and the basin, where yesterday morning I had bathed in still water and sunshine with my boys. I wandered on and found a sheltered nook in a mass of rock where I sat with the wind howling and the waves bursting around me. There I fell into a sort of brown study—almost half asleep.

But I had not sat long before I came broad awake, for I heard voices, low and earnest. One I recognized as Joe's voice. The other was a woman's. In a lull of the wind, I heard the woman say (I could fancy with a sigh), "I'm sure you'll du what is right, Joe. Don't 'e think o' me, Joe."

"It's just of you that I do think, Aggy. You know it ben't for my sake. Surely you know that?"

There was no answer for a moment. I was doubting what I had best do—go away quietly or let them know I was there—when she spoke again. There was a momentary lull now in the noises of both wind and water, and I heard what she said well enough.

"It ben't for me to contradict you, Joe. But I don't think you be going to die. You be no worse than last year. Be you now, Joe?"

Once before, a stormy night and darkness had brought me close to a soul in agony. Then I was in agony myself, and now the world was all fair and hopeful around me. But here were two souls straying in a mist which faith might roll away and leave them walking in the light. The moment was come for me to speak.

"Joe!" I called out.

"Who's there?" he cried, and I heard him start to his feet.

"Only Mr. Walton. Where are you?"

"We can't be very far off," he answered, not in a tone of any pleasure.

I rose, and peering about through the darkness, found that they were a little higher up on the same rock by which I was sheltered.

"You mustn't think," I said, "that I have been eavesdropping.

153

I had no idea anyone was near me till I heard your voices."

"I saw someone go up the Castle Rock," said Joe, "but I thought he was gone away again. It will be a lesson to me."

"I'm no telltale, Joe," I returned, as I scrambled up the rock. "You will have no cause to regret that I happened to overhear a little. I am sure you will never say anything you need be ashamed of. But what I heard was sufficient to let me into the secret of your trouble. Will you let me talk to Joe, Agnes? I've been young myself, and to tell the truth, I don't think I'm old yet."

"I am sure, Sir," she answered, "you won't be hard on Joe and me. I don't suppose there be anything wrong in liking each other, though we can't be . . . married."

She spoke in a low tone, and her voice trembled very much, yet there was a certain womanly composure in her utterance. "I'm sure it's very bold of me to talk so," she added, "but Joe will tell you all about it."

I was close beside them now, and fancied I saw through the dusk the motion of her hand stealing into his.

"Well, Joe, this is just what I wanted," I said. "A woman can be braver than a big smith sometimes. Agnes has done her part. Now you do yours, and tell me all about it."

No response followed my adjuration. I must help him.

"I think I know how the matter lies, Joe. You think you are not going to live long, and that therefore you ought not to marry. Am I right?"

"Not far off it, Sir," he answered.

"Now, Joe," I said, "can't we talk as friends about this matter? I have no right to intrude into your affairs—none in the least— except what friendship gives me. If you say I am not to talk about it, I shall be silent. To force advice upon you would be as impertinent as useless."

"My mind has been made up for a long time. What right have I to bring other people into trouble? But I take it kind of you, though I mayn't look overpleased. Agnes wants to hear your way of it. I'm agreeable."

This was not very encouraging, but I thought it sufficient ground for proceeding. "I suppose that you will allow that the root of all Christian behavior is the will of God?"

"Surely, Sir."

"Is it not the will of God then, that when a man and a woman love each other, they should marry?"

"Where there be no reasons against it."

"Of course. And you judge you see reason for not doing so, else you would?"

"I do see that a man should not bring a woman into trouble for the sake of being comfortable himself for the rest of a few weary days."

Agnes was sobbing gently behind her handkerchief. I knew how gladly she would be Joe's wife, if only to nurse him through his last illness.

"Not except it would make her comfortable too, I grant you, Joe. But listen to me. In the first place, you don't know, and you are not required to know, when you are going to die. In fact, you have nothing to do with it. Many a life has been injured by the constant expectation of death. It is life we have to do with, not death. The best preparation for the night is to work diligently while the day lasts. The best preparation for death is life. Besides, I have known delicate people who have outlived all their strong relations and have been left alone in the earth. Marriage and death are both God's will, and you have no business to set the one over against the other. For anything you know, the gladness and the peace of marriage may be the very means intended for your restoration to health and strength. I suspect your desire to marry, yet fighting against the idea that you ought not to marry, has a good deal to do with the state of health in which you now find yourself. If a man were happy, he would get over many things that he could not get over if he were miserable."

"But it's for Aggy. You forget that."

"I do not forget that. What right have you to seek for her another kind of welfare than you would have yourself? Are you to treat her as if she were worldly when you are not, to provide for her a comfort which you yourself would despise? Why should you not marry because you have to die soon? If you are thus doomed, which to me is by no means clear, why not have what happiness you may? You may find at the end of twenty years that here you are after all."

"And if I find myself dying at the end of six months?"

"Thank God for those six months. The whole thing, my dear fellow, is a want of faith in God. I do not doubt you think you are doing right, but, I repeat, the whole thing comes from want of faith in God. You will take things into your own hands and order them after a preventive and self-protective fashion, lest God should have ordained the worst for you—which is truly no evil, and would be best met by doing His will. Death is no more an evil than marriage is."

"But you don't see it as I do," persisted the blacksmith.

"Of course I don't. I think you see it as it is not."

He remained silent for a little. A shower of spray fell upon us. He started. "What a wave!" he cried. "That spray came over the top of the rock—we shall have to run for it!"

I fancied that he only wanted to avoid further conversation. "There's no hurry," I said. "It was high water an hour and a half ago."

"You don't know this coast, Sir," returned he, "or you wouldn't talk like that." As he spoke he rose. "For God's sake, Aggy!" he cried in terror, "Come at once! Every other wave be rushing across the breakwater as if it were on the level!"

He hurried back, caught her by the hand, and began to draw her along.

"Hadn't we better stay where we are?" I suggested.

"It's not the tide, Sir. It's a ground swell—from a storm somewhere at sea—and that never asks no questions about tide or no tide."

"Come along, then," I said. "But just wait one minute more. It is better to be ready for the worst."

I had seen a crowbar lying among the stones, and thought now it might be useful. I found it and gave it to Joe, then took the girl's disengaged hand. She thanked me in a voice perfectly calm and firm. Joe took the bar in haste, and drew Agnes toward the breakwater.

Any thought of real danger had not yet crossed my mind. But when I looked at the outstretched back of the breakwater, and saw a dim sheet of white sweep across it, I prepared myself for a struggle.

"Do you know what to do with the crowbar, Joe?" I asked, grasping my own stout oak stick more firmly.

"To stick between the stones and hold on. We must watch our time between the waves."

"You take the command then, Joe," I returned. "You see better than I do, and you know that raging wild beast there. I will obey orders, one of which will be not to lose hold of Agnes—eh, Joe?"

Joe gave a grim enough laugh in reply, and we started, he

carrying his crowbar in his right hand against the advancing sea, and I my oak stick in my left toward the still water within.

"Quick march!" said Joe, and away we went. Now the back of the breakwater was very rugged, for it was formed of huge stones, with wide gaps between where the waters had washed out the cement and worn their edges. But what impeded our progress secured our safety.

"Halt!" cried Joe, when we were but a few yards beyond the shelter of the rocks. "There's a topper coming."

A huge wave rushed against the far outsloping base and flung its heavy top right over the middle of the mass, a score of yards in front of us.

"Now for it," cried Joe. "Run!"

We did run. In my mind there was just sense enough of danger to add to the pleasure of the excitement. I did not know how much danger there was. Over the rough worn stones we sped, stumbling.

"Halt!" cried the smith once more, and we did halt, but this time, as it turned out, in the middle front of the coming danger.

"God be with us!" I exclaimed, when the huge billow showed itself through the night. The smith stuck his crowbar between two great stones. To this he held on with one hand, and threw the other arm around Agnes' waist. I too had got my oak firmly fixed, held on with the other hand, and threw the other arm round Agnes. It took but a moment.

"Now then!" cried Joe. "Here she comes! Hold on, Sir. Hold on, Aggy!"

But when I saw the height of the water as it rushed on us, I cried out, "Down, Joe! Down on your face, and let it over us easy! Down, Agnes!"

They obeyed. We threw ourselves across the breakwater, with our heads to the coming foe, and I grasped my stick close to the stones. Over us burst the mighty wave, floating us up from the stones where we lay. But we held on, the wave passed, and we sprung gasping to our feet.

"Now, now!" cried Joe and I together and, heavy as we were, with the water pouring from us, we flew across the remainder of the heap and arrived, panting and safe, at the other end, ere one wave more had swept the surface. The moment we were in safety we turned and looked back, and saw a huge billow sweep the breakwater from end to end. We looked at each other for a moment without speaking.

"I believe, Sir," said Joe at length, with slow and solemn speech, "if you hadn't taken the command at that moment we should all have been lost. We were awfully near death."

"Nearer than you thought, Joe, and yet we escaped it. Things don't go all as we fancy, you see. Faith is as essential to manhood as foresight. Believe me, Joe. It is very absurd to trust God for the future, and not trust Him for the present. The man who is not anxious is the man most likely to do the right thing. He is cool and collected and ready. Our Lord told His disciples that when they should be brought before kings and rulers, they were to take no thought what answer they should make, for it would be given them when the time came."

We were climbing the steep path up the downs. Neither of my companions spoke.

"You have escaped one death together," I said. "Dare another."

Neither of them returned an answer. When we came near the parsonage, I said, "Now, Joe, you must go in and go to bed at once. I will take Agnes home. You can trust me not to say anything against you."

Joe laughed rather hoarsely, and replied, "As you please, Sir. Good night, Aggy. Mind you get to bed as soon as you can."

When I returned from giving Agnes over to her parents, I made haste to change my clothes and put on my warm dressing gown. (I may as well mention that not one of us was the worse for our ducking.) I then went up to Connie's room.

"Here I am to see you, Connie, quite safe."

"I've been lying listening to every blast of wind since you went out, Papa. But all I could do was trust in God."

"Do you call that *all*, Connie? Believe me, there is more power in that than any human being knows the tenth part of yet. It is indeed all."

I said no more then. Though I told my wife about it that night, we were well into another month before I told Connie.

When I left her, I went to Joe's room to see how he was, and found him having some gruel. I sat down on the edge of his bed, and said, "Well, Joe, this is better than under water. I hope you won't be the worse for it."

"I don't much care what comes of it—it will all be over soon."

"But you ought to care what comes of you, Joe. I will tell you why. You are an instrument out of which ought to come praise to

God, and, therefore, you ought to care for the instrument."

"That way, yes, I ought."

"And you have no business to be like some children, who say, 'Mamma won't give me so and so,' instead of asking her to give it to them."

"I see what you mean. But, really, you put me out before the young woman. I couldn't say before her what I meant. Suppose, you know, Sir, there was to come a family. It might be, you know."

"Of course. What else would you have?"

"But if I was to die, where would she be then?"

"In God's hands, just as she is now."

"But I ought to take care that she is not left with a burden like that to provide for."

"O Joe! How little you know of a woman's heart! It would just be the greatest comfort she could have for losing you, that's all. Many a woman has married a man she did not care enough for, just that she might have a child of her own to let out her heart upon. I don't say that is right, you know, for such love cannot be perfect. A woman ought to love her child because it is her husband's more than because it is her own, and because it is God's more than either's. If Agnes really loves you, as no one can look in her face and doubt, she will be far happier if you leave her a child—yes, she will be happier if you only leave her your name for hers—than if you died without calling her your wife."

I took Joe's basin from him, and he lay down. He turned his face to the wall. I waited a moment, but finding him silent, bade him good-night, and left the room.

My words must have found their intended mark, for only a month after that storm-tossed night I married the two of them.

TWENTY-SIX

A WALK WITH MY WIFE

It was some time before we got the old church bells to work. The worst of it was to get the cranks, which at first required strong pressure on the keys, to work easily enough. But neither Joe nor his cousin spared any pains to perfect the attempt, and at length we succeeded. I took Wynnie down to the instrument, and she made the old tower discourse loudly and eloquently.

One of the nights after that I had a walk and a talk with my wife. It had rained a good deal during the day, but as the sun went down the air began to clear. And when the moon shone out near the full, she walked the heavens, not "like one that hath been led astray," but as "queen and huntress, chaste and fair."

"What a lovely night it is!" said Ethelwyn, who had come into my study—where I always sat with unblinded windows that the night and her creatures might look in upon me—and she had stood gazing out for a moment.

"Shall we go for a little turn?" I said.

"I should like it very much," she answered. "I will go and put on my bonnet."

In a minute or two she looked in again, all ready. I rose, laid aside my Plato, and went with her. We turned our steps along the edge of the down, and descended upon the breakwater where we seated ourselves on the same spot where, in the darkness, I had heard the voices of Joe and Agnes. What a different night it was from that! The sea lay as quiet as if it could not move for the moonlight that lay upon it. The glory over it was so mighty in its

160

peacefulness, that the wild element beneath was afraid to toss itself even with the motions of its natural unrest. The moon was like the face of a saint before which the stormy people have grown dumb. The rocks stood up solid and dark, and the pulse of the ocean throbbed against them with a lapping gush, soft as the voice of a passionate child soothed into shame of its vanished petulance. But the sky was the glory. Although no breath moved below, there was a gentle wind abroad in the upper regions.

We sat and watched the marvelous depth of the heavens, covered with a stately procession of ever-appearing and ever-vanishing cloud forms—great sculpturesque blocks of a shattered storm, the icebergs of the upper sea. These were not far off against a blue background, but floating near us in the heart of a blue-black space, gloriously lighted by a golden rather than a silvery moon.

At length my wife spoke. "I hope Mr. Percivale is out tonight," she said. "How he must be enjoying it if he is!"

"I wonder the young man is not returning to his professional labors," I said. "Few artists can afford such long holidays as he is taking."

"He is laying in stock, though, I suppose," she answered. "And he must paint better the more familiar he gets with the things God cares to fashion."

"Doubtless. But I am afraid the work of God he is chiefly studying at present is our Wynnie."

"Well, is she not a worthy object of his study?" returned Ethelwyn, looking up into my face with an arch expression.

"Doubtless, again. But I hope she is not studying him quite so much in her turn. I have seen her eyes following him about."

My wife made no answer for a moment. Then she said, "Don't you like him, Harry?"

"Yes. I like him very much."

"Then why should you not like Wynnie to like him?"

"I should like to be surer of his principles, for one thing."

"I should like to be surer of Wynnie's."

I was silent. Ethelwyn resumed, "Don't you think they might do each other good? They both love the truth, I am sure—only they don't perhaps know what it is yet. I think if they were to fall in love with each other, it would very likely make them both more desirous of finding it."

"Perhaps," I said at last. "But you are talking about awfully serious things, Ethelwyn."

"Yes, as serious as life," she answered.

"You make me very anxious," I said. "The young man has not, I fear, any means of gaining a livelihood for more than himself."

"Why should he, before he wanted it? I like to see a man who can be content with an art and a living by it."

"I hope I have not been to blame in allowing them to see so much of each other," I said, hardly heeding my wife's words.

"It came about quite naturally," she rejoined. "If you had opposed their meeting, you would have been interfering, just as if you had been Providence. And you would have only made them think more about each other."

"He hasn't said anything—has he?" I asked in positive alarm.

"Oh, dear no. It may be all my fancy. I am only looking a little ahead. I confess I should like him for a son-in-law. I approve of him," she added, with a sweet laugh.

"Well," I said, "I suppose sons-in-law are the possible, however disagreeable, results of having daughters." I tried to laugh, but hardly succeeded.

"Harry," said my wife, "I don't like you in such a mood. It is not like you at all. It is unworthy of you."

"How can I help being anxious when you speak of such dreadful things as the possibility of having to give away my daughter, my precious wonder that came to me through you out of the infinite— the tender little darling!"

" 'Out of the heart of God,' you used to say, Harry. Yes, and with a destiny He had ordained. It is strange to me how you forget your best and noblest teaching sometimes. You are always telling us to trust God. Surely it is a poor creed that will only allow us to trust in God for ourselves—a very selfish creed. There must be something wrong there. I should say that the man who can only trust God for himself is not half a Christian. Either he is so selfish that that satisfies him, or he has such a poor notion of God that he cannot trust Him with what most concerns him. The former is not your case, Harry. Is it the latter, then? For I must take my turn at the preaching sometimes, mayn't I, Dearest?"

She took my hand in both of hers, and the truth arose in my heart. I never loved my wife more than at that moment, but now I could not speak for other reasons. I saw that I had been faithless to my God, and the moment I could command my speech, I hastened to confess it.

"You are right, my dear," I said, "quite right. I have been

wicked, for I have been denying my God. I have been putting my providence in the place of His, trying like an anxious fool to count the hairs on Wynnie's head, instead of being content that the grand, loving Father should count them. My love, let us pray for Wynnie, for what is prayer but giving her to God and His holy, blessed will?"

We sat hand in hand. Neither of us spoke aloud, but we spoke in our hearts to God, talking to Him about Wynnie. Then we rose together and walked homeward, still in silence. But my heart and hand clung to my wife as to the angel whom God had sent to deliver me out of the prison of my faithlessness. And as we went, lo, the sky was glorious again. It had faded from my sight, had grown flat as a dogma and uninteresting; the moon had been but a round thing with the sun shining upon it, and the stars were only minding their own business. But now the solemn march toward an unseen, unimagined goal had again begun. Wynnie's life was hid with Christ in God. Away strode the cloudy pageant with its banners blowing in the wind. Solitary stars, with all their sparkles drawn in, shone quiet as human eyes in the deep solemn clefts of dark blue air. The moon saw the sun, and therefore made the earth glad.

"You have been a moon to me this night, my wife," I said. "You were looking full at the truth, while I was dark. I saw its light in your face, and believed, and turned my soul to the sun. And now I am both ashamed and glad. God keep me from sinning so again."

"My dear husband, it was only a mood, a passing mood," said Ethelwyn, seeking to comfort me.

"It was a mood, and thank God, it is now past; but it was a wicked one. It was a mood in which the Lord might have called me a devil, as He did St. Peter. Such moods have to be grappled with and fought the moment they appear. They must not have their way for a single thought even."

"But we can't always help it, can we?"

"We can't help it out and out, because our wills are not yet free with the freedom God is giving us as fast as we will let Him. When we are able to will thoroughly, then we shall do what we will. At least, I think we shall. But there is a mystery in it God understands. All we know is that we can struggle and pray. But a mood is an awful oppression sometimes, when you least believe in it and most wish to get rid of it. It is like a headache in the soul."

"What *do* the people do who don't believe in God?" said Ethelwyn.

Then Wynnie, who had seen us pass the window, opened the door of the bark house for us. We passed into Connie's chamber and found her lying in the moonlight, gazing at the same heavens as had her father and mother.

TWENTY-SEVEN

OUR LAST SHORE DINNER

The next day there was to be an unusually low tide about two o'clock, and we resolved to dine upon the sands. All morning the children were out playing on the threshold of old Neptune's palace—for in his quieter mood, he will, like a fierce mastiff, let children do with him what they will. I gave myself a whole holiday and wandered about on the shore. The sea was so calm, and the shore so gently sloping that you could hardly tell where the sand ceased and the sea began—the water sloped to such a thin pellicle, thinner than any knife edge, upon the shining brown sand, and you saw the sand underneath the water to such a distance out. Yet this depth, which would not drown a red spider, was the ocean.

In my mind I followed that bed of shining sand, bared of its hiding waters, out and out, till I was lost in an awful wilderness of chasms, precipices, and mountain peaks, in whose caverns the sea serpent may dwell with his breath of pestilence, and the kraken with "his scaly rind" may be sleeping "his ancient dreamless, uninvaded sleep."

I lifted my eyes and saw how the autumn sun hung above the waters, oppressed with a mist of his own glory. Far away to the left a man who had been gathering mussels on a low rock—inaccessible save in such a tide—threw himself into the sea and swam ashore. Above his head the storm tower stood in the stormless air, and the sea glittered and shone. The long-winged birds knew not which to choose, the balmy air or the cool deep, now flitting like arrowheads through the one, now alighting eagerly upon the other, to forsake it anew for the thinner element. I thanked God for His glory.

"O Papa, it's so jolly! So jolly!" shouted the children as I passed them again.

"What is it that's so jolly, Charlie?" I asked.

"My castle," screeched Harry in reply, "only it's tumbled down. The water *would* keep coming in underneath."

"I tried to stop it with a newspaper," cried Charlie, "but it wouldn't. So we were forced to let it be, and down it went into the ditch."

"We blew it up rather than surrender," said Dora. "We did. Only Harry always forgets, and says the water did it."

I drew near the rock that held the bath. I had never approached it from this side before. It was high above my head, and a stream of water was flowing from it. I scrambled up, undressed and plunged into its dark hollow, where I felt like one of the sea beasts of which I had been dreaming, down in the caves of the unvisited ocean. But the sun was over my head, and the air with an edge of the winter was about me. I dressed quickly, descended on the other side of the rock, and wandered again on the sands to sea-ward of the breakwater. How different was the scene when a rav-ing mountain of water filled all the hollow where I now wandered, and rushed over the top now so high above me, where I had to cling to its stones to keep from being carried off like a bit of floating seaweed! Here and there rose a well-known rock, but now changed in look by being lifted all the height between the base on the waters, and the second base in the sand.

But the chief delight of the spot, closed in by rocks from the open sands, was the multitude of fairy rivers that flowed across it to the sea. The gladness these streams gave me I cannot communi-cate. The tide had filled thousands of hollows in the breakwater, hundreds of cracked basins in the rock, huge sponges of sand. From all of these—from cranny and crack and oozing sponge—the water flowed in restricted haste back to the sea, tumbling in tiny cataracts down the faces of the rocks, bubbling from their roots as from wells, gathering in tanks of sand, and overflowing in broad, shallow streams, curving and sweeping in their sandy channels just like the great rivers of a continent—here spreading into smooth, silent lakes and reaches, here babbling along in ripples and waves innumerable. All their channels were of golden sand, and the gold-en sunlight was above and through and in them all: gold and gold met with the waters between. And all the ripples made shadows. The eye could not see the rippling on the surface, but the sun saw it, and drew it in shadowy motion upon the sand beneath—with gold burnished and trembling, melting, curving, blending, vanishing ever, ever renewed. It was as if all the watermarks upon a web of golden silk had been set in wildest yet most graceful motion. My eye could not be filled with seeing. I stood in speechless delight for a while, gazing at the "endless ending" which was "the humor of the game."

"Father," I murmured half aloud, "Thou alone art, and I am because Thou art. Thy will shall be mine."

I know that I must have spoken aloud, because I remember the start of consciousness and discomposure occasioned by the voice of Percivale greeting me.

"I beg your pardon," he added, "I did not mean to startle you, Mr. Walton. I thought you were only looking at Nature's childplay—not thinking."

"I know few things more fit to set one to thinking than what you have very well called Nature's childplay," I returned. "Is Nature very heartless now, do you think, to go on with this kind of thing at our feet, when away up yonder lies the awful London with so many sores festering in her heart?"

"You must answer your own question, Mr. Walton. You know I cannot. I confess I feel the difficulty deeply. I will go further and confess that the discrepancy makes me doubt many things I would gladly believe. I know *you* are able to distinguish between a glad unbelief and a sorrowful doubt."

"How will you go back to your work in London after seeing all this? Suppose you had had nothing here but rain and high winds and sea fogs, would you have been better fitted for doing something to comfort those who know nothing of such influences than you will be now? One of the most important qualifications of a sick nurse is a ready smile. A long-faced nurse in a sick room is a visible embodiment and presence of the disease against which the life of the patient is fighting in agony. What a power of life and hope has a woman—young or old, I do not care—with a face of the morning, a dress like the spring, and in her hand a bunch of wild flowers with the dew upon them! That is sympathy, not the worship of darkness. And she, looking death in the face with a smile, brings a little health, a little strength to fight, a little hope to endure, actually lapt in the folds of her gracious garments. For the

167

soul itself can do more healing than any medicine, if it be fed with the truth of life."

"But is life such an affair of sunshine and gladness?"

"If life is not, then I confess all this show of Nature is worse than vanity; it is a vile mockery. Life is gladness; it is the death in it that makes the misery. But our Lord has conquered death—the moral death that He called the world—and Nature has God at her heart. God wears His singing robes in a day like this, and says to His children, 'Be not afraid: your brothers and sisters up there in London are in My hands; go and help them. I am with you. Bear to them the message of joy. Tell them to be of good cheer; I have overcome the world. Tell them to endure hunger and not sin, to endure passion and not yield, to admire and not desire. Sorrow and pain are serving My ends, for by them will I slay sin, and save My children.' "

"I wish I could believe as you do, Mr. Walton."

"I wish you could. But God will teach you if you are willing to be taught."

"I desire the truth, Mr. Walton."

"God bless you. God is blessing you," I said.

"Amen," returned Percivale devoutly, and we strolled away together in silence toward the cliffs, where the recession of the tide allowed us to get far enough away from the face of the rocks to see the general effect.

"Who could imagine, in weather like this, and with this baby of a tide lying behind us, low at our feet, that those grand cliffs before us bear on their front the scars and dints of centuries of passionate contest with this same creature that is at this moment unable to rock the cradle of an infant? Look behind you, at your feet, Mr. Percivale; look before you at the chasms, rents, caves, and hollows, of those rocks."

"I wish you were a painter, Mr. Walton," he said.

"And *I* wish I were," I returned. "At least, I know I should rejoice in it, if it had been given me to be one. But why do you say so now?"

"Because you have always some individual predominating idea, which would give interpretation to nature while it gave harmony, reality, and individuality to your representation."

"I know what you mean," I answered, "but I have no gift whatever in that direction. I have no idea of drawing, or of producing the effects of light and shade, though I think I have a little notion of color."

"Even so, I wish I could ask your opinion of some of my pictures."

"That I should never presume to give. I could only tell you what they made me feel or think. Some day I may have the pleasure of looking at them."

"May I offer you my address?" he said, and took a card from his pocketbook. "It is a poor place, but if you should happen to think of me when you are in London, I shall be honored by your paying me a visit."

"I shall be most happy," I returned, taking his card. "Did it ever occur to you, in reference to the subject we were upon a few moments ago, how little you can do without shadow in making a picture?"

"Little indeed," answered Percivale. "In fact, it would be no picture at all."

"I doubt if the world would fare better without its shadows."

"But it would be a poor satisfaction with regard to the nature of God, to be told that He allowed evil for artistic purposes."

"It would, indeed, if you regard the world as a picture. But if you think of His art as expended, not upon the making of a history or drama, but upon the making of an individual, a being, a character, then I think a great part of the difficulty vanishes. So long as a creature has not sinned, sin is possible to him. Does it seem inconsistent with the character of God that, in order that sin should become impossible, He should allow sin to come? That, in order that His creatures should choose the good and refuse the evil, in order that they might turn from sin with a perfect repugnance of the will, He should allow them to fall? That, in order that from being sweet childish children they should become noble, childlike men and women, He should let them try to walk alone? Why should He not allow the possible in order that it should become impossible?"

"I think I understand you," returned Percivale. "I will think over what you have said. These are very difficult questions."

As we spoke, we turned from the cliffs and wandered back across the salt streams to the sands beyond. From the direction of the house came a little procession of servants, with Walter at their head, bearing the preparations for our dinner over the gates of the lock, down the sides of the embankment of the canal, and across the sands.

"Will you join our early dinner?" I asked.

"I shall be delighted," he answered, "if you will let me be of some use first. I presume you mean to carry Connie out."

"Yes, and you shall help me carry her, if you will."

"That is what I hoped," said Percivale, and we went together toward the parsonage.

As we approached, I saw Wynnie sitting at the drawing room window, but when we entered the room, only my wife was there.

"Where is Wynnie?" I asked.

"She saw you coming," she answered, "and went to get Connie ready, for I guessed Mr. Percivale had come to help you carry her out."

But I could not help thinking there might be more than that in Wynnie's disappearance. "What if she should fall in love with him," I thought, "and he should never say a word? That would be dreadful for us all."

They had been repeatedly together of late, and if they did fall in love, it would be very natural on both sides. There was evidently a great mental resemblance between them, so that they could not help sympathizing with each other's peculiarities and would make a fine couple.

Why should not two such walk together along the path to the gates of the light? And yet I could not help some anxiety. I did not know anything of his history. I had no testimony concerning him from anyone who knew him, and his past life was a blank to me. His means of livelihood was probably insufficient—certainly, I judged, precarious; and his position in society—but there I checked myself. I had had enough of that kind of thing already.

All this passed through my mind in about three turns of the winnowing fan of thought. Mr. Percivale had begun talking to my wife, who took no pains to conceal that his presence was pleasant to her; and I went upstairs, almost unconsciously, to Connie's room.

When I opened the door, forgetting to announce my approach as I ought to have done, I saw Wynnie leaning over Connie, and Connie's arm round her waist. Wynnie started back, and Connie gave a little cry, for the jerk hurt her. Wynnie turned her head at Connie's cry, and I saw a tear on her face.

"My darlings, I beg your pardon," I said. "It was very stupid of me not to knock at the door."

Connie looked up at me with large eyes and said, "It's nothing,

Papa. Wynnie is in one of her gloomy moods, and didn't want you to see her crying. She gave me a little pull, that was all. It didn't hurt me much, only I'm such a goose! I'm in terror before the pain comes. Look at me," she added. "I'm all right now." And she smiled in my face perfectly.

I turned to Wynnie, put my arm about her, kissed her cheek, and left the room. I looked round at the door, and saw that Connie was following me with her eyes, but Wynnie's were hidden in her handkerchief.

I went back to the drawing room, and in a few minutes Walter announced dinner. The same moment Wynnie came to say that Connie was ready. She did not lift her eyes, or approach to give Percivale any greeting, but went again as soon as she had given her message. I saw that he looked first concerned, and then thoughtful.

Percivale and I ascended to Connie's room. Wynnie was not there, but Connie lay, looking lovely, all ready for going. We lifted her, and carried her out the window and down by the path to the breakwater.

As we reached the breakwater, I found that Wynnie was following behind us. We stopped in the very middle of it and set Connie down, as if I wanted to take breath. But I had thought of something to say to her, which I wanted Wynnie to hear without its being addressed to her.

"Do you see, Connie," I said, "how far off the water is?"

"Yes, Papa, it is a long way off. I wish I could get up and run down to it."

"You can hardly believe that all between, all those rocks, and all that sand, will be covered before sunset."

"I know it will be. But it doesn't *look* likely, does it, Papa?"

"Not in the least, my dear. Do you remember that stormy night when I came through your room to go out for a walk in the dark?"

"Remember it, Papa? I cannot forget it. Every time I hear the wind blowing when I wake in the night, I fancy you are out in it."

"Well, Connie, look down into the great hollow there, with rocks and sand at the bottom of it."

"Yes, Papa."

"Now, look over the side of your litter. You see these holes all about between the stones?"

"Yes, Papa."

"Well, one of these little holes saved my life that night, when

171

the great gulf there was full of huge mounds of roaring water, rushing across this breakwater with force enough to sweep a whole cavalry regiment off its back."

"Papa!" exclaimed Connie, turning pale.

Then I told her all the story while Wynnie listened behind.

"Then I *was* right in being frightened!" cried Connie.

"You were right in trusting in God, Connie."

"But you might have been drowned, Papa!"

"Nobody has a right to say that anything might have been other than what has been. Before a thing has happened, we can say might or might not, but that has to do only with our ignorance. Think what a change, from the dark night and roaring water, to this fullness of sunlight and the bare sands with the water lisping on their edge away there in the distance. Now, troubles will come in life which look as if they would never pass away, just as the night and the storm look as if they would last forever. But the calm and the morning cannot be stayed, and the storm in its very nature is transient. The effort of Nature, as that of the human heart, ever is to return to its repose, for God is peace."

"But if you will excuse me, Mr. Walton," said Percivale, "you say that from your experience. But you can hardly expect experience to be of use to any but those who have had it. It seems to me that its influences cannot be imparted."

"That depends. Of course, as experience, it can have no weight with another, for it is no longer experience. One remove, and it ceases. But faith in the person who *has* experienced can draw over or derive some of its benefits to him who has the faith. Experience may thus, in a sense, be accumulated, and we may go on the fresh experience of our own. At least I can hope that the experience of a father may take the form of hope in the minds of his daughters. Hope never hurt anyone, never yet interfered with duty. It always strengthens to the performance of duty, gives courage and clears the judgment. St. Paul says we are saved by hope. Hope is the most rational thing in the universe. Even the ancient poets, who believed it was delusive, yet regarded it as an antidote given by the mercy of the gods against some of the least of life's ills."

"But they counted it delusive. A wise man cannot consent to be deluded."

"Assuredly not. The sorest truth rather than a false hope! But what is a false hope? Only one that ought not to be fulfilled. The old poets could give themselves little room for hope, and less for its fulfillment, for what were their gods? One thing I repeat—the waves that foamed across the spot where we now stand are gone away, have sunk, and vanished."

"But they will come again, Papa," faltered Wynnie.

"And God will come with them, my love," I said, as we lifted the litter.

In a few minutes more, we were all seated on the sand around a tablecloth spread upon it. The tide had turned, and the waves were creeping up over the level, soundless almost as thought, but it would be time to go home long before they had reached us. The sun was in the western half of the sky, and now and then a breath of wind came from the sea, with a slight saw-edge in it, but not enough to hurt. Connie could stand much more in that way now. And when I saw how she could move herself on her couch, hope for her kept fluttering joyously in my heart. I could not help fancying even that I saw her move her legs a little.

Charles and Harry were every now and then starting up from their dinner and running off with a shout, to return with apparently increased appetite for the rest of it. Neither their mother nor I cared to interfere with the indecorum. Wynnie was very silent, but looked more cheerful. Connie seemed full of quiet bliss. My wife's face was a picture of heavenly repose. The nurse was walking about with the baby, occasionally with one hand helping the other servants to wait upon us. They too seemed to have a share in the gladness of the hour and, like Ariel, did their spiriting gently.

"This is the will of God," I said, after the things were removed, and we had sat for a few moments in silence.

"What is the will of God, Harry?" asked Ethelwyn.

"Why, this, my love," I answered, "this living air and wind and sea and light and land all about us—this consenting, consorting harmony of Nature that mirrors a like peace in our souls. The perfection of such visions, the gathering of them all in one, was— is, I should say—in the face of Christ Jesus. You will say His face was troubled sometimes. Yes, but with a trouble that broke not the music but deepened the harmony. When He wept at the grave of Lazarus, you do not think it was for Lazarus himself, or for His own loss of him? That could not be, seeing He had the power to call him back when He would. The grief was for the poor troubled hearts left behind, to whom it was so dreadful because they had not faith enough in His Father, the God of life and love.

"It was the aching, loving hearts of humanity for which He

173

wept—the hearts that needed God so awfully and could not yet trust Him. Their brother was only hidden in the skirts of their Father's garment, but they could not believe that. They said he was dead, lost, away, all gone, as the children say. And it was so sad to think of a whole world full of the grief of death, that He could not bear it without the human tears to help His heart, as they help ours.

"It was for our dark sorrows that He wept. But the peace could be no less plain on the face that saw God. Did you ever think of that wonderful saying, 'Again a little while, and ye shall see Me, because I go to the Father'? The heart of man would have joined the 'because I go to the Father' with the former result, the not seeing of Him. The heart of man is not able, without more and more light, to understand that all vision is in the light of the Father. Because Jesus went to the Father, the disciples saw Him tenfold more. His body was no longer before their eyes, but His very Being, His very Self was in their hearts—not in their affections only—in their spirits, their heavenly consciousness.

"People find it hard to believe grand things, but why? If there be a God, is it not likely everything ought to be grand, simple, and noble? The ages of eternity will go on showing that such they are and ever have been. God will yet be victorious over our wretched unbeliefs."

I was sitting facing the sea, but with my eyes fixed on the sand, boring holes in it with my stick, for I could talk better when I did not look at my familiar faces. (I did not feel thus in the pulpit. There I sought the faces of my flock to assist me in speaking to their needs.) As I drew near to the close of my last monologue, a colder and stronger blast from the sea blew in my face. I lifted my head, and saw that the tide had crept up a long way, and was coming in fast. A luminous fog had sunk down over that western horizon, had almost hidden the sun, had obscured half the sea, and destroyed all our hopes of a sunset. A certain commonplace veil had dropped over the face of nature, and the wind came in little bitter gusts across the dull waters.

It was time to lift Connie and take her home. We did so, and that was the last time we ate together on the open shore.

TWENTY-EIGHT
A PASTORAL VISIT

The next morning rose in a rainy mist, which the wind mingled with salt spray torn from the tops of the waves. Every now and then the wind blew a blast of larger drops against the window of my study with an angry clatter and clash, as if daring me to go out and meet its ire. Earth, sea, and sky were possessed by a gray spirit that threatened wrath.

The breakfast bell rang and I went down. Wynnie stood at the window, looking out upon the restless tossing of the waters, but with no despondent answer to the trouble of nature. On the contrary, her cheeks were luminous, and her eyes flashed. Had Percivale said something to her? Or had he just passed the window, and given her a look which she might interpret as she pleased? No, it was only that she was always more peaceful in storm than in sunshine. I said to myself: "She must marry a poor man someday. She is a creature of the north, not of the south; the hot sun of prosperity would wither her up. Give her a bleak hillside, with a glint or two of sunshine between the hailstorms, and she will live and grow. Give her poverty and love, and life will be interesting to her as a romance. Give her money and position and she will grow dull and haughty; she will believe in nothing that poet can sing or architect build. She will, like Cassius, "scorn her spirit for being moved to smile at anything."

She turned and saw me, and came forward. "Don't you like a day like this, Papa?"

"I always have. And you take after me in that, as in a good

many things besides. That is how I understand you so well."

"Do I really take after you, Papa? Are you sure that you understand me so well?" she asked, brightening up.

"Yes. And I know I do," I returned.

"Even better than I do myself?" she asked, with an arch smile.

"Considerably, if I mistake not."

"How delightful! To think that I am understood even when I don't understand myself!"

"But even if I am wrong, you are yet understood. The blessedness of life is that we can hide nothing from God. If we could hide anything from God, that hidden thing would by and by turn into a terrible disease. It is the sight of God that keeps and makes things clean. But as we are both fond of this kind of weather, what do you say to going out with me? I have to visit a sick woman."

"You don't mean Mrs. Coombes, Papa?"

"No, my dear. I did not hear she was ill."

"Oh, I daresay it is nothing much. Only Old Nursey said yesterday she was in bed with a bad cold."

"We'll call and inquire as we pass. I have just had a message from that cottage that stands all alone on the corner of Mr. Barton's farm—over the cliff, you know—that the woman is ill, and would like to see me. So the sooner we start, the better, that is, if you are inclined to go with me."

"How can you put an *if* to that, Papa? I shall have done my breakfast in five minutes, Papa. Oh! Here's Mamma. Mamma, I'm going out for a walk in the rain with Papa. You won't mind, will you?"

"I don't think it will do you any harm, my dear."

Wynnie left the room to put on her long cloak and her bonnet, and after that we went out into the weather. We called at the sexton's cottage and found him sitting gloomily by the low window, looking seaward.

"I hope your wife is not *very* poorly, Coombes," I said.

"No, Sir. She be very comfortable in bed. Bed's not a bad place to be in such weather," he answered, turning again a dreary look toward the Atlantic. "Poor things!"

"What a passion for comfort you have, Coombes! How does that come about, do you think?"

"I suppose I was made so."

"To be sure you were. God made you so."

"Surely. Who else?"

176

"Then I suppose He likes *making* people comfortable if He makes people *like* to be comfortable."

"It du look likely enough."

"Then when He takes it out of your hands, you mustn't think He doesn't look after the people you would make comfortable if you could."

"I must mind my work, you know."

"Yes, surely. And you mustn't want to take His out of His hands, and go grumbling as if you would do it so much better if He would only let you get *your* hand to it."

"I daresay you be right," he said. "I must just go and have a look about though. Here's Agnes. She'll tell you about her mother."

He took his spade from the corner and went out. He often brought his tools into the cottage, and he had carved the handle of his spade all over with the names of the people he had buried.

"Tell your mother, Agnes, that I will call in the evening and see her, if she would like to see me. We are going now to see Mrs. Stokes. She is very poorly, I hear."

Wynnie turned to me outside and said, "Let us go through the churchyard, Papa, and see what the old man is doing."

"Very well, my dear. It is only a few steps round."

"Why do you humor the sexton's foolish fancy so much, Papa? It is such nonsense! You taught us about the resurrection."

"Most certainly, my dear. But it would be of no use to try to get it out of his head by any argument. He has a kind of craze in that direction. To get people's hearts right is of much more importance than convincing their judgments. Right judgment will follow. All such fixed ideas should be encountered from the deepest grounds of truth, and not from the outsides of their relations. Coombes has to be taught that God cares for the dead more than he does, and therefore it is unreasonable for him to be anxious about them."

When we reached the churchyard, we found the old man kneeling on a grave before its headstone. It was very old, with a death's skull and crossbones carved upon the top of it in high relief. With his pocketknife, he was removing the lumps of green moss out of the hollows of the eyes of the carven skull. We did not interrupt him, but walked past with a nod.

Then we were on the downs, and the wind was buffeting us, and every other minute assailing us with a blast of rain. Wynnie drew her cloak closer about her, bent her head toward the blast, and struggled on bravely by my side. No one who wants to enjoy a walk in the rain must carry an umbrella—it is pure folly. We came to one of the stone fences, cowered down by its side for a few moments to recover our breath, and then struggled on again.

When we reached the house, I left Wynnie seated by the kitchen fire, and was shown into the room where Mrs. Stokes lay. She was a hard-featured woman, with cold, troubled black eyes that rolled restlessly about. She lay on her back, moving her head from side to side. She looked at me, and turned her eyes away toward the wall, and I guessed that something was on her mind. I approached the bedside and seated myself by it. I always do so at once, for the patient feels more at rest than if I stand up tall. I laid my hand on hers.

"Are you very ill, Mrs. Stokes?" I said.

"Yes, very," she answered with a groan. "It be come to the last with me."

"I hope not indeed, Mrs. Stokes. It's not come to the last with us, so long as we have a Father in heaven."

"Ah, but it be with me. He can't take any notice of the like of me."

"But indeed He does, whether you think it or not. He takes notice of every thought we think, and every deed we do, and every sin we commit."

I said the last words with emphasis, for I suspected something more than usual upon her conscience. She gave another groan, but made no reply. I therefore went on. "Our Father in heaven is not like some fathers on earth, who so long as their children don't bother them, let them do anything they like. He will not have us do what is wrong. He loves us too much for that."

"He won't look at me," she said, half murmuring, half sighing it out, so that I could hardly hear what she said.

"It is because He is looking at you that you are feeling uncomfortable," I answered. "He wants you to confess your sins. I don't mean to me, but to Himself—though if you would like to tell me anything, and I can help you, I shall be very glad. You know Jesus Christ came to save us from our sins, and that's why we call Him our Saviour. But He can't save us from our sins if we won't confess that we have any."

"I'm sure I never said but what I be a great sinner, as well as other people."

"You don't suppose that's confessing your sins?" I said. "I

once knew a woman of very bad character, who allowed to me she was a great sinner. But when I said, 'Yes, you have done so and so,' she would not allow any of those deeds to be worthy of being reckoned amongst her sins. When I asked her what great sins she had been guilty of—seeing these counted for nothing—I could get no more out of her than that she was a great sinner, like other people, as you have been saying."

"I hope you don't be thinking I ha' done anything of that sort!" she said, with wakening energy. "No man or woman dare say I've done anything to be ashamed of."

"Then you've committed no sins," I returned. "But why did you send for me? You must have something to say to me."

"I never did send for you. It must ha' been my husband."

"Ah, then, I'm afraid I've no business here!" I returned, rising. "I thought you had sent for me."

She returned no answer. I hoped that by retiring I should set her thinking, and make her more willing to listen the next time I came. I think clergymen may do much harm by insisting when people are in a bad mood, as if they had everything to do, and the Spirit of God nothing at all. I bade her good-day, hoped she would be better soon, and returned to Wynnie.

As we walked home together, I said, "Mrs. Stokes had not sent for me herself, and rather resented my appearance. But I think she will send for me before many days are over."

TWENTY-NINE

THE SORE SPOT

We had a week of hazy weather after this, which I spent chiefly in my study and in Connie's room. A world of mist hung over the sea which, as if ill-tempered or unhappy, folded itself in its mantle, and lay still. It refused to hold any communion with mortals.

One morning Dora knocked at the door saying that Mr. Percivale had called, that Mamma was busy, and would I mind if she brought him up to the study.

"Not in the least, my dear," I answered, "I shall be very glad to see him."

"Unfavorable weather for your sacred craft, Percivale," I said, as he entered. "I presume you are thinking of returning to London now, as there seems so little to be gained by remaining here. When this weather begins to show itself, I could wish myself in my own parish. But I am sure the change, even through the winter, will be good for my daughter."

"I must be going soon," he answered. "But it would be too bad to take offense at the old lady's first touch of temper. I mean to wait and see whether we shall not have a little bit of St. Martin's Summer, as Shakespeare calls it, after which, hail London, queen of smoke and—"

"And what?" I asked, seeing he hesitated.

" 'And soap,' I was fancying you would say. For you never will allow the worst of things, Mr. Walton."

"No, surely I will not. For one thing, the worst has never been seen by anybody yet. We have no experience to justify it."

We were chatting in this loose manner, when Walter came to tell me that Mr. Stokes was asking for me. I went down to see him.

"My wife be very bad, Sir," he said. "I wish you could come and see her."

"Does she want to see me?" I asked.

"She's been more uncomfortable than ever since you were there last," he said.

"But," I repeated, "has she said she would like to see me?"

"I can't say it, Sir."

"Then *you* want me to see her?"

"Yes, Sir. But I be sure she do want to see you. I know her way, you see. She never would say she wanted anything in her life. She would always leave you to find it out. So I got sharp at that."

"And then, would she allow she had wanted it when you got it?"

"No, never. She be peculiar, my wife. She always be."

"Does she know that you have come to ask me now?"

"No."

"Have you courage to tell her?"

The man hesitated.

"If you haven't courage to tell her," I resumed, "I have nothing more to say. I can't go—or, rather, I will not go."

"I will tell her."

"Then tell her that I refuse to come until she sends for me herself."

"Ben't that rather hard on a dying woman?"

"I have my reasons. Except she send for me herself, the moment I go she will take refuge in the fact that she did not send for me. I know your wife's peculiarity too, Mr. Stokes."

"Well, I *will* tell her. It's time to speak my own mind."

"When she sends for me, if it be in the middle of the night, I shall be with her at once."

He left, and I returned to Percivale. We went on talking for some time. Indeed, we talked so long that the dinner hour was approaching, and one of the maids came with the message that Mr. Stokes had called again. I could not help smiling inwardly at the news. I went down at once, and found him smiling too.

"My wife do send me for you this time, Sir," he said. "Between you and me, I cannot help thinking she have something on her mind she wants to tell you."

"Why shouldn't she tell you, Mr. Stokes? That would be most natural. And then if you wanted any help about it, why, of course here I am."

"She don't think well enough of my judgment for that. And I daresay she be quite right. She always do make me give in before she have done talking. But she have been a right good wife to me."

"Perhaps she would have been a better wife if you hadn't given in quite so much. It is very wrong to give in when you think you are right."

"But I never be sure of it when she talk to me awhile."

"Ah, then, I have nothing to say, except that you ought to have been surer—*sometimes*. I don't say *always*."

"But she do want you very bad now, Sir. I don't think she'll behave to you as she did before. Do come."

"Of course I will—instantly."

I returned to the study, and said to Percivale, "I do not know how long I may have to be with the poor woman. Why don't you wait here and take my place at the dinner table? I promise not to depose you if I should return before the meal is over."

He thanked me very heartily. I showed him into the drawing room, told my wife where I was going, and not to wait dinner for me—I would take my chance—and joined Mr. Stokes.

"You have no idea, then," I said, after we had gone about half-way, "what makes your wife so uneasy?"

"No, I haven't," he answered. "Except it be," he resumed, "that she was too hard, as I thought, upon our Mary, when she wanted to marry beneath her, as my wife thought."

"How beneath her? Who was it she wanted to marry?"

"She did marry him. She has a bit of her mother's temper, you see, and she would take her own way."

"Ah! There's a lesson to mothers, is it not? If they want to have their own way, they mustn't give their own temper to their daughters."

"But how are they to help it?"

"Ah, how indeed? But what is your daughter's husband?"

"A laborer. He works on a farm out by Carpstone."

"But you have worked on Mr. Barton's farm for many years, if I don't mistake."

"I have. But I am a foreman now, you see."

"But you weren't so always, and your son-in-law, whether he

works his way up or not, is, I presume, much where you were when you married Mrs. Stokes."

"True as you say. But it's not me that has anything to say about it. I never gave the man a nay. But you see my wife, she always do be wanting to get her head up in the world, and since she took to the shopkeeping—"

"The shopkeeping!" I said, with some surprise. "I didn't know that."

"Well, you see, it's only for a quarter or so out of the year. This is a favorite walk for the folks as comes here for the bathing—past our house, to see the great cave down below. And my wife she got a bit of a sign put up, and put a few ginger-beer bottles there in the window, and—"

"A bad place for the ginger beer," I said.

"They were only empty ones with corks and strings, you know. My wife she know better than to put the ginger beer its own self in the sun. But she do carry her head higher after that, and a farm-laborer was none good enough for her daughter."

"And hasn't she been kind to her since she married, then?"

"She's never done her no harm."

"But she hasn't gone to see her very often, or asked her to come and see you very often, I suppose."

"There's ne'er a one o' them crossed the door of the other," he answered, with some evident feeling of his own in the matter.

"Ah! But you don't approve of that yourself, Stokes?"

"Approve of it? No, Sir. I be a farm laborer once myself. But she take after her mother, she do. I don't know which of the two it is as does it, but there's no coming and going between Carpstone and this."

We were approaching the house. I told Stokes he had better let her know I was there. If she had changed her mind, it was not too late for me to go home again without disturbing her. He came back saying she was still very anxious to see me.

"Well, Mrs. Stokes, how do you feel today? You don't look much worse."

"I be much worse. You don't know what I suffer, or you wouldn't make so little of it. I be very bad."

"I know you are very ill, but I hope you are not too ill to tell me why you are so anxious to see me. You *have* something to tell me, I suppose."

With pale and deathlike countenance, she appeared to be fight-

ing more with herself than with the disease which had nearly
overcome her. The drops stood upon her forehead, and she did not
speak.

"Was it about your daughter you wanted to speak to me?"

"No," she muttered. "I have nothing to say about my daughter.
She was my own, and I could do as I pleased with her."

I thought that we must have a word about that by and by, but
meantime she must relieve her heart of the one thing whose pressure she felt.

"Then," I said, "you want to tell me about something that was
not your own?"

"Who said I ever took what was not my own?" she returned
fiercely. "Did Stokes dare to say I took anything that wasn't my
own?"

"No one has said anything of the sort. Only I cannot help
thinking, from your own words and from your own behavior, that
such must be the cause of your misery."

"It is very hard that the parson should think such things," she
muttered again.

"My poor woman," I said, "you sent for me because you had
something to confess to me. I want to help you, if I can. But you
are too proud to confess it yet, I see. There is no use in my staying
here, for it only does you harm. So I will bid you good-morning. If
you cannot confess to me, confess to God."

"God knows it, I suppose, without that."

"Yes. But that does not make it less necessary for you to confess
it. How is He to forgive you, if you won't allow that you have done
wrong?"

"It be not so easy as you think. How would you like to say you
had took something that was not your own?"

"Well, I shouldn't like it, certainly. But if I had it to do, I think
I should make haste and do it, and so get rid of it."

"But that's the worst of it—I can't get rid of it."

"But," I said, laying my hand on hers, and trying to speak as
kindly as I could, although her whole behavior would have been
exceedingly repulsive but for her evidently great suffering, "you
have now confessed taking something that did not belong to you.
Why don't you summon courage and tell me all about it? I want to
help you out of the trouble as easily as ever I can, but I can't if
you don't tell me what you've got that isn't yours."

"I haven't got anything," she muttered.

"You had something then, whatever may have become of it now."

She was again silent.

"What did you do with it?"

"Nothing."

I rose and took up my hat. She stretched out her hand, as if to lay hold of me, with a cry, "Stop, stop. I'll tell you all about it. I lost it again. That's the worst of it. I got no good of it."

"What was it?"

"A sovereign," she said, with a groan. "And now I'm a thief, I suppose."

"No more a thief than you were before. Rather less, I hope. But do you think it would have been any better for you if you hadn't lost it, and had got some good of it, as you say?"

She was silent yet again.

"If you hadn't lost it, you would most likely have been a great deal worse for it than you are—a more wicked woman altogether."

"I'm not a wicked woman."

"It is wicked to steal, is it not?"

"I didn't steal it."

"How did you come by it, then?"

"I found it."

"Did you try to find out the owner?"

"No. I knew whose it was."

"Then it was very wicked not to return it. And, I say again, that if you had not lost the sovereign, you would have been most likely a more wicked woman than you are."

"It was very hard to lose it. I could have given it back. And then I wouldn't have lost my character as I have done this day."

"Yes, you could—but I doubt if you would."

"I would."

"Now, if you had it, you are sure you would give it back?"

"Yes, that I would," she said, looking me so full in the face that I was sure she meant it.

"How would you give it back? Would you get your husband to take it?"

"No! I wouldn't trust him."

"With the story, you mean? You do not wish to imply that he would not restore it."

"I don't mean that. He would do what I told him."

"How would you return it, then?"

"Make a parcel of it and send it."

"Without saying anything about it?"

"Yes. Where's the good? The man would have his own."

"No, he would not. He has a right to your confession, for you have wronged him. That would never do."

"You are too hard upon me." She began to weep angrily.

"Do you want to get the weight of this sin off your mind?"

"Of course I do. I am going to die. Oh, dear! Oh, dear!"

"That is just how I want to help you. You must confess, or the weight of it will stick there."

"But if I confess, I shall be expected to pay it back."

"Of course. That is only reasonable."

"But I haven't got it, I tell you. I have lost it."

"Have you not a sovereign in your possession?"

"No, not one."

"Can't you ask your husband to let you have one?"

"There! I knew it was no use. I knew you would only make matters worse. I do wish I had never seen that wicked money."

"You ought not to abuse the money. It was not wicked. You ought to wish that you had returned it. But that is no use. The thing is to return it now. Has your husband a sovereign?"

"No. He may ha' got one since I be laid up. But I never can tell him about it. And I should be main sorry to spend one of his hard earnings in that way, poor man."

"Well, I'll tell him. And we'll manage it somehow."

I thought for a few moments she would break out in opposition, but she hid her face with the sheet instead, and burst into a great weeping.

I took this as permission, and went to the door and called her husband. He came in looking scared. His wife did not look up, but lay weeping. I hoped much for her and him too from this humiliation before him, for I had little doubt she needed it.

"Your wife, poor woman," I said, "is in great distress because—I do not know when or how—she picked up a sovereign that did not belong to her, and instead of returning it, put it away somewhere, and lost it. This is what is making her so miserable."

"Deary me!" said Stokes, in the tone with which he would have spoken to a sick child. Going up to his wife he sought to draw down the sheet from her face, apparently that he might kiss her, but she kept tight hold of it, and he could not. "Deary me!" he went on. "We'll soon put that to rights. When was it, Jane, that you found it?"

"When we wanted so to have a pig of our own; and I thought I could soon return it," she sobbed from under the sheet.

"Deary me! Ten years ago! Where did you find it?"

"I saw Squire Tresham drop it, as he paid me for some ginger beer he got for some ladies that was with him. I do believe I should ha given it back at the time, but he made faces at the ginger beer, and said it was very nasty, and I thought, well, I would punish him for it."

"It was your temper that made a thief of you, then," I said.

"My old man won't be so hard on me as you. I wish I had told him first."

"I wish that too," I said, "were it not that I am afraid you might have persuaded him to be silent about it, and so have made him miserable and wicked too. But now, Stokes, what is to be done? This money must be paid. Have you got it?"

The poor man looked blank.

"She will never be at ease till this money is paid," I insisted.

"Well, I ain't got it, but I'll borrow it of someone. I'll go to master and ask him."

"No, my good fellow, that won't do. Your master would want to know what you were going to do with it, perhaps, and we mustn't let more people know about it than just ourselves and Squire Tresham. There is no occasion for that. I'll tell you what. I'll give you the money, and you must take it—or, if you like, I will take it to the squire—and tell him all about it. Do you authorize me to do this, Mrs. Stokes?"

"Please, Sir. It's very kind of you. I will work hard to pay you again, if it please God to spare me. I am very sorry I was so cross-tempered to you, but I couldn't bear the disgrace of it," she said from under the bedclothes.

"Well, I'll go," I said, "and as soon as I've had my dinner, I'll go over to Squire Tresham's, then come back tonight and tell you about it. And now I hope you will be able to thank God for forgiving you this sin. But you must not hide and cover it up, but confess it clean out to Him, you know."

She made me no answer, but went on sobbing.

I hastened home, and when I went into the dining room, I found that they had not sat down to dinner. I expostulated that it was against the rule of the house, when my return was uncertain.

"But, my love," said my wife, "why should you not let us

please ourselves sometimes? Dinner is so much nicer when you are with us."

"I am very glad you think so," I answered. "But there are the children."

"The children have had their dinner."

"Always in the right, Ethelwyn—but there's Mr. Percivale."

"I never dine till seven o'clock—to save daylight," he said.

"Then I am beaten on all points. Let us dine."

During dinner I could scarcely help observing how Percivale's eyes followed Wynnie, or, rather, every now and then settled down upon her face. That she was aware, almost conscious of this, I could not doubt. One glance at her satisfied me of that. But certain words of the Apostle Paul kept coming again and again into my mind, for they were winged words those, and even when they did not enter, they fluttered their wings at my window: "Whatsoever is not of faith is sin." And I kept reminding myself that I must heave the load of sin off me, as I had been urging poor Mrs. Stokes to do. For surely, all fear is sin, and one of the most oppressive sins from which the Lord came to save us.

After dinner I set out for Squire Tresham's. He was a rough but kindhearted elderly man. When I told him the story of the poor woman's misery, he was quite concerned at her suffering. When I produced the sovereign, he would not receive it at first, but requested me to take it back to her, and say she must keep it by way of an apology for his rudeness about her ginger beer—for I took care to tell him the whole story, thinking it might be a lesson to him too. But I begged him to take it, for it would, I thought, not only relieve her mind more thoroughly, but keep her from thinking lightly of the affair afterward. Of course, I could not tell him I had advanced the money, for that would have quite prevented him from receiving it.

I then returned straight to the cottage.

"Well, Mrs. Stokes," I said, "it's all over now. That's one good thing done. How do you feel yourself now?"

"I feel better now, Sir. I hope God will forgive me."

"God does forgive you. But there are more things you need forgiveness for. It is not enough to get rid of one sin. We must get rid of all our sins, you know. They're not nice things, are they, to keep in our hearts? It is just like shutting up nasty corrupting things, dead carcasses, under lock and key in our most secret drawers, as if they were precious jewels."

"I wish I could be good, like some people, but I wasn't made so. There's my husband now. I do believe he never do anything wrong in his life. But then, you see, he would let a child take him in."

"And far better too. Infinitely better to be taken in. Indeed there is no harm in being taken in—but there is awful harm in taking in."

She did not reply, and I went on. "You would feel a good deal better yet, if you would send for your daughter and her husband now, and make up with them."

"I will. I'm tired of having my own way. But I was made so."

"You weren't made to continue so, at all events. God gives us the necessary strength to resist what is bad in us. But you must give in to Him, else He cannot get on with it. I think it very likely He made you ill now, just that you might think, and feel that you had done wrong."

"I have been feeling that for many a year."

"That made it the more needful to make you ill, for you had been feeling your duty and yet not doing it, and that was worst of all. You know Jesus came to lift the weight of our sins, our very sins themselves, off our hearts, by forgiving them and helping us to cast them away from us. Everything that makes you uncomfortable must have sin in it somewhere, and He came to save you from it. Send for your daughter and her husband. And, when you have done that, you will think of something else to set right that's wrong."

"But there would be no end to that way of it, Sir."

"Certainly not, till everything was put right."

"But a body might have nothing else to do, that way."

"Well, that's the very first thing that has to be done. It is our business in this world. We were not sent here to have our own way and try to enjoy ourselves."

"That is hard on a poor woman that has to work for her bread."

"To work for your bread is not to take your own way, for it is God's way. But you have wanted many things your own way. And because you would not trust Him with His own business, but took it into your hands, you have not enjoyed your own life. If you will but do His will, He will take care that you have a life to be very glad of and very thankful for. And the longer you live, the more blessed you will find it. But I will leave you with that for now, for

189

I have talked long enough. I will come and see you again tomorrow, if you like."

"Please do. I shall be very grateful."

As I headed home, I thought, if the lifting of one sin off the human heart was like a resurrection, what would it be when every sin was lifted from every heart! Every sin, then, discovered in one's own soul must be a pledge of renewed bliss in its removing. And when St. Paul's words came to me—"Whatsoever is not of faith is sin"—I thought what a weight of sin had to be lifted from the earth. But what could I do for it? I could just begin with myself, and pray to God for that inward light which is His Spirit.

THIRTY

THE GATHERING STORM

The weather cleared up again the next day, and for a fortnight it was lovely. In this region we saw less of the sadness of the dying year than in our own parish, for there being so few trees in the vicinity of the ocean, the autumn had nowhere to hang out her mourning flags. There the air is so mild, and the temperature so equable, that the bitterness of the season is almost unknown. That is, however, no guarantee against furious storms.

Turner paid us another visit, and brought good news from home. Everything was going on well. Weir was working as hard as usual, and everybody agreed that I could not have found a better man to take my place.

Connie was much improved, and was now able to turn a good way from one side to the other. Finding her health so steady, Turner encouraged her in making gentle and frequent use of her strength, impressing upon her, however, that everything depended upon avoiding a jerk or twist of any sort. I was with them when he said this. She looked up at him with a happy smile.

"I will do all I can, Mr. Turner," she said, "to get out of people's way. I want to help—and not be helped more than other people—as soon as possible. I will therefore be as gentle as Mamma and as brave as Papa, and see if I don't get well, Mr. Turner. I mean to have a ride on old Sprite next summer, I do," she added, nodding her pretty head up from the pillow, when she saw the glance the doctor and I exchanged. "Look here," she went on, poking the eider-down quilt up with her foot.

191

"Magnificent," said Turner, "but mind, you must do nothing out of bravado. That won't do at all."

"I have done," said Connie, putting on a face of mock submission.

That day we carried her out for a few minutes, but it was to be the last time for many weeks.

One day I was walking home from a visit I had been paying to Mrs. Stokes. She was much better—indeed, on her way to recovery—and her mental health was improved as well. Her manner to me was certainly very different, and the tone of her voice, when she spoke to her husband especially, was changed—a certain roughness in it was much modified.

It was a cold and gusty afternoon. The sky eastward and overhead was tolerably clear when I set out from home, but when I left the cottage to return, I could see that some change was at hand. Shaggy vapors of light gray were blowing rapidly across the sky from the west. A wind was blowing fiercely up there, although the gusts down below came from the east. Away to the west, a great thick curtain of luminous yellow fog covered all the horizon. A surly secret seemed to lie in its bosom, though now and then I could discern the dim ghost of a vessel through it. I was glad when I seated myself comfortably by the drawing room fire and saw Wynnie making tea.

"It looks stormy, I think, Wynnie," I said.

Her eyes lightened, as she looked out to sea from the window.

"You seem to like the idea of it," I added.

"You told me I was like you, Papa, and you look as if you liked the idea of it too."

"In itself, certainly, a storm is pleasant to me. I should not like a world without storms any more than I should like that Frenchman's idea of the perfection of the earth, when all was to be smooth as a trim shaven lawn: rocks and mountains banished, and the sea breaking on the shore only in wavelets of ginger beer or lemonade, I forget which. But the older you grow, the more sides of a thing will present themselves to your contemplation. The storm may be grand and exciting, but you cannot help thinking of the people who are in it. Think for a moment of the multitude of vessels, great and small, which are gathered within the skirts of that angry vapor out there."

"But," said Wynnie, "you say *everybody* is in God's hands."

"Yes, surely, my dear, as much out in yon stormy haze as here beside the fire."

"Then we ought not to be miserable about them, even if there comes a storm, ought we?"

"No, surely. And, besides, I think if we could help any of them, the very persons that enjoyed the storm the most would be the busiest to rescue them from it. At least, I fancy so. But isn't the tea ready?"

"Yes, Papa. I'll just go and tell Mamma."

She returned with her mother, and the three children also joined us. Turner had just come in from a walk over the hills, and was now standing looking out at the sea.

"She looks uneasy, does she not?" I said.

"You mean the Atlantic?" he returned, looking round. "Yes, I think so. I am glad she is not a patient of mine. I fear she is going to be very feverish, probably delirious before morning. She won't sleep much, and will talk rather loudly when the tide comes in."

"You will not care to go out again. What shall we do this evening? Shall we go to Connie's room and have some Shakespeare?"

"I could wish nothing better. What play shall we have?"

"Let us have the *Midsummer Night's Dream*," said Ethelwyn.

"Oh, yes!" said Wynnie with a roguish look. "There is one reason why I like that play."

"I should think there might be more than one, Wynnie."

"But one reason is enough for a woman at once—isn't it, Papa?"

"I'm not sure of that. But what is your reason?"

"The fairies are not allowed to play any tricks with the women. *They* are true throughout."

"I might choose to say that was because they were not tried."

"And I might venture to answer that Shakespeare, being true to nature always, as you say, Papa, knew very well how absurd it would be to represent a woman's feelings as under the influence of the juice of a paltry flower."

"Capital, Wynnie!" said her mother, and Turner and I chimed in with our approbation.

So we sat in Connie's room, delighting ourselves with the reflex of the poet's fancy, while the sound of the rising tide kept mingling with the fairy talk and the foolish rehearsal.

"Musk roses," said Titania—and the first of the blast, going round south to west, rattled the window.

"Good hay, sweet hay, hath no fellow," said Bottom—and the roar of the waves was in our ears.

"So doth the woodbine the sweet honeysuckle gently entwist," said Titania—and the blast poured the rain in a spout against the window.

"Slow in pursuit, but matched in mouth like bells," said Theseus—and the wind whistled shrill through the chinks of the bark house.

We drew the curtains closer, made up the fire higher, and read on. It was time for supper before we finished, and when we left Connie to go to sleep, it was with the hope that through all the rising storm, she would dream of breeze-haunted summer woods.

THIRTY-ONE

THE GATHERED STORM

I woke in the middle of the night and the darkness to hear the wind howling. It was wide awake now and up with intent. It seized the house and shook it furiously, and the rain kept pouring, only I could not hear it save in the *rallentando* passages of the wind. But through all the wind, I could hear the roaring of the big waves on the shore. I did not wake my wife, but put on my dressing gown and went softly to Connie's room to see whether she was awake. I feared if she were, she would be frightened, even though Wynnie was with her, for Wynnie always slept in a little bed in the same room.

I opened the door very gently, and peeped in. The fire was burning, for Wynnie was an admirable stoker and could generally keep the fire wakeful all night. There was just light enough to see that Connie was fast asleep, and that her dreams were not of storms. But as I turned to leave the room, Wynnie's voice called me in a whisper. Approaching her bed, I saw her eyes, like the eyes of the darkness, for I could scarcely see anything of her face.

"Awake, darling?" I said.

"Yes, Papa. I have been awake a long time. But isn't Conni sleeping delightfully? She does sleep so well! Sleep is surely very good for her."

"It is the best thing for us all, next to God's Spirit, I sometimes think, my dear. But are you frightened by the storm? Is that what keeps you awake?"

"No, but sometimes the house shakes so that I do feel a little nervous. I don't know how it is. I never felt afraid of anything natural before."

"What our Lord said about not being afraid of anything that could only hurt the body applies here. In all the terrors of the night, think about Him."

"I do try, Papa. But don't you stop—you will get cold. It is a dreadful storm, is it not? Suppose there should be people drowning out there now!"

"There may be, my love. People are dying every moment on the face of the earth, and drowning is only an easy way of dying. Mind, they are all in God's hands."

"Yes, Papa. I will turn round and shut my eyes, and fancy that His hand is over them, making them dark with His care."

"And it will not be fancy, my darling, if you do. Good night."

Dark, dank, weeping, the morning dawned. All dreary was the earth and sky, and the wind was still hunting the clouds across the heavens. It lulled a little as we sat at breakfast, but soon the storm was up again, and the wind raved. I went out, and the wind caught me and shook me as if with invisible human hands I fought with it, and made my way into the deserted streets of the village. Not a man or horse was to be seen, no doors were open, and the little shops looked as if nobody had crossed their thresholds for a week.

One child came out of the baker's with a big loaf in her apron, and the wind threatened to blow the hair off her head, or her into the canal. I took her by the hand, and she led me to her home while I kept her from being carried away by the wind. Having landed her safely inside her mother's door, I went on, climbed the heights above the village, and looked abroad over the Atlantic.

What a waste of aimless tossing to and fro! Gray mist above full of falling rain—gray, wrathful waters underneath, foaming and bursting as billow broke upon billow. The tide was ebbing now, but almost every other wave swept the breakwater. They burst on the rocks at the other end of it, and rushed in shattered spouts and clouds of spray far into the air over their heads.

The solitary form of a man stood at some distance gazing, as I was, out upon the ocean. I walked toward him, suspecting who this might be who loved Nature so well that he did not shrink from her, even in her most uncompanionable moods. I soon found I was right—it was Percivale.

"What a clashing of waterdrops!" I said. "They are but

waterdrops, after all, that make this great noise upon the rocks, only there are a great many of them."

"Yes," said Percivale. "But look out yonder. You see a single sail, close-reefed, away in the mist there? As soon as you think of the human struggle with the elements, as soon as you know that hearts are in the midst of it, it is a clashing of waterdrops no more. It is an awful power, which the will and all that it rules have to fight for the mastery, or at least for freedom."

"Surely you are right. But as I have now seen how matters are with the elements, and have had a good pluvial bath as well, I think I will go home and change my clothes."

"I have hardly had enough of it yet," returned Percivale. "I shall have a stroll along the heights here. And when the tide has fallen a little way from the foot of the cliffs, I shall go down on the sands, and watch a while there. But I will go with you as far as the village, and then turn and take my way along the downs for a mile or two. I don't mind being wet."

"I didn't once."

We reached the brow of the heights, and here we parted. A fierce blast of wind rushed at me, and I hastened down the hill. How dreary the streets did look—how much more dreary than the stormy down! I saw no living creature as I returned but a terribly draggled dog, a cat that seemed to have a bad conscience, and a lovely little-girl face flattening the tip of its nose against a window-pane. Every rain pool was a mimic sea, and had a mimic storm within its own narrow bounds. The water went hurrying down the kennels like a long brown snake anxious to get to its hole and hide from the tormenting wind; and every now and then the rain came in full rout before the conquering blast.

When I got home I peeped in at Connie's door, and saw that she was raised a little more than usual—that is, the end of the couch against which she leaned was at a more acute angle. She was sitting staring (rather than gazing) out at the wild tumult. Her face was paler and keener than usual.

"Why, Connie, who set you up so straight?"

"Mr. Turner, Papa. I wanted to see out, and he raised me himself. He says I am so much better, I may have it in the seventh notch as often as I like."

"But you look too tired for it. Hadn't you better lie down again?"

"It's only the storm, Papa."

"The more reason you should not see it if it tires you so."

"It does not tire me, Papa. Only I keep constantly wondering what is going to come out of it. It looks as if *something* must follow."

"You didn't hear me come into your room last night, Connie. The storm was raging then as loud as it is now, but you were out of its reach, fast asleep. Now it is too much for you. You must lie down."

"Very well, Papa."

I lowered the support, and when I returned from changing my wet garments she was already looking much better.

After dinner I went to my study. Then evening began to fall, and I went out again, for I wanted to see how the sexton and his wife were faring. The wind had already increased in violence, and threatened to blow a hurricane. The old mill shook its foundations as I passed through it to reach the lower part where they lived. When I peeped in from the bottom of the stair, I saw no one; but, hearing steps overhead, I called out.

Agnes answered, as she descended an inner stair which led to the bedrooms above, "Mother's gone to church."

"Gone to church!" I said, a vague pang darting through me as I thought I had forgotten some service. But the next moment I recalled the old woman's preference for the church during a storm.

"Oh, yes, Agnes! I remember," I said. "Your mother thinks the weather bad enough to take to the church, does she? How do you come to be here now? And where is your husband?"

"He'll be here in an hour or so. He don't mind the wet. You see, we don't like the old people to be left alone when it blows what the sailors call 'great guns.' "

"And what becomes of his mother then?"

"There don't be any sea out there. Leastways," she added with a quiet smile, and stopped.

"You mean, I suppose, Agnes, that there is never any perturbation of the elements out there?"

She laughed, for she understood me well enough. The temper of Joe's mother was proverbial.

"But really," she said, "she don't mind the weather a bit. And though we don't live in the same cottage with her, for Joe wouldn't hear of that, we see her far oftener than we see my mother, you know."

"I'm sure it's quite fair, Agnes. Is Joe very sorry that he

married you, now?"

She hung her head, blushing deeply, and replied, "I don't think he be, Sir. I do think he gets better. He's been working very hard the last week or two, and he says it agrees with him."

"And how are you?"

"Quite well, thank you."

I had never seen her look half so well. Life was evidently a very different thing to both of them now. I left her and took my way to the church.

When I reached the churchyard, there in the middle of the rain and the gathering darkness was the old man busy with the duties of his calling. A certain headstone stood right under a drip from the roof, and this drip had caused the mold at the foot of the stone to sink, so that there was a considerable crack between the stone and the soil. The old man had cut some sod from another part of the churchyard, and was now standing, with the rain pouring on him from the roof, beating this sod down in the crack. He was sheltered from the wind by the church, but was as wet as could be.

"This will never do, Coombes," I said. "You will get your death of cold. You must be as full of water as a sponge. Old man, there's rheumatism in the world!"

"It be only my work, Sir, but I believe I ha' done now for a night. I think he'll be a bit more comfortable now. The very wind could get at him through that hole."

"Do go home, then," I said, "and change your clothes. Is your wife in the church?"

"She be, Sir. This door—this door," he added, as he saw me going round to the usual entrance. "You'll find her in there."

I lifted the great latch and entered. I could not see her at first, for it was much darker inside the church. It felt very quiet in there somehow, although the place was full of the noise of winds and waters. Mrs. Coombes was sitting at the foot of the chancel rail, knitting as usual.

Her sweet old face, lighted up by a moonlike smile, and seen in the middle of the ancient dusk filled with the sounds (but only the sounds) of tempest, gave me a sense of one dwelling in the secret place of the Most High.

"How long do you mean to stay here, Mrs. Coombes?" I asked. "Not all night?"

"No, not all night, surely. But I hadn't thought o' going yet for a bit."

"Why, there's Coombes out there, wet to the skin, and I'm afraid he'll go on pottering at the churchyard bedclothes till he gets his bones as full of rheumatism as they can hold."

"Deary me! I didn't know as my old man was there. He tould me he had them all comfortable for the winter a week ago. But to be sure there's always some mendin' to do."

I heard Joe speaking outside, and the next moment he came into the church. After speaking to me he turned to Mrs. Coombes.

"You be comin' home with me, Mother. This will never do. Father's wet as a mop. I ha' brought something for your supper, and Aggy's a-cookin' of it, and we're going to be comfortable over the fire, and have a chapter of the New Testament to keep down the noise of the sea. There! Come along."

The old woman drew her cloak over her head, put her knitting carefully in her pocket, and stood aside for me to lead the way.

"No, no," I said, "I'm the shepherd and you're the sheep, so I'll drive you before me—at least you and Coombes. Joe here will be offended if I take on me to say I am *his* shepherd."

"Nay, nay, don't say that. You've been a good shepherd to me, when I was a very sulky sheep. But if you'll please to go, I'll lock the door behind, for you know in them parts the shepherd goes first, and the sheep follow the shepherd. And I'll follow like a good sheep," he added laughing.

"You're right, Joe," I said, and took the lead without more ado. I was struck by his saying *them parts,* which indicated a habit of pondering on the places as well as circumstances of the Gospel story.

Coombes joined us at the door, and we all walked to his cottage, Joe taking care of his mother-in-law, and I taking what care I could of Coombes by carrying his tools for him. But as we went, I feared I had done ill in that, for the wind blew so fiercely that I thought the thin feeble little man would have got on better if he had been more heavily weighted against it. But I made him take hold of my arm, and so we got in. When we opened the inner door, the welcome of a glowing fire burst up the stair, and I went down with them. Coombes departed to change his clothes, and the rest of us stood round the fire where Agnes was busy cooking something like white puddings for their supper.

"Did you hear," said Joe, "that the coast guard is off to the Goose-pot? There's a vessel ashore there, they say. I met them on the road with the rocket cart."

"How far off is that, Joe?"

"Some five or six miles, I suppose, along the coast nor'ards."

"What sort of vessel is she?"

"That I don't know. Some say she be a schooner, others a brigantine. The coast guard didn't know themselves."

"Poor things!" said Mrs. Coombes. "If any of them come ashore, they'll be sadly knocked to pieces on the rocks in a night like this." She had caught a little infection of her husband's mode of thought.

"It's not likely to clear up before morning, I fear, is it, Joe?"

"I don't think so. There's no likelihood."

"Will you condescend to sit down and take a share with us, Sir?" said the old woman.

"There would be no condescension in that, Mrs. Coombes. I will another time with all my heart. But in such a night I ought to be at home with my own people. They will be more uneasy if I am away."

"Of coorse, of coorse."

"So I'll bid you good-night. I wish this storm were well over."

I buttoned my greatcoat, pulled my hat down on my head, and set out. The roaring of the waves on the shore was terrible. All I could see of them now was the whiteness of their breaking, but they filled the earth and the air with their furious noises.

I found the whole household full of the storm. The children kept pressing their faces to the windows trying to pierce as by force of will through the darkness, and discover what the wild thing out there was doing. They could see nothing—all was one mass of blackness and dismay and ceaseless roaring. I ran up to Connie's room, and found that she was left alone. She looked restless, pale, and frightened. The house quivered, and still the wind howled and whistled through the adjoining bark hut.

"Connie, darling, have they left you alone?"

"Only for a few minutes, Papa. I don't mind it."

"Don't be frightened at the storm, my dear. He who could walk on the Sea of Galilee and still the storm of that little pool, can rule the Atlantic just as well. Jeremiah says, 'He divideth the sea when the waves thereof roar.' "

The same moment Dora came running into the room. "Papa!" she cried. "The spray—such a lot of it—came dashing on the windows. Will it break them?"

"I hope not, my dear. Stay with Connie while I run down."

"O Papa! I do want to see."

"What do you want to see, Dora?"

"The storm, Papa."

"It is as black as pitch. You can t see anything."

"Oh, but I want to—to—be beside it."

"Well, you shan't stay with Connie, if you are not willing. Go along, and ask Wynnie to come here."

The child was so possessed by the commotion outside that she did not seem even to see my rebuke, much less feel 't. She ran off, and Wynnie presently came. I left her with Connie and went down. The dining room was dark, for they had put out the lights that they might see better from the windows. The children and some of the servants were there looking out.

There came a lull in the wind, and I thought I heard a gun. I listened, but heard nothing more. When I went up to the drawing room, I found that Percivale had joined our party. He and Turner were talking together at one of the windows.

"Did you hear a gun?" I asked them.

"No. Was there one?"

"I'm not sure. I half fancied I heard one, but no other followed. There will be a good many fired tonight though, along this awful coast."

"I suppose they keep the lifeboat always ready," said Turner.

"No lifeboat, I fear, would live in such a sea," I said.

"They would try, though, I suppose," said Turner.

"I do not know," said Percivale, "for I don't know the people. But I have seen a lifeboat out in as bad a night—whether in as bad a sea, I cannot tell."

Then Wynnie joined us, and I asked her, "How is Connie, now, my dear?"

"Very restless and excited, Papa. I came down to say that if Mr. Turner didn't mind, I wish he would go up and see her."

"Of course, instantly," said Turner, and moved to follow Wynnie.

But the same moment, as if it had been beside us in the room, so clear, so shrill was it, we heard Connie's voice shrieking, "Papa! Papa! There's a great ship ashore down there. Come, come!"

Turner and I rushed from the room toward the narrow stairs that led directly up to the bark hut. The door at the top of it was open, as was the door from Connie's room. Enough light shone in to show a figure by the farthest window with its face pressed against the glass. "Papa! Papa! Quick, quick! The waves will knock her to pieces!"

It was Connie standing there.

THIRTY-TWO

THE SHIPWRECK

Turner and I both rushed at the stair, though there was not room for more than one upon it. I was first, but stumbled on the lowest step and fell. Turner put his foot on my back, jumped over me, sprang up the stair, and when I reached the top, he was meeting me with Connie in his arms, carrying her back to her room. But she kept crying, "Papa, Papa! The ship, the ship!"

My duty woke in me—Turner could attend to Connie far better than I could. I made one spring to the window. The moon was not to be seen, but the clouds were thinner, and enough light was soaking through them to show a wave-tormented mass some little way out in the bay, and in that moment a shriek pierced the howling of the wind like a knife. I rushed bareheaded from the house and flew straight to the sexton's, snatched the key from the wall, crying only, "Ship ashore!" and rushed to the church.

My hand trembled so that I could hardly get the key into the lock, but I opened the door, felt my way to the tower, knelt before the keys of the hammer bells, opened the chest, and struck them wildly, fiercely. An awful jangling, out of tune and harsh, burst into the storm-vexed air. I struck repeatedly at the keys, wanting noise, outcry, *reveille*.

In a few minutes I heard voices and footsteps. From some parts of the village, out of sight of the shore, men and women gathered to the summons. Through the door of the church, which I had left open, came voices in hurried question. "Ship ashore!" was all I could answer.

I wondered that so few appeared at the cry of the bells. After those first nobody came for what seemed a long time. I believe, however, I was beating the alarm for only a few minutes altogether. Then a hand was laid on my shoulder.

"Who is there?" I said, for it was far too dark to know anyone.

"Percivale. What is to be done? The coast guard is away. Nobody seems to know anything. It is no use to go on ringing more. Everybody is out, even to the maidservants. Come down to the shore and you will see."

"But is there no lifeboat?"

"Nobody seems to know anything about it, except that 'it's no manner of use to go trying *that* with such a sea on.' "

"But someone must be in command of it," I said.

"Yes," returned Percivale. "But none of the crew are amongst the crowd. All the sailor-like fellows are going about with their hands in their pockets."

"Let us make haste, then," I said. "Perhaps we can find out. Are you sure the coast guard have nothing to do with the lifeboat?"

"I believe not. They have enough to do with their rockets."

"Roxton has far more confidence in his rockets than in anything a lifeboat could do, on this coast at least."

While we spoke, we came to the bank of the canal. To my surprise, the canal itself was in a storm, heaving and tossing and dashing over its banks.

"Percivale!" I exclaimed. "The gates are gone! The sea has torn them away."

"Yes, I suppose so. Would God I could get six men to help me. I have been doing what I could, but I have no influence amongst them."

"What do you mean?" I asked. "What could you do if you had a thousand men at your command?"

He made no answer for a few moments, during which we were hurrying on for the bridge over the canal. Then he said, "They regard me only as a meddling stranger, I suppose, for I have been able to get no useful answer. They are all excited, but nobody is doing anything."

"They must know about it a great deal better than we," I returned, "and we must not do them the injustice of supposing they are not ready to do all that can be done."

All this time the ocean was raving in our ears, and the awful tragedy was going on in the dark behind us. The wind was almost as loud as ever, but the rain had quite ceased, and when we reached the bridge the moon had succeeded in pushing the clouds aside. There was little shore left, for the waves had rushed up almost to the village. The sand and the roads, every garden wall, every window that looked seaward—all were crowded with gazers. But it seemed a wonderfully quiet crowd, for the noise of the wind and the waves filled the whole vault, and what was spoken was heard only in the ear to which it was spoken.

Out there in the moonlight lay a mass of something, made discernible by the flashing waves bursting over it. She was far above the low-water mark, nearer the village by a furlong than the spot where we had taken our last dinner on the shore. It was strange to think that yesterday the spot lay bare to human feet, where now so many men and women were isolated in a howling waste of angry waters. The cries came plainly to our ears, and we were helpless to save them.

Percivale went about hurriedly, talking to this one and that one, as if he still thought something might be done. He turned to me. "Do try, Mr. Walton, and find the captain of the lifeboat."

I turned to a sailor-like man who stood at my elbow and asked him.

"It's no use, I assure you," he answered. "No boat could live in such a sea. It would be throwing away the men's lives."

"Do you know where the captain lives?" Percivale asked.

"If I did, I tell you it is of no use."

"Are you the captain yourself?" returned Percivale.

"What is that to you?" he answered, surly now. "I know my own business."

The same moment several of the crowd nearest the edge of the water made a simultaneous rush into the surf and laid hold of the body of a woman—alive or dead I could not tell. I could just see the long hair hanging from the white face as they bore her up the bank.

"Run, Percivale," I said, "and fetch Turner. She may not be dead yet."

"I can't," answered Percivale. "You had better go yourself, Mr. Walton."

He spoke hurriedly, and I saw he must have some reason for answering me so abruptly. He was talking to Jim Allen, one of the village's most dissolute young fellows, and as I turned to go they strode away together.

I sped home as fast as I could, for it was easier to get along now that the moon shone. I found that Turner had given Connie a composing draught, and she was asleep exhausted. In her sleep she kept on talking about the ship.

We hurried back to see if anything could be done for the woman. As we went up the side of the canal, we perceived dark shadows before us—a body of men hauling something along. Yes, it was the lifeboat, afloat on the troubled waves of the canal, each man seated in his own place, his hands quiet upon his oar, his cork jacket braced about him, his feet out before him, ready to pull the moment they should pass beyond the broken gates of the lock out on the awful tossing waves. They sat very silent, and the men on the path towed them swiftly along. The moon uncovered the faces of two of the rowers.

"Percivale! Joe!" I cried.

"Right, Sir!" said Joe.

"I've nothing to lose," Percivale called out, "but Joe has his wife."

"I've everything to win," Joe returned. "The only .ning that makes me feel a bit fainthearted is that I'm afraid it's not my duty that drives me to it, but the praise of men, leastaways, a woman. What would Aggy think of me if I was to let them drown out there and go to my bed and sleep? I must go. And it's the first chance I've had of returning thanks for her. Please God, I shall see her again tonight."

"That's good, Joe. Trust in God, my men, whether you sink or swim."

"Ay, ay, Sir," they answered as one man.

"This is your doing, Percivale," I said, turning and walking alongside of the boat for a little way.

"It's more Jim Allen's," said Percivale. "Without him I couldn't have done anything."

"God bless you, Jim," I said. "You'll be a better man after this."

"Donnow, Sir," returned Jim, cheerily. "That's harder work than pulling an oar."

And even the captain himself was on board. Percivale had persuaded Jim Allen, and the two had gone about in the crowd until they had found almost all the crew. The captain, protesting against the folly of it, at last gave in; and once having yielded, he was, like a true Englishman, as much in earnest as any of them. Two missing men were replaced by Percivale and Joe.

"God bless you, my men!" I called after them, and turned again to follow the doctor. I found Turner in the little public house whither they had carried the body. The woman was quite dead.

"It is an emigrant vessel," he said. "Look at the body."

It was that of a woman about twenty, tall and finely formed. The face was very handsome, but it did not need the evidence of the hands to prove that she was one of our sisters who have to labor for their bread.

"What should such a girl be doing on board ship but going out to America or Australia? To her lover, perhaps," said Turner. "You see she has a locket on her neck. I hope nobody will dare take it off. Some of these people are not far derived from those who thought a wreck a godsend."

A sound of many feet was at the door just as we turned to leave the house. They were bringing another body, that of an elderly woman—dead, quite dead. Turner had ceased examining her, and we were going out together when, through all the tumult of the winds and waves, a fierce hiss—vindictive, wrathful—tore the air over our heads. Far up seaward, something like a fiery snake shot from the high ground on the right side of the bay, over the vessel, and into the water beyond it.

"Thank God! That's the coast guard," I cried.

We rushed through the village and up onto the heights where they had planted their rocket apparatus. How dismal the sea looked in the struggling moonlight! I approached the cliff and saw down below the great mass of the vessel's hulk, with the waves breaking every moment upon her side. Now and then there would come a lull in the wild sequence of rolling waters, and then I saw now she rocked on the bottom. Her masts had all gone by the board, and a perfect chaos of cordage floated and swung in the waves that broke over her. But her bowsprit remained entire, and shot out into the foamy dark, crowded with human beings.

The first rocket missed, and its trailing lifeline fell uselessly to the water. They prepared to fire another. Roxton stood by with his telescope, ready to watch the result.

"This is a terrible job," he said when I approached him. "I doubt if we shall save one of them."

"There's the lifeboat!" I cried, as a dark spot approached the vessel from the other side.

"The lifeboat!" he returned with contempt. "You don't mean to say they've got *her* out! She'll only add to the mischief. We'll have to save her too."

She was still some way from the vessel, and in comparatively smooth water; but between her and the hull the sea raved in madness. The billows rode over each other in pursuit of some invisible prey. Another hiss, as of concentrated hatred, and the second rocket was shooting its parabola through the dusky air. Roxton raised his telescope to his eye the same moment.

"Over her starn!" he cried. "There's a fellow getting down from the cathead to run aft—Stop, stop!" he shouted. "There's an awful wave on your quarter!"

His voice was swallowed in the roaring of the storm. A dark something shot from the bow toward the stern, but then the huge wave fell upon the wreck. The same moment Roxton exclaimed— so cooly as to amaze me, forgetting how men must come to regard familiar things without discomposure—"He's gone! I said so. The next'll have better luck, I hope."

(That man came ashore alive, though, for I was to hear his story later.)

But now my attention was fixed on the lifeboat in the wildest of the broken water. At one moment she was down in a huge cleft, the next balanced like a beam on the knife-edge of a wave, tossed about as the waves delighted in mocking the rudder. As yet she had shipped no water, but then a huge wave rushed up, towered over her, toppled, and fell upon her with tons of water. The boat vanished. The next moment, there she was, floating helplessly about like a living thing stunned by the blow of the falling wave. The struggle was over. As far as I could see, every man was in his place, but the boat drifted away before the storm shoreward, and the men let her drift. Were they all killed as they sat? I thought of my Wynnie, and turned to Roxton.

"That wave has done for them," he said. "I told you it was no use. There they go."

"But what is the matter?" I asked. "The men are sitting every man in his place."

"I think so," he answered. "Two were swept overboard, but they caught the ropes and got in again. But don't you see they have no oars?"

That wave had broken every one of them off at the rowlocks, and now they were helpless.

I turned and ran. Before I reached the brow of the hill another rocket was fired and fell wide shoreward, partly because the wind blew with fresh fury at that very moment. I heard Roxton say, "She's breaking up. It's no use. That last did for her." I hurried off for the other side of the bay, to see what became of the lifeboat. I heard a great cry from the vessel as I reached the brow of the hill, and so turned for a parting glance. The dark mass had vanished, and the waves were rushing at will over the space.

The crowd was less on the shore, and many were running toward the other side, anxious about the lifeboat. I hastened after them, for Percivale and Joe filled my heart. The crowd led the way to the little beach in front of the parsonage, where it would be well for the crew if they were driven ashore, for it was the only spot where they could escape being dashed on the rocks.

There was a crowd before the garden wall, a bustle, and great confusion of speech. The people, men and women, boys and girls, were all gathered about the crew of the lifeboat, which already lay exhausted on the grass.

"Percivale!" I cried, making my way through the crowd.

There was no answer.

"Joe!" I cried again, searching with eager eyes amongst the crew, to whom everybody was talking.

Still there was no answer, and from the disjointed phrases I heard, I could gather nothing. All at once I saw Wynnie looking over the wall, despair in her face, her wide eyes searching wildly through the crowd. I could not look at her till I knew the worst. The captain was talking to Old Coombes, but as soon as he saw me, he gave me his attention.

"Where is Mr. Percivale?" I asked, with all the calmness I could assume.

He took me by the arm, and drew me nearer to the mouth of the canal. He pointed in the direction of the Castle Rock. "If you mean the stranger gentleman—"

"And Joe Harper, the blacksmith," I interposed.

"They're there."

"You don't mean those two—just those two—are drowned?" I said.

"No, I don't say that, but God knows they have little chance."

I could not help thinking that God might know they were not in the smallest danger. However, I only begged him to tell me where they were.

"Do you see that schooner there, just between you and Castle Rock? The gentleman you mean and Joe Harper too are on board the schooner."

"No," I answered, "I can't say I see it. Is she aground?"

"Oh, dear no. She's a light craft, and can swim there well enough. If she'd be aground, she'd ha' been ashore in pieces hours ago. But whether she'll ride it out, God only knows, as I said afore."

"How ever did they get aboard of her? I never saw her from the heights opposite."

"You were all taken up with the ship ashore, you see. And she don't make much show in this light. But there she is, and they're aboard of her."

He gave me his part of the story, and the rest of it I was able to piece together later. Two men had been swept overboard, as Roxton said—one of them was Percivale—but they had got on board again, to drift, oarless, with the rest, now in a windless valley, and now aloft on a tempest-swept hill of water.

A little out of the full force of the current, and not far from the channel of the small stream, lay the little schooner, where it had been driven into the bay. The master, however, knew the ground well. The current carried him a little out of the wind, and would have thrown him upon the rocks next, but he managed to drop anchor just in time. The cable held and there the little schooner hung in the skirts of the storm, with the jagged teeth of the rocks within an arrow flight. In the excitement of the great wreck, no one had observed the danger of the little coasting bird. If their cable held till the tide went down, and the anchor did not drag, she would be safe. If not, she would surely be dashed to pieces.

In the schooner were two men and a boy: two men had been washed overboard an hour or so before they reached the bay. When they had dropped their anchor, they lay exhausted on the deck. Indeed they were so worn out that they had been unable to drop their sheet anchor, and were holding on only by their best bower. Had they not been a good deal out of the wind, this would have been useless. Even if it held, she was in danger of having her bottom stove in by bumping against the sands as the tide went out, but that they had not to think of yet. The moment they lay down, they fell asleep in the middle of the storm, and while they slept it increased in violence.

Suddenly one of them awoke, and thought he saw a vision of

angels. For over his head faces looked down upon him from the air—that is, from the top of a great wave. The same moment he heard a voice, two of the angels dropped on the deck beside him, and the rest vanished. Those angels were Percivale and Joe. And angels they were, for they came just in time, as all angels do—the schooner *was* dragging her anchor.

But it did not take them many minutes now to drop their strongest anchor, and they were soon riding in perfect safety.

I thanked the captain, and returned to the garden wall, for I could do nothing by staring out in the direction of the schooner. Only one little group of the crowd remained, and at its center stood a woman. Wynnie had disappeared. The woman who remained was Agnes Harper.

"Agnes," I said, "the storm is breaking up."

"Yes, Sir," she answered, and looked up as if waiting for a command. There was no color in her cheeks or in her lips—at least it seemed so in the moonlight—only in her eyes. But she was perfectly calm. She was leaning against the low wall, with her hands clasped and hanging quietly down before her. Then, after just a moment's pause, in the same still tone, she spoke out her heart. "Joe's at his duty?"

"Yes," I returned. "At all events, he's not taking care of his own life. And if one is to go wrong, I would ten thousand times rather err on that side. But I am sure Joe has been doing right, and nothing else."

"Then there's nothing to be said, is there?" she returned, with a sigh of relief.

I presume some of the surrounding condolers had been giving her Job's comfort by blaming her husband.

"Do you remember, Agnes, what the Lord said to His mother when she reproached Him with having left her and His father?"

"I can't remember anything at this moment," was her touching answer.

"Then I will tell you. He said, 'Why did you look for Me? Didn't you know that I must be about something My Father had given Me to do?' Now Joe was and is about his Father's business, and you must not be anxious about him. There could be no better reason for not being anxious."

Without a word Agnes took my hand and kissed it. I did not withdraw my hand, for I knew that would be to rebuke her love for Joe.

"Will you come in and wait?" I asked.

"No, thank you. I must go to my mother. God will look after Joe, won't He?"

"As sure as there is a God, Agnes," I said, and she went away without another word.

I put my hand on the top of the wall and jumped over, and almost alighted on a woman lying there, my own Wynnie.

She had not fainted, but was lying with her handkerchief stuffed into her mouth to keep from screaming. She rose, and without looking at me, walked away toward the house, straight to her own room, and shut the door. I found her mother with Connie who was now awake, pale, and frightened. I told Ethelwyn that Percivale and Joe were on board the little schooner, that Wynnie was in terror about Percivale, that I had found her lying on the wet grass, and that she must get her into a warm bath and to bed.

We went together to Wynnie's room. She was standing in the middle of the floor, with her hands pressed against her temples.

"Wynnie," I said, "our friends are not drowned. I think you will see them quite safe in the morning. Pray to God for them."

She did not hear a word.

"Leave her with me," said Ethelwyn, proceeding to undress her, "and tell Nurse to bring up the large bath. There is plenty of hot water in the boiler: I gave orders to that effect, not knowing what might happen."

Wynnie shuddered as her mother said this, but I waited no longer, for when Ethelwyn spoke, everyone felt her authority. I obeyed her and then went to Connie's room.

"Do you mind being left alone a little while?" I asked her.

"No, Papa. Only—are they all drowned?" she said with a shudder.

"I hope not, my dear. But be sure of the mercy of God, whatever you fear. You must rest in Him, my love, for He is Life, and He will conquer death both in the soul and in the body."

Dora and the boys were all fast asleep, for it was very late. Telling Nurse to be on the watch because Connie was alone, I went again to the beach. I called first, however, to inquire after Agnes. I found her quite composed, sitting with her parents by the fire, none of them doing anything, scarcely speaking, only listening intently to the sounds of the storm now beginning to die away.

I next went to the place where I had left Turner. Five bodies lay there, and he was busy with a sixth. The surgeon of the place was with him, and they quite expected to recover this man.

The morning began to dawn with a pale ghastly light, and the sea raged on, although the wind had gone down. There were many strong men about, with two surgeons and all the coast guard, and the houses along the shore were at the disposal of any who wanted aid. The parsonage was at some distance, and I was glad to think there was no necessity for carrying thither any of those whom the waves cast on the shore.

When I reached home and found Wynnie quieter, and Connie again asleep, I walked out along our own downs till I could see the little schooner still safe at anchor. She was clearly out of all danger now, and if Percivale and Joe were safe on board, we might confidently expect to see them before many hours were past. I went home with the good news.

For a few moments I doubted whether I should tell Wynnie, for I could not know with any certainty that Percivale was in the schooner. But I reflected that we have no right to modify God's facts for fear of what may be to come. A little hope founded on a present appearance, even if that hope should never be realized, may be the very means of enabling a soul to bear the weight of a sorrow past the point at which it would otherwise break down. I would therefore tell Wynnie, and let her share my expectation.

I think she had been half asleep, for when I entered her room, she started up in a sitting posture, looking wild, and put her hands to her head.

"I have brought you good news, Wynnie," I said. "The little schooner is quite safe."

"What schooner?" she asked listlessly, and lay down again, her eyes still staring unappeased.

"Why the schooner they say Percivale got on board."

"He isn't drowned then!" she cried with a choking voice, and she put her hands to her face and burst into tears.

"Wynnie," I said, "everybody but you has known all night that Percivale and Joe Harper are probably quite safe. They may be ashore in a couple of hours."

"But you don't know it. He may be drowned yet."

"Of course, there is room for doubt—but none for despair. See what a poor helpless creature hopelessness makes you."

"But how can I help it, Papa?" she asked piteously. "I am made so." But as she spoke, the dawn was clear upon the height of her forehead.

"You are not made yet, as I am always telling you. And God has ordained that you shall have a hand in your own making. You have to consent, to desire that what you know for a fault shall be set right by His loving will and Spirit."

"I don't know God, Papa."

"Ah, my dear! That is where it all lies. You do not know Him, or you would never be without hope."

"But what am I to do to know Him?" she asked, rising on her elbow.

The saving power of hope was already working in her. She was once more turning her face toward the Life.

"Read as you have never read before about Christ Jesus, my love. Read with the express object of finding out what God is like, that you may know Him and trust Him. And give yourself to Him, and He will give you peace."

"What are we to do," I said to my wife later, "if Percivale continues silent? For even if he be in love with her, I doubt if he will speak."

"We must leave all that, Harry," she answered.

She was turning on me the counsel I had given Wynnie. It is strange how easily we can tell our brother what he ought to do, and yet do ourselves precisely as we rebuked him for doing. I lay down and fell fast asleep.

THIRTY-THREE

THE FUNERAL

It was a lovely morning when I woke once more. The sun was flashing back from the sea which was still tossing, but no longer furiously, only as if it wanted to turn itself every way to flash the sunlight about. The madness of the night was over and gone; the light was abroad; and the world was rejoicing. And there was the schooner lying dry on the sands, her two cables and anchors stretching out yards behind her. But halfway between the two sides of the bay rose a mass of something shapeless, drifted over with sand. It was all that remained together of the great ship. The wind had ceased altogether, only now and then a little breeze arose which murmured, "I am very sorry," and lay down again. And I knew that in the houses on the shore, there lay at least fifteen dead men and women.

I went down to the dining room. The three youngest children were busy at their breakfast, but neither Ethelwyn, Wynnie, nor Turner had yet appeared. I made a hurried meal and was just rising to go and inquire further into the events of the night, when the door opened and in walked Percivale, looking very solemn, but in perfect health and well-being.

I grasped his hand warmly. "Thank God," I said, "that you are returned to us, Percivale!"

"I doubt if that is much to give thanks for," he said.

"We are the judges of that," I rejoined. "Tell me about it.'

Percivale's account of the matter was that as they drifted helplessly along, he suddenly saw, from the top of a huge wave, the

216

little vessel below him. They were, in fact, almost upon the rigging, and the wave on which they rode swept the quarterdeck of the schooner.

Percivale said the captain of the lifeboat called out, "Aboard!" even though the captain said he remembered nothing of the sort—if he did, he must have meant the men on the schooner to board the lifeboat. But Percivale, fancying the captain meant them to board the schooner, sprang at her foreshrouds. When the wave swept along the schooner's side, Joe sprang on the mainshrouds, and so they dropped on the deck together.

While he was narrating the events, Wynnie entered. She started, turned pale and then very red, and for a moment hesitated in the doorway.

"Here is another to rejoice at your safety, Percivale," I said.

Thereupon he stepped forward to meet her, and she gave him her hand with evident emotion, looking more lovely than I had ever seen her. Then she sat down and began to busy herself with the teapot, though her hand trembled. I requested Percivale to begin his story once more, and excused myself to go to the village. As I left, he was recounting to her—with evident enjoyment—the adventures of the night.

I went first to the mill to see how Joe was, but there was no one there but the old woman.

She greeted me with a beaming face. "Oh Sir! My Willie's come home!"

"Home? In this storm?"

"Did ye see that schooner there last night aridin' out the weather? He were on it, he were, though two on 'em were swept o'er and drowned, and two men o' the lifeboat had to come out to rescue 'em. Only drenched, he were, and wore out a bit, and now he's out wi' his Mary for a walk, and right glad she were to see him too."

I rejoiced with her, and told her the rest of the story, and how Percivale and Joe had come from the wet sky like sea-angels to deliver her Willie. "And where are Joe and Agnes?" I concluded.

"You see, Sir, Joe had promised a little job of work to be ready today, and so he couldn't stop. He did say Agnes needn't go with him, but she thought she couldn't part with him so soon, you see."

"She had received him too from the dead—raised to life again," I said. "It was most natural. But that Joe—will nothing make him lay aside his work?"

"I tried to get him to stop, saying he had done quite enough last night for all next day. But he told me it was his business to get the tire put on Farmer Wheatstone's cartwheel today just as much as it was his business to go in the lifeboat yesterday. So he would go, and Aggy wouldn't stay behind."

"Fine fellow, Joe!" I said, and took my leave of the happy woman.

As I drew near the village, I heard the sound of hammering and sawing, and apparently everything at once in the way of joinery, for they were making coffins in the joiner's shops.

The county magistrate sent a notice of the loss of the vessel to the Liverpool papers, requesting those who might wish to identify or claim any of the bodies, to appear within four days at Kilkhaven. As this threw the fourth day upon Saturday, and it was clear that the dead must not remain above ground over Sunday, I therefore arranged that they should be buried late on the Saturday night.

On the Friday morning, a young woman and an old man (unknown to each other) arrived by the coach from Barnstaple. They had come to look, if they might, at the shadow left behind by the departing souls of their friends. That afternoon, with the approbation of the magistrate, I had all the bodies removed to the church. Some in their coffins, others on stretchers, they were laid in front of the Communion rail. In the evening the two visitors went to see them, and I took care to be present.

The old man soon found his son. I was at his elbow as he walked between the rows of the dead. He turned to me and said quietly, "That's him. He was a good lad. God rest his soul. He's with his mother, and if I'm sorry, she's glad."

With that he smiled, or tried to smile. I could only lay my hand on his arm. He walked out of the church, sat down upon a stone, and stared at the mold of a new-made grave in front of him. It was well to see with what a sober sorrow the dignified old man bore his grief—as if he felt that the loss of his son was only for a moment.

But the young woman had taken on the hue of the corpse she had come to seek. Her eyes were sunken as if with the weight of the light she cared not for, and her cheeks had already pined away as if to be ready for the grave. She never even told us whom she came seeking, and after one involuntary question, which simply received no answer, I was very careful not to even approach another. I do not think the form she sought was there, and she may have left the church with the lingering hope that, after all, that one had escaped.

But God had them in His teaching, and all I could do was to ask them to be my guests till the funeral and the following Sunday were over. To this they kindly consented, and I took them to my wife who received them like herself, and had in a few minutes made them at home with her.

The next morning a Scotchman appeared, seeking the form of his daughter, and so I went with him to the church. He was a tall, gaunt, bony man, with long arms and huge hands, a rugged granitelike face, and a slow ponderous utterance which I had some difficulty in understanding. He treated the object of his visit with a certain hardness (and at the same time lightness) which I also had some difficulty in understanding.

"You want to see the—" I said, and hesitated.

"Ow ay—the boadies," he answered. "She winna be there, I daursay, but I jist like to see, for I wadna like her to be beeried gin sae be 'at she was there, wi'oot biddin' her good-by like."

When we reached the church, I opened the door and entered. An awe fell upon me fresh and new, for the beautiful church had become a tomb. Solemn, grand, ancient, it rose as a memorial of the dead who lay in peace before her altar rail, as if they had fled for sanctuary from a sea of troubles. And by the vestry door sat Mrs. Coombes, like an angel watching the dead, with her sweet solemn smile, and her constant ministration of knitting.

He glanced at one and another of the dead and passed on. He had looked at ten or twelve ere he stopped, and stood gazing on the face of the beautiful form which had been the first to come ashore. He stooped, and stroked the white cheeks, taking the dead in his great rough hands, and smoothing the brown hair tenderly, saying, as if he had quite forgotten that she was dead, "Eh, Maggie! Hoo cam ye here, Lass?"

Then, as if for the first time the reality had grown comprehensible, he put his hands before his face, and burst into tears. His huge frame was shaken with sobs for one long minute, while I stood looking on with awe and reverence. He ceased suddenly, pulled a blue cotton handkerchief from his pocket, rubbed his face with it as if drying it with a towel, put it back, turned, and said, without looking at me, "I'll awa' hae."

"She came ashore with a locket on," I said. "Would you like to take it with you, or would you rather she be laid away with it on?"

"Gin ye please," he said softly, "it wur her own mother's, and I wadna like to beery it too."

I gently unfastened the locket and laid it on the palm of his huge hand. He opened it, gazed inside at whatever picture was there, and then put it silently and tenderly in his pocket.

"Would you like a piece of her hair as well?" I asked.

"Gin ye please," he answered gently, as if his daughter's form had been mine now, and her effects and hair were mine to give.

I turned to Mrs. Coombes. "Have you a pair of scissors there?" I asked.

"Yes, to be sure," she answered, rising, and lifting a huge pair by the string suspending them from her waist.

"If you please, cut off a nice piece of her beautiful hair for her father," I said.

She lifted the lovely head, chose, and cut off a long piece, and handed it respectfully to him.

He took it without a word, sat down on the step before the Communion rail, and began to smooth out the wonderful sleave of dusky gold. He drew it out a yard long, passing his big fingers through and through it tenderly, as if it had been still growing on the live lovely head, and stopping every moment to pick out the bits of seaweed and shells, and shake out the sand that had been wrought into its mass. He sat thus for nearly half an hour, and we stood looking on with something closely akin to awe. At length he folded it up, drew from his pocket an old black leather book, laid it carefully in the innermost pocket, and rose. I led the way from the church, and he followed me.

Outside the church, he laid his hand on my arm, and said, groping with his other hand in his trousers pocket, "She'll hae putten ye to some expense—for the coffin an' sic like."

"We'll talk about that afterward," I answered. "Come home with me now, and have some refreshment."

"Na, I thank ye. I hae putten ye to eneuch o' tribble already. I'll jist awa' hame."

"We are going to lay them down this evening. You won't go before the funeral. Indeed, I think you can't get away till Monday morning. My wife and I will be glad of your company till then."

"I'm no company for gentle fowk, Sir."

"Come and show me in which of these graves you would like to have her laid," I said.

He yielded and followed me.

Coombes had not dug many spadefuls before he saw that ten such men as he could not dig the graves in time. But there was plenty of help to be had from the village and the neighboring farms, and most of the graves were ready now. The brown hillocks lay about the churchyard—the moleheaps of burrowing death.

The stranger looked around him and his face grew critical. He stepped a little hither and thither, and at length turned and said, "I wadna like to be greedy, but gin ye wad lat her lie next the kirk there—i' that neuk—I wad tak' it kindly. And syne gin ever it cam' aboot that I cam' here again, I wad kne whaur she was. Could ye get a sma' bit heidstane putten up? I wad leave the siller wi' ye to pay for't."

"To be sure I can. What will you have on the stone?"

"Ow jist—lat me see—'Maggie Jamieson'—nae Marget, but jist Maggie. She was aye Maggie at hame. 'Maggie Jamieson, frae her father.' It's the last thing I can gie her. Maybe ye micht put a verse o' Scripter aneath't, ye ken."

"What verse would you like?"

He thought for a while. "Isna there a text that says, 'The deid shall hear His voice'?"

"Yes. 'The dead shall hear the voice of the Son of God.' "

"Ay. That's it. Weel, jist put that on. They canna do better than hear His voice."

I led the way home, and he accompanied me without further objection or apology. After dinner, I proposed that we should all go on the downs, for the day was warm and bright. We sat on the grass. I felt that I could not talk to them as from myself. I knew nothing of the possible gulfs of sorrow in their hearts. To me their forms seemed each like a hill in whose unseen bosom lay a cavern of dripping waters, perhaps with a subterranean torrent of anguish raving through its hollows and tumbling down hidden precipices, whose voice only God heard, and only God could still. I would speak no words of my own. The Son of God had spoken words of comfort to His mourning friends, when He was the present God and they were the forefront of humanity. I would read some of the words He spoke. From them the human nature in each would draw what comfort it could.

I took my New Testament from my pocket and said, without any preamble, "When our Lord was going to die, He knew that His friends loved Him enough to be very wretched about it. He knew that they would be overwhelmed for a time with trouble. He knew too that they could not believe that glad end of it all, to which end He looked across the awful death that awaited Him—a death to which that of our friends in the wreck was ease itself. I will just read to you what He said."

I read from the fourteenth to the seventeenth chapter of John's Gospel. I knew there were words of meaning in the words into which I could hardly hope any of them would enter. But I knew likewise that the best things are just those from which the humble will draw the truth they are capable of seeing. Therefore I read as for myself, and left it to them to hear for themselves. Nor did I add any word of comment, fearful of darkening counsel by words without knowledge, for the Bible is awfully set against what is not wise.

When I had finished, I closed the book, rose from the grass, and walked toward the brow of the shore. They rose likewise and followed me. Little of any sort was said. The sea lay still before us, knowing nothing of the sorrow it had caused. We wandered a little way along the cliff.

The bell began to toll, and we went to church for the burial service. My companions placed themselves near the dead, while I went into the vestry till the appointed hour. I thought, as I put on my surplice, how in all religions but the Christian, the dead body was a pollution to the temple. Here the church received it as a holy thing, for a last embrace ere it went to the earth.

As the dead were already in the church, the usual form could not be carried out. I therefore stood by the Communion table and began to read. " 'I am the resurrection and the life,' saith the Lord; 'he that believeth in Me, though he were dead, yet shall he live: and whosoever liveth and believeth in Me shall never die.' "

I advanced as I read, till I came outside the rails and stood before the dead. There I read the psalm, "Lord, Thou hast been our refuge," and the glorious lesson, "Now is Christ risen from the dead, and become the firstfruits of them that slept." Then the men of the neighborhood came forward, and in long solemn procession bore the bodies out of the church, each to its grave. At the church door I stood and read, "Man that is born of woman," then went from one to another of the graves and read over each, as the earth fell on the coffin lid, "Forasmuch as it hath pleased Almighty God of His great mercy." Then I went back to the church door and read, "I heard a voice from heaven," and so to the end of the service.

When I returned to the house, I found that one of the surviving sailors wished to see me—the very man, in fact, who had been washed from the deck before my eyes, and cast up on the shore with a broken leg. I went, and found him very pale and worn.

"I think I am going," he said, "and I wanted to see you before I die."

"Trust in Christ, and do not be afraid," I returned.

"I prayed to Him to save me when I was hanging to the rigging, and if I wasn't afraid then, I'm not going to be afraid now, dying quietly in my bed. But just look here."

He took from under his pillow something wrapped up in paper, unfolded the envelope, and showed a lump of something—I could not at first tell what. He put it in my hand, and then I saw that it was part of a Bible, with nearly the upper half of it worn or cut away, and the rest partly in a state of pulp.

"That's the Bible my mother gave me when I left home first," he said. "I don't know how I came to put it in my pocket, but I think the rope that cut through them when I was lashed to the shrouds would a'most have cut through my ribs if it hadn't been for it."

"Very likely," I returned. "The body of the Bible has saved your bodily life: may the spirit of it save your spiritual life."

"I think I know what you mean," he panted out. "My mother was a good woman, and I know she prayed to God for me."

"We will pray for you in church today, and I will come in afterward and see how you are."

I knelt and offered the prayers for the sick. He thanked me, and I took my leave.

As for my own family, Turner insisted on Connie's remaining in bed for two or three days. She looked worse in face—pale and worn—but it was clear, from the way she moved in bed, that the fresh power called forth by the shock had not vanished with the moment. Wynnie was quieter, almost, than ever, but there was a constant secret light in her eyes. Percivale was at the house every day, always ready to make himself useful.

THIRTY-FOUR
CHANGED PLANS

In a day or two Connie was permitted to take to her couch once more. It seemed strange that she should look so much worse, and yet be so much stronger. Whenever they carried her, she begged to be allowed to put her feet to the ground. Turner yielded, though without quite ceasing to support her. He was satisfied, however, that she could have stood upright for a moment at least. He would not, of course, risk it.

The time of his departure was nearing, and he seemed anxious. Connie continued worn-looking and pale, and her smile, though ever ready to greet me when I entered, had lost much of its light. She had arranged the curtain of her window to shut out the sea, and I said something to her about it once. Her reply was "Papa, I can't bear it. I was so fond of the sea when I came down. It lay close to my window, with a friendly smile ready for me every morning when I looked out. I daresay it is all from want of faith, but I can't help it. It looks so far away now, like a friend that had failed me, and I would rather not see it."

I saw that the struggling life within her was grievously oppressed, and that the things which surrounded her were no longer helpful. Her life had been driven to its innermost cave, and now when it had been enticed to venture forth and look abroad, a sudden pall had descended upon Nature. I could not help thinking that the good of our visit to Kilkhaven had come, and that evil, from which I hoped we might escape, was following. I left her, and sought Turner.

224

"It strikes me, Turner," I said, "that the sooner we leave, the better it will be for Connie."

"I agree. The very prospect of leaving the place would do something to restore her."

"Would it be safe to move her?"

"Far safer than to let her remain. At the worst, she is now far better than when she came. Try her. Hint at the possibility of going home, and see how she will take it."

"Well," I said, "I shan't like to be left alone, but if she goes, they must all go, except, perhaps, I might keep Wynnie. But I don't know how her mother would get on without her."

"I don't see why you should stay behind. Mr. Weir would be as glad to come as you would be to go, and it can make no difference to Mr. Shepherd."

It seemed a very sensible suggestion. Certainly it was a desirable thing for both my sister and her husband. They had no such reasons as we had for disliking the place, and it would enable Martha to avoid the severity of yet another winter. I said as much to Turner, and went back to Connie's room.

The light of a lovely sunset was lying outside her window, but she was sitting so that she could not see it. I asked, without any preamble, "Would you like to go back to Marshmallows, Connie?"

Her countenance flashed into light. "Oh! Dear Papa! Do let us go," she said. "That would be delightful."

"Well, I think we can manage it, if you will only get a little stronger for the journey. The weather is not as good for travel as when we came down."

"No. But I am ever so much better, you know, than I was then."

The poor girl was already stronger from the mere prospect of going home again. She moved restlessly on her couch, half mechanically put her hand to the curtain, pulled it aside, looked out, faced the sun and the sea, and did not draw it back.

I left her and went to find Ethelwyn. She heartily approved of the proposal for Connie's sake, and said that it would be scarcely less agreeable to herself. I could see a certain troubled look above her eyes, however.

"You are thinking of Wynnie," I said.

"Yes. It is hard to make one sad for the sake of the rest."

"True. But it is one of the world's recognized necessities."

225

"No doubt."

"Besides, you don't suppose Percivale can stay here the whole winter. They must part sometime."

"Of course. Only they did not expect it so soon."

But here my wife was mistaken.

I went to my study to write to Weir. I had hardly finished my letter when Walter came to say that Mr. Percivale wished to see me.

I said as he was shown in, "I am just writing home to say that I want my curate to change places with me here, which I know he will be glad enough to do. I see Connie had better go home."

"You will all go then, I presume," returned Percivale.

"Yes, of course."

"Then I need not regret that I can stay no longer. I came to tell you that I must leave tomorrow."

"Ah! Going to London?"

"Yes. I don't know how to thank you for all your kindness. You have made my summer something like a summer."

"We have had our share of the advantage, and that a large one. We are all glad to have made your acquaintance, Mr. Percivale. Now, we shall be passing through London within a week or ten days, in all probability. Perhaps you will allow us the pleasure of looking at some of your pictures then?"

His face flushed. What did the flush mean? It was not one of mere pleasure, for there was confusion and perplexity in it. But he answered at once, "I will show you them with pleasure. I fear, however, you will not care for them."

Would this fear account for his embarrassment? I hardly thought it would, but I could not for a moment imagine that he had any serious reason for shrinking from a visit.

"I shall be sure to pay you a visit. But you will dine with us today, of course?" I said.

"With pleasure," he answered, and took his leave.

I finished my letter to Weir and went out for a walk. I wandered on the downs till I came to the place where a solitary rock stands upon the top of a cliff looking seaward, in the suggested shape of a monk praying. I seated myself, and looked out over the Atlantic. How faded the ocean appeared! It seemed as if all the sunny dyes of summer had been diluted and washed with the fogs of the coming winter.

The thought of seeing my own people again filled me with gladness. I would leave those I had here learned to love with regret, yet trusting I had taught them something. They had taught me much, and therefore there could be no end in our relation in the Lord, who alone gives security to any tie. I should not, therefore, sorrow as if I were to see their faces no more.

I took my farewell of that sea and those cliffs. I should see them often enough ere we went, but I should not feel so near them again. Even this parting said that I must "sit loose to the world," an old Puritan phrase. I could gather up only its uses, treasure its best things, and let all the rest go; those things I called mine— earth, sky and sea, home, books, the treasured gifts of friends—had all to leave me, belong to others and help to educate them. I should not need them. I should have my people, my souls, my beloved faces, and could well afford to part with these.

So my thoughts went on as I turned from the sea.

I found Wynnie looking very grave when I went into the drawing room. Her mother was there too, and Mr. Percivale. It seemed rather a moody party. They wakened up a little, however, after I entered, and before dinner was over, we were chatting together merrily.

"How is Connie?" I asked Ethelwyn.

"Better already," she answered.

"Everybody seems better," I said. "The very idea of going home seems reviving to us all."

Wynnie darted a quick glance at me, caught my eye (which was more than she had intended), and blushed. She sought refuge in a bewildered glance at Percivale, caught his eye in turn, and blushed yet deeper. He plunged instantly into conversation, not without a certain involuntary sparkle in his eyes.

"Did you go see Mrs. Stokes this morning?" he asked.

"No," I answered. "She does not want much visiting now. She is going about her work, apparently in good health. Her husband says she is not the same woman, and I hope he means that in more senses than one."

I did my best to keep up the conversation, but every now and then it fell like a wind that would not blow. I withdrew to my study. Percivale and Wynnie went out for a walk. The next morning he and Turner left by the early coach.

Wynnie did not seem very much dejected. I thought that perhaps the prospect of meeting Percivale again in London kept her up.

THIRTY-FIVE
THE STUDIO

I will not linger over our preparations or leave-takings. The two boys, who had wanted to bring down the chest, now wanted to take home two or three boxes filled with pebbles, great oyster shells, and seaweed.

Weir was also quite pleased to make the unexpected exchange. Before he came, I went about among the people to tell them a little about my successor, that he might not appear among them quite as a stranger.

It was a bright cold morning when we started, and the first part of our railway journey was very pleasant. But as we drew near London we entered a thick fog, and before we arrived, a small dense November rain was falling. Connie looked a little dispirited, partly from weariness, but no doubt from the change in the weather.

"Not very cheerful, this, Connie, my dear," I said.

"No, Papa," she answered, "but we *are* going home, you know."

Going home. I lay back in the carriage and thought how this November London fog was like the valley of the shadow of death we had to pass through on the way *home*. A shadow like this would fall upon me, and the world would grow dark and life grow weary—but I should know it was the last of the way home.

As the thought of water is to the thirsty soul, such is the thought of home to the wanderer in a strange country. And my own soul had always felt the discomfort of strangeness in the very midst of

228

its greatest blessedness. In the closest contact of one human soul with another, when all the atmosphere of thought was rosy with love, again and yet again on the far horizon, the dim, lurid flame of unrest would shoot for a moment through the enchanted air, and the soul would know that she was not yet home. But did I know where or what that home was?

I lifted my eyes, and saw those of my wife and Connie fixed on mine, as if they were reproaching me for saying in my soul that I could not be quite at home with them. Then I said in my heart, "Come home with me, Beloved; there is but one home for us all. When we find that home we shall be gardens of delight to each other, little chambers of rest, galleries of pictures, wells of water."

Again, what was this home? God Himself. His thoughts, His will, His love, His judgments, are man's home. To think His thoughts, to choose His will, to love His loves, to judge His judgments, and thus to know that He is in us—this is to be at home. It is the father, the mother, that make for the child his home. Indeed, I doubt if the *home* idea is complete to the parents of a family themselves, when they remember that their fathers and mothers have vanished.

At this point something rose in me seeking utterance.

"Won't it be delightful, Ethelwyn," I began, "to see our fathers and mothers such a long way back in heaven?"

But her face betrayed that I had pained her, and I felt at once how dreadful a thing it was not to have had a good father or mother. I do not know what would have become of me but for a good father. I wonder how anybody ever can be good who has not had a good father. Every father or mother who is not good makes it just as impossible to believe in God as it can be made. But He is our one good Father and does not leave us, even when our fathers and mothers have forsaken us and left Him without a witness.

Then the evil odor of brick-burning invaded my nostrils, and I knew that London was about us. A few moments after, we reached the station where a carriage was waiting to take us to our hotel.

Dreary was the change from the stillness and sunshine of Kilkhaven to the fog and noise of London. But Connie slept better that night than she had for a good many nights before.

After breakfast the next morning, I said to Wynnie, "I am going to see Mr. Percivale's studio, my dear. Have you any objection to going with me?"

"No, Papa," she answered blushing. "I have never seen an

artist's studio in my life."

"Get your bonnet and come along then."

She ran off and was ready in a few minutes. We gave the cab driver directions, and set out. It was a long drive, but at length we stopped in front of a very common-looking house on a very dreary street, in which no man could possibly identify his own door except by the number. I knocked under the number given on Percivale's card. A woman who looked at once dirty and cross (the former probably the cause of the latter) opened the door and gave bare assent to my question whether Mr. Percivale was at home. Then she withdrew with the words "Second floor," and left us to find our own way up the stairs.

We knocked at the door of the front room. A well-known voice cried, "Come in," and we entered. Percivale, in a short velvet coat, with his palette on his thumb, advanced to meet us. His face wore a slight flush, which I attributed solely to pleasure, and nothing to any awkwardness in receiving us in such a poor place as he occupied.

I cast my eyes round the room. Any romantic notions Wynnie might have indulged concerning the marvels of a studio must have paled considerably at the first glance around Percivale's room. It was plainly the abode, if not of poverty then of self-denial, although I suspected both. It was a common room, with no carpet save a square in front of the fireplace; no curtains except a piece of something like a drugget nailed flat across the lower half of the window to make the light fall from upward; two or three horsehair chairs, nearly worn out; a table in a corner, littered with books and papers; a horrible lay figure, at the present moment dressed apparently for a scarecrow; and a large easel, on which stood a half-finished oil painting. These constituted almost the whole furniture of the room.

With his pocket handkerchief, Percivale dusted one chair for Wynnie and another for me. Standing before us, he said, "This is a very shabby place to receive you in, Miss Walton, but it is all I have."

"A man's life consists not in the abundance of the things he possesses," I ventured to say.

"Thank you," said Percivale. "I hope not. It is well for me it should not."

"It is well for the richest man in England that it should not," I returned. "If it were not so, the man who could eat most would be the most blessed."

"Have you been very busy since you left us, Mr. Percivale?" asked Wynnie.

"Tolerably," he answered, "but I have not much to show for it. That on the easel is all. I hardly like to let you look at it, though."

"Why?" asked Wynnie.

"First, because the subject is painful. Next, because it is so unfinished."

"But why should you paint subjects you do not like people to look at?"

"I very much want people to look at them."

"Why not us, then?" said Wynnie.

"Because you do not need to be pained."

"Are you sure it is good for you to pain anybody?" I said.

"Good is done by pain; is it not?" he asked.

"Undoubtedly. But whether *we* are wise enough to know when and where and how much is the question."

"Of course, I do not make the pain my object."

"If it comes only as a necessary accompaniment, that may alter the matter greatly," I said. "But still I am not sure that anything in which the pain predominates can be useful in the best way."

"Perhaps not," he returned. "Will you look at the daub?"

"With much pleasure," I replied, and we rose and stood before the easel. Percivale made no remark, but left us to find out what the picture meant. Nor had I long to look before I understood it—in a measure at least.

It represented a wretchedly ruinous garret. The plaster had come away in several places, and between the laths in one spot hung the tail of a great rat. In a dark corner lay a man dying. A woman sat by his side with his hand in hers. Her eyes were fixed not on his face, but on the open door, where in the gloom you could just see the struggles of two undertaker's men to get the coffin past the turn of the landing toward the door. Through the window there was one peep of the blue sky, whence a ray of sunlight fell on the one scarlet blossom of a geranium in a broken pot on the windowsill outside.

"I do not wonder you did not like to show it," I said. "How can you bear to paint such a dreadful picture?"

"It is a true one. It only represents a fact."

"Not all facts have a right to be represented."

"Surely you would not get rid of painful things by huddling

them out of sight?"

"No, nor yet by gloating upon them."

"You will believe me that it gives me anything but pleasure to paint such pictures, as far as the subject goes," he said with some discomposure.

"Of course. I know you well enough by this time to know that. But no one could hang it on his wall who would not either gloat on suffering or grow callous to it. Whence then would come the good in painting the picture? If it had come into my possession, I would—"

"Put it in the fire," suggested Percivale, with a strange smile.

"No. Still less would I sell it. I would hang it up with a curtain before it, and only look at it now and then when I thought my heart was in danger of growing hardened to the sufferings of my fellowmen and forgetting that they need the Saviour."

"I could not wish it a better fate. That would answer my end."

"Would it now? Is it not rather those who care little or nothing about such matters that you would like to influence? Would you be content with one solitary person like me? And, remember, I wouldn't buy it. I would rather not have it, and could hardly bear to know it was in my house. I am certain you cannot do people good by showing them *only* the painful. Make it as painful as you will, but put some hope into it, something to show that action is worth taking in the affair. People will turn away from mere suffering, and you cannot blame them. Every show of it, without hinting at some door of escape, only urges them to forget it all. Why should they be pained if it can do no good?"

"For the sake of sympathy, I should say," answered Percivale.

"They would rejoin, 'It is only a picture. Come along.' No. Give people hope, if you would have them act at all, in anything."

"I was almost hoping you would read the picture rather differently. There is a bit of blue sky up there, and a bit of sunshiny scarlet in the window." He looked at me curiously as he spoke.

"I have read it so for myself. But you only put in the sky and the scarlet to heighten the perplexity and make the other look more terrible."

"Now I know that as an artist I have succeeded, however I may have failed otherwise. I did so mean it. But knowing you would dislike the picture, I almost hoped, in my cowardice, that you would read your own meaning into it."

Wynnie had not said a word. As I turned away from the picture,

I saw that she was quite distressed, but whether by the picture, or the freedom with which I had remarked upon it, I do not know. My eyes fell upon a little sketch in sepia, and I began to examine it, in the hope of finding something more pleasant to say. It was nearly the same thought, however, only treated in a gentler and more poetic mode. A girl lay dying on her bed, as a youth held her hand. A torrent of summer sunshine fell through the window, and made a lake of glory upon the floor.

I turned away.

"You like that better, don't you, Papa?" said Wynnie, tremulously.

"It is beautiful, certainly," I answered. "And if it were only one, I should enjoy it, as a mood. But coming after the other, it seems but the same thing more weakly embodied."

I confess I was a little vexed. I was much interested in Percivale, for his own sake, as well as for my daughter's, and I had expected better things from him. But I saw that I had gone too far.

"I beg your pardon, Mr. Percivale," I said. "I fear I have been too free in my remarks. I know, likewise, that I am a clergyman and not a painter, and therefore incapable of giving the praise which I have little doubt your art at least deserves."

"I trust that honesty cannot offend me, however much and justly it may pain me."

"But now I have said my worst, I should much like to see what else you have at hand to show me."

"Unfortunately, I have too much at hand. Let me see."

He strode to the other end of the room where several pictures were leaning with their faces against the wall. From these he chose one and fitted it into an empty frame, then brought it forward and set it on the easel.

In it a dark hill rose against the evening sky which shone through a few thin pines on its top. Along a road on the hillside, four squires bore a dying knight—a man past middle age. One behind carried his helm, and another led his horse whose fine head only appeared in the picture. The head and countenance of the knight were very noble, telling of many a battle, and ever for the right. The last had doubtless been gained, for one might read victory as well as peace in the dying look. The party had just reached the edge of a steep descent, and in the valley below, the last of the harvest was just being reaped, while the shocks stood all about the fields under the face of the sunset. There was no gold left in the sky, only a little dull saffron, but plenty of that lovely liquid green of the autumn sky, divided with a few streaks of pale rose. The sky overhead (which could not be seen in the picture) was mirrored in a piece of water in the center of the valley.

"My dear fellow!" I cried. "Why did you not show me this first, and save me from saying so many unkind things? Here is a picture to my own heart. It is glorious. Look here, Wynnie," I went on. "It is evening, and the sun's work is done—he has set in glory, leaving his good name behind him in a lovely harmony of color. The old knight's work is done too—his day has set in the storm of battle, and he is lying lapt in the coming peace. They are bearing him home to his couch and his grave, mourning for and honoring the life that is ebbing away. But he is gathered to his fathers like a shock of corn fully ripe, and so the harvest stands golden in the valley beneath. The picture would not be complete, however, if it did not tell us of the deep heaven overhead, the symbol of that heaven where the knight is bound. What a lovely idea to represent it by means of the water, the heaven embodying itself in the earth, as it were, that we may see it! And that dusky hillside, and those tall slender mournful-looking pines, with that sorrowful sky between, lead the eye and point the heart upward toward that heaven. It is indeed a grand picture, full of feeling, a picture and a parable."

I looked at the girl. Her eyes were full of tears called forth either by the picture or by the pleasure of finding something of Percivale's work appreciated by me, who had spoken so hardly of his other pictures.

"I cannot tell you how glad I am that you like it," she said.

"Like it!" I returned. "I am simply delighted with it—more than I can express—so much delighted that, if I could have this alongside of it, I should not mind hanging that other, that hopeless garret, on the most public wall I have."

"Then," said Wynnie bravely, though in a tremulous voice, "you confess, don't you, Papa, that you were too hard on Mr. Percivale at first?"

"Not too hard on his picture, my dear, and that was all he had given me to judge by. No man should paint a picture like that. You are not bound to disseminate hopelessness, for where there is no hope, there can be no sense of duty."

"But surely, Papa, Mr. Percivale has *some* sense of duty," said Wynnie, in an almost angry tone.

"Assuredly, my love. Therefore I argue that he has some hope, and therefore again that he has no right to publish such a picture."

At the word *publish* Percivale smiled. But Wynnie went on with her defense.

"But you see, Papa, that Mr. Percivale does not paint such pictures only. Look at the other."

"Yes, my dear. But pictures are not like poems, lying side by side in the same book, so that the one can counteract the other. The one of these might go to the stormy Hebrides, and the other to the vale of Avalon. But even then, I should be strongly inclined to criticize the poem that had nothing, positively nothing, of the aurora in it."

"He could refuse to let the one go without the other," said Wynnie.

"He might sell them together, but the owner would part them." I turned to Percivale. "If you would allow me, I will come and see your other pictures another time. I do hope, however, that we can persuade you to dine with us this evening."

We could, and he did. But though our meal was pleasant, the soon-to-be-fulfilled promise of home lay close to our hearts. We left early the next day, then, and the last segment of the journey to Marshmallows was accomplished in a rain and fog that could not dampen our spirits.

THIRTY-SIX

HOME AGAIN

Oldcastle Hall opened wide to welcome us. We laid Connie once more in her own room, and then I left the others to explore while I went up to my study. The familiar faces of my books welcomed me. I threw myself in my reading chair, and gazed around me with pleasure. I felt it so *homey* here. All my old friends—whom somehow I hoped to see someday—were present there in the spirit ready to talk with me any moment when I was in the mood, making no claim upon my attention when I was not! I felt as if I should like, when the hour should come, to die in that chair, and pass into the society of the witnesses in the presence of the tokens they had left behind.

I heard shouts on the stairs, and in rushed the two boys.

"Papa! Papa!" they were crying together.

"What is the matter?"

"We've found the big chest just where we left it!"

'Well, did you expect it would have taken itself off?"

"But there's everything in it just as we left it."

"Were you afraid that it would turn itself upside down, and empty all its contents on the floor the moment you turned your backs?"

"Well, Papa, we did not think anything about it, but—but—there everything is as we left it."

With this triumphant answer, they turned and hurried a little abashed out of the room. But not many more moments elapsed before the sounds that arose from them sufficiently reassured me of the state of their spirits.

When they were gone, I forgot my books in the attempt to penetrate and understand my boys' thoughts. And soon I came to see that they were right and I was wrong. Theirs was the wonder of the discovery of the existence of *law*. There was nothing that they had experienced, until now, that would lead them to believe that any such thing should remain where it was left. There *was* a reason in the nature of God, but as far as the boys had previously understood, no one could expect to find anything where he had left it. I began to see yet further into the truth—even the laws of nature reveal the character of God, being of necessity fashioned after His own being and will.

I rose and went down to see if everybody was getting settled, and how the place looked. Ethelwyn was already going about the house as if she had never left it, and as if we all had just returned from a long absence, and she had to show us home-hospitality.

Wynnie had vanished, but I soon found her in her mother's favorite old haunt—beside the little pond called Bishop's Basin, for the fascination and horror of this mysterious spot had laid hold on Wynnie. The frost lay thick in the hollow when I went down there, and the branches, lately clothed with leaves, stood bare and icy around her.

I resolved that night to tell Wynnie, in her mother's presence, all the legend of the place, and the whole story of how I won her mother. But for now I left her there. I was so pleased to be at home again that I could not rest, but went wandering everywhere, into places even which I had not entered for ten years at least, and found fresh interest in everything. For this was home, and here I was.

EPILOGUE

And with our return to Marshmallows, our adventures in the Seaboard Parish came to an end.

And what has happened in the years that have followed after? Perhaps I have roused curiosity without satisfying it, but out of a life one cannot always cut complete portions and serve them up in nice shapes. I am well aware that I have not told the *fate* of any of my family. This I cannot relate, for their *fates* are not yet determined.

But, if it is any satisfaction, Connie has had a quiet happy life as Mrs. Turner. She has never grown strong, but has very tolerable health, as her husband watches her with the utmost care and devotion.

Harry has gone home, but Charlie is a barrister of the Middle Temple. And Dora puts up with the society of her old father and mother, and is something else than unhappy.

Nor did we leave our Kilkhaven friends entirely behind us. The Scotchman and the young lady, who were our guests for the funeral after the shipwreck, have since come to visit us here at Oldcastle Hall. And the seaman I went to see, he who had survived that same shipwreck by the protection of his mother's Bible—he did not die but recovered as I expected—and came after us to Marshmallows, where he still works for us in our garden and stables.

But of Wynnie and Mr. Percivale and Connie's baby? Ah! The rest of their story is long and must be left for another volume and another author. My hand is tired, and I promised my Ethelwyn an evening walk.

The story that began in *A Quiet Neighborhood* and continued in *The Seaboard Parish* concludes with *The Vicar's Daughter*.

EDITOR'S AFTERWORD

A good *story* will last almost forever. A particular writing style or fashion will scarcely last a half century.

Which explains both why George MacDonald's novels have not been widely read in the last sixty years, and why they are now once more coming to the public attention.

MacDonald's novels suffered from the same excesses that plagued the other novels of his generation: verbosity, repetition, and digression. But buried beneath the archaic and quaint style and mannerisms of the preceding century, embedded within what we see as "historical romances," lie a series of novels that still deserve to be in the hands of readers.

The Seaboard Parish was not written as a historical novel—it was a contemporary work as published (after a popular magazine serialization) in 1868. MacDonald's works were written from life, and reflect his deep insight into the nature of God, and of fallen and redeemed man. The places and people were handily taken from places and people around him; he wrote of all that was near at hand, from all that he knew best.

The Marshmallows of *A Quiet Neighborhood* and *The Seaboard Parish* is a real place; it is MacDonald's name for the village of Arundel, situated directly south of London and only a few miles north of the English Channel. Arundel was the scene of MacDonald's first pastorate, lasting from 1850 to 1853. He served a small Congregational assembly, whose chapel still stands (though disused) almost in the shadow of the grand castle that was MacDonald's model for Oldcastle Hall.

Kilkhaven and Tintagel and St. Nectan's Glen are all real places as well, and may be seen today. Kilkhaven was MacDonald's name for Bude, a town on the northern Cornish coast where MacDonald and his family spent the summer of 1867.

My wife and I visited Bude in the summer of 1984, and found much of it exactly as described—the marvelous cobbled breakwater protecting the harbor from the daily ravages of the sea; the curious cottages at the end of the quay near the canal; and even the ornate boathouse—not the one used now (at the head of the canal) but the one which still stands a few hundred yards away from the sea.

Tintagel is exactly as MacDonald saw it, except that wide stone steps with sturdy handrails ease the climb to the top, making an otherwise perilous ascent possible even for the visitors (such as myself) who have no head for heights. The stone arch through which Connie saw the sea still stands, affording an unparalleled view of the waves crashing between the cliffs hundreds of feet below.

Merlin's Cave burrows under the peninsula where the castle stands, and the old church and graveyard still huddle atop the land's edge overlooking the castle ruins. St. Nectan's Glen, a few miles away, is also preserved as a tourist stop and tea garden.

(MacDonald's son Greville recollected the family's time in the area of Bude as among the happiest of his childhood—and largely because his father was more involved in the lives and play of his children then than at any other time within his memory.)

The Seaboard Parish (along with its prequel *A Quiet Neighborhood* and its sequel *The Vicar's Daughter*) was reprinted in numerous editions throughout MacDonald's lifetime. But after he died in Surrey in 1905, his novels began a slow descent from public acclaim. Old copies of the books traded hands quietly over the ensuing years, but no major attempt was made to reprint them.

His novels are so scarce today that I could not find a copy of *The Seaboard Parish* for sale. Only five library copies exist in the Midwest—most of them tucked away securely in universities. The copy used to prepare this edition came from the Wade Collection at Wheaton College, Wheaton, Illinois, through the kindness of Dr. Lyle Dorsett and Brenda Phillips. The Wade Collection houses one of the finest groupings of MacDonald's works on this side of the Atlantic, along with the works and memorabilia of G.K. Chesterton, C.S. Lewis, J.R.R. Tolkien, Owen Barfield, and Dorothy L. Sayers.

As in the previous volume, the aim of the editing and abridgement process has been to strike a balance between brevity and breadth that will be economical to print, interesting to the reader of the 1980s, and faithful to the heart of MacDonald's vision. I make no pretense that this edited version is *better* than the original, merely shorter and easier to read. If anyone who has read this far in this edition should happen across an original copy of *The Seaboard Parish,* he or she should not miss the chance to enjoy it in its original breadth, richness, and entirety.

Dan Hamilton
Indianapolis, Indiana
December 1984